D0783151

THE History TEACHER

A NOVEL

SUSAN BACON

Porter Street Press

MEMPHIS / AUSTIN

Articles that appeared in *The New York Times*, *Time* magazine and *The Atlantic Monthly* are quoted in the text. Citations for these articles appear in the Endnotes.

The History Teacher is a work of fiction. All dialogue and specific events, and all characters except for certain well-known historical figures, are products of the author's imagination and are not to be interpreted or construed as real. Where actual historical figures do appear, the situations, incidents, and dialogue concerning those figures are fictional and *not* intended to depict actual events or to suggest that this work is anything other than fiction. In all other respects, any resemblance to actual persons, living or dead, events, or locations is entirely coincidental.

Book design by Design Positive
Jacket design by Taylor Martin
Portrait by Fran Doggrell

Library of Congress Cataloging-in-Publication Data has been applied for.
Library of Congress Control Number: 2019907781

ISBN: 9781733082709
ISBN: 9781733082716 (ebook)

 **Porter Street Press**
MEMPHIS / AUSTIN

For Evie and Owen

No historian lines up all the dots. Every work of history is a ridiculously selective selection from the universe of possible dots.

—Louis Menand

A Chronology of Events

May 1945 Germany surrenders and the Cold War effectively begins.

August 1945 United States drops atomic bomb on Hiroshima ending the war in the Pacific.

March 1947 President Truman signals a new interventionist foreign policy aimed at keeping the world safe from totalitarianism.

July 1947 Central Intelligence Agency (CIA) established.

June 1948 Office of Special Projects created to subvert Soviet expansion through propaganda and covert military operations. Subsequently renamed the Office of Policy Coordination (OPC), it is rolled into the CIA in 1951.

August 1948 Alger Hiss accused of being a Communist before the House Un-American Activities Committee (HUAC).

September 1949 Russia tests its own atomic bomb.

January 1950 Alger Hiss convicted of perjury and sentenced to five years in prison.

March 1951 Ethel and Julius Rosenberg convicted of providing atomic secrets to Soviet Union and sentenced to death.

August 1953 CIA orchestrates overthrow of Iranian Government and puts the pro-Western Reza Shah Pahlavi back in power.

THE SEVENTIES

August 1974 Nixon announces his resignation in the wake of Watergate.

December 1974 Seymour Hersh's investigative report on illegal CIA operations under Nixon—including domestic spying—breaks on the front page of *The New York Times*.

1975-1976 Church Committee investigates the intelligence community, exposing a range of illegal and covert activities that occurred from the 1950s to the mid-1970s.

January 1977 Jimmy Carter's presidency begins. He implements cutbacks at the CIA and vows to reduce the sale of arms to foreign nations including Iran.

April 1978 Publication of Allen Weinstein's *Perjury* draws attention to the Alger Hiss case.

January 1978 Civil unrest begins to escalate in Iran culminating in the overthrow of the Shah the following January.

PART I

Friday, February 3, 1978. The National Weather Service has issued a major storm warning for the eastern seaboard. It's the third such forecast in recent weeks. The first two snows failed to materialize. This latest one appears to be yet another meteorologist's blunder. The skies remain clear through Sunday. On Monday morning, people fall into their normal routines. Schools open, highways in motion, business as usual. Then, round about mid-morning, the storm blasts in as if out of nowhere. Hurricane-force winds. Massive accumulations of snow, unremitting, falling at rates of up to four inches an hour. By nightfall Monday, the northeastern seaboard from the Delmarva Peninsula up the coast to Cape Cod is experiencing one of the worst snowstorms of the 20th century. It continues into the night Monday and all day Tuesday. That is where our story begins.

No. 1

Miller's Lane

A statuesque woman in a full-length camel hair coat and a large angular mink hat walks her boxer down Miller's Lane. It is a narrow road, no more than a mile long, and deceptively rural, although it's well within the city limits. Walk up Miller's Lane to the top of the hill and it ends at a traffic light, a main thoroughfare that leads deeper into the city. Walk in the other direction, and it takes you into the woods along a ravine and out toward the old Balfour Mill. There are no sidewalks on Miller's Lane. And there is no traffic on this Monday morning. She is walking toward the woods, holding the fold of her coat against the wind. The dog seems to struggle with every step. Staying close to the steep incline that marks the edge of an adjacent estate, her estate, they move downhill, slow and steady. She is obviously not a young woman, but she's sure-footed enough. It's below freezing, and the sky is a purple white. The smell of ice is in the air.

Roy Howard is waiting for her in the woods beyond. He's stashed his black Bronco at the old mill and walked the half-mile up along the ravine toward Miller's Lane. He wears a ball cap, a standard issue

Carhartt, jeans, work boots so as not to attract attention and carries a tripod, a surveyor's instrument, under his arm as he makes his way to an old truss bridge that lurches over the ravine. There is natural forest all around, tall stalks of trees with bare branches black against the winter sky. A low fieldstone wall—aged, craggy, all browns and greys— stretches along the edge of the road, above the ravine. "Medieval," he thinks. He stations himself at the bridge, a relic with wooden slats and a canopy of rusted iron. He knows that she'll come on foot, that she's in her eighties. He figures it will take her maybe 20 minutes, 30 tops to get to him.

A heavy wind is barreling in from the west. Had anyone been watching from the row of cottages along Miller's Lane or from the woods beyond where Roy Howard stands waiting beside his tripod, it would have seemed odd to see a bicycle appear at the top of the lane. A man in a flak jacket and grey wool cap riding down the hill as if it were a bright fall day, heading toward the woods, coming at Margaret Quinn from behind, hardly pedaling, moving fast. But no one is watching. And no one would have expected foul play. "Such an awful day," they would say later. "What on earth was she doing out in that mess? And how did she not see it coming?"

As the snow begins to fall, Roy Howard folds back his glove to check the time. It's almost ten. He hears the crack of a tree branch and reflexively reaches for his weapon, buried under the Carhartt in a halter over his left breast. "Sitting duck," he thinks. He considers moving the weapon to his pocket but doesn't want to spook the old lady. He holds the tripod in one gloved hand and secures his cap with the other, watching the entrance to Miller's Lane, alert, standing on a mound of dirt, crystals falling on his boots like white ash, melting as they hit. She should be here any second, he is thinking when the front of an old brown pickup pokes out from Miller's Lane, turning toward him, heading north along the narrow road. Reaching for his breast, his weapon, he steps back, nudging up against the fieldstone wall, snow striking him in the face as the truck approaches and he sees the passenger window roll down, the dark muzzle of a gun.

***

Margaret Quinn had been planning this outing for weeks. At breakfast that morning, she sat at the head of the long oak table in the formal dining room and ate two coddled eggs, listening intently to the news report—"Anwar Sadat arrived last night at Camp David to meet with President Carter and the Secretary of State heralding a new push for peace in the Middle East"—then more closely to the weather outlining the trajectory of a winter storm. She smoked a cigarette and took a good, long look at the sky through the windows that ran the length of the east wall of the expansive room. Once she'd made up her mind, she headed straight from the table to the coat closet in the front hall. She found Flip near the fireplace in the library, nudged him from a deep sleep, ushered him through the living room and the dining room, where her breakfast plate sat streaked with runny yolk, then to the rear hall, a windowless, grey corridor beyond the back stairs that led to the mudroom. "Blizzard my foot," she said to the dog as she clipped on his leash. "Rubbish." Then, almost as an afterthought, she fished around in a battered creel for a pair of gloves and left without a word to anyone and nothing more than her keys in her coat pocket. Surprised by her own determination and the strength of the wind as she closed the door behind her, she hesitated only to pull her hat tight around her ears, moving along the brick walkway past the frozen boxwoods, down the front drive and through the fieldstone gates of the estate, turning left down Miller's Lane.

When she failed to return, a woman named Annie Daniels called the police. She identified herself as Mrs. James Quinn's housekeeper and reported only that Mrs. Quinn was missing and no, there was no way she could have gone out in the car. "She doesn't go out," she said. "And her lunch…her soup is on the table. I've looked everywhere. She's not here." It was just after noon when she made the call. By then, Margaret Quinn had been gone for several hours.

They might not have found her had it not been for the dog, half-alive by her side. She lay frozen, face down, swaddled in snow, wedged at the edge of the Quinn estate where Miller's Lane meets the forest beyond, a blizzard swirling all around. Roy Howard, who had been only 28 years old, lay at the bottom of the ravine with a hole in his head.

No. 2

Upper West Side, Manhattan

On this Monday morning, the day of the killer blizzard, Emma Quinn stands half-dressed in a pair of faded brown corduroy pants and a loose-fitting mohair sweater drinking black coffee from a hand-thrown mug, surveying her living room. The paint on the old windows is chipped, but the walls are a clean, bright white and the room sparsely furnished—a grand piano, a leather sofa, a big old pine coffee table. Five vintage posters, framed, perfectly aligned on one wall, Soviet propaganda posters. A woman in a babushka. The magnified face of a man in black-rimmed circular glasses, flanked by some blocky red Cyrillic text. Vladimir Ilych Lenin in an overcoat, his arm raised against the backdrop of the Soviet flag. Across the room, over the sofa, a softer, gentler lithograph, the image of a woman in a long dress and festive feathered hat, a mix of creamy yellows and greens. A Toulouse-Lautrec, signed and numbered, an original.

Piles of books lie open and stacked one upon another on the sofa. Typewritten pages, some torn and crumpled, are scattered about on the floor. Beside the typewriter, an ashtray the size of a saucer, noxious, full. "Nasty," she says, sticking her tongue out, uttering a long guttural slur. "Blaouck." Walking to the window, she cranes to see the sky beyond the brick wall a few feet away and out to West End Avenue below. There is no snow. There is no sign of snow. Disappointed, she walks down a narrow hall to the bedroom, the bath. "Jesus," she says, looking at herself, brushing her teeth, her hair, putting on a pair of silver hoop earrings, adding a scarf, removing the scarf, fastening a leather watch on her slim wrist.

She puts on snow boots, just in case, fills her backpack and walks the 20-some blocks to the Columbia campus. She's forgotten her gloves. Reflexively, she jams her hands in her pockets, but she's barely conscious of the cold, obsessing over a detail, a missing piece that will tie the book together, knowing that if she doesn't finish she won't get tenure. She hits Broadway, oblivious to the crowds around her in their rush to buy staples, to stock up in advance of the storm. Batteries. Milk. Jugs of water, as if somehow the plumbing itself will be compromised.

In contrast, stillness pervades the Columbia campus. She wonders if classes have been cancelled. "Lucky devils are all asleep," she says to herself, speaking the words out loud, and heads up the imposing marble stone steps toward Low Library. On the marble plaza that over-looks the campus, as she turns toward a cluster of brick buildings that rise above Amsterdam Avenue like a fortress buttressing the univer-sity from the city beyond, she has a feeling she's missed something, a sensation that's not unknown to her. Out of sync with the outside world, she lives alone without a television, reads the newspaper late in the day, forgets to turn on the radio. As she exits the elevator, she calls out to the woman at the front desk of the History Department. "We closed?" The woman rolls her eyes. "Not yet. But it's supposed to get bad." Emma pauses for an instant as if she's unsure how to proceed. "We should know within the hour," the woman says in a patronizing tone, expressing a deep, exasperated "Geeez" under her breath that Emma barely notices.

In the hours that follow, Professor Quinn delivers her Western Civ 101 lecture to a roomful of freshmen eager for a shutdown. By the time she's finished, it's snowing buckets, and the wind has picked up and getting over to the research desk at Butler is going to be a challenge without gloves or a hat or an umbrella. But she has this thing, this detail she needs to pursue, and she's determined to get there before it shuts down. "Manny," she calls out, as she arrives, running toward the research desk, her hair stuck to her head like a bizarre, blondish do-rag flecked with ice chips. The room itself is massive, its ceilings stretching high above the milky windows that line the south wall. There is rich, dark wood everywhere—card catalogues, benches, tables, shelves—yet the space reads cold and grey, the terrazzo floor as linoleum. It's deserted, a few staffers here and there pushing carts of books, clearing things up. Behind the research desk, Manny is putting on his jacket, pulling his long greying ponytail over his back collar. "Thank God you're still here," she says, approaching. Reaching for his backpack, he looks up at her. "You just want me for my database," he says, smiling and throwing his backpack over his shoulder. He's wearing wire-rimmed glasses and his skin has a grey cast to it so he seems to blend with the room. He could be 30. Could be 50. Hard to tell. Like half the overage men in the neighborhood, students from the '60s who got stuck somehow, radicalized, cast free from their family's expectations and their own but unable to free themselves from the safety of the university, he looks like he maybe slept in his clothes. "Jesus, Quinn," he says, putting on his baseball cap. "Did you miss the weather report? Can you not see we're closing?"

Emma makes a face, half grimace, half apology. "But it's important," she says. He responds sarcastically. "No doubt," turning to the bulky computer. "I think they've already shut down the mainframe." But he sets his backpack on the floor, clicks the keyboard, watches the computer screen light up, standing. "You still working on that Rosa Luxemburg thingy?"

"Thingy?" she says, then speaks in a rush of breath, moving around behind the desk, looking over his shoulder as he sits. "I need the August Bebel correspondence from Hamburg in 1906." As Emma moves in closer, his palms start sweating. But she's oblivious. "Anything around the time of the Polish Congress. Actually, everything. Could be in an obscure communication. I have a new theory."

"Earth-shattering, I'm sure," Manny says. He strikes a few more keys, feigns bewilderment as he reads the screen, looks up at Emma, finally speaking, "Says here I've already given you the Bebel bibliography." He smiles. "Hmmmmmm," he says as if to himself, drawing it out, turning off the machine, grinning up at her. "Looks like you're going to have to go to Poland."

No. 3

Quinn Estate

Annie Daniels fears that she has made a terrible mistake. She tries to reassure herself. There is a routine, she tells herself. Every day, the same. Since Mr. Quinn died, the same. Mrs. Quinn takes her breakfast in the dining room at 8:30. And while she drinks her second cup of coffee and smokes her second cigarette and lingers over the news broadcast, Annie is upstairs, straightening, going from one room to the next, making her bed, emptying the ashtrays in her sitting room, wiping down the bathroom beyond, the one that used to be Mr. Quinn's, the one the size of a bedroom with two sinks and aging pink and green tiles. By the time Mrs. Quinn leaves the table, Annie's finished. She's moved through the three rooms—bedroom, sitting room, bath, each connected to the other—smoothly, tending to the details. She doesn't touch the table in the sitting room, the stacks of papers, the newspaper clippings under all the paperweights. When she is finished, she moves down the back stairway to the laundry room or the kitchen.

Mrs. Quinn always uses the front stairs, always. They don't pass in the hall, or see each other at all until lunch, which is at noon, always. "It's usual," she thinks. Even today, when Annie retreated to her own room, set off from the rest of the house, upstairs, in the back, that was normal. That was not unusual. But at noon, there's no sign of Mrs. Quinn. Annie searches the house, casual at first, then frantic. She cannot find her and there is no sign of the dog. "Surely, on a day like this, she wouldn't have taken Flip out for a walk," she thinks. And she can't remember a time when Mrs. Quinn left without saying goodbye.

Now she's been waiting for more than an hour for some word from the police. She's called 911 three times. A slight woman, Annie wears a grey cotton uniform with a white Peter Pan collar ruffled at its edge, an old green sweater thrown over her shoulders. Her long, grey, twizzly hair is knotted on the back of her head. Stationed in the library near the phone, she moves from window to window, wrapping the sweater tight across her chest like a shawl, watching the snow spinning in circles around the front of the house. She can barely make out the stone columns at the foot of the drive across the expansive lawn. The sky, the air, the yard itself enveloped in a fuzzy grey-white mist, vaporous, as if possessed.

There had been sirens, she's certain she heard them when she was searching the upper rooms one last time, nosing through the closet that runs like a corridor from one end of Mrs. Quinn's bedroom to the other, walking the gauntlet of summer dresses, silk blouses that tie at the neck, woolen slacks, smoky sweaters and jackets, overwhelmed by the musty, cooped-up smell of well-worn clothes, brushing their sleeves, pulling them aside, examining the floor. "Maybe she had a stroke, a heart attack, fell in the dark," she is thinking. Still, the police have not arrived.

She's certain that she's done everything right. She had risen at 6 a.m. Cold as it was, bone-chilling cold, she walked the 100-whatever yards down to the foot of the drive, to the front gates to fetch the paper before she served breakfast. She let Flip out so he could do his business. And she checked the sky. It was not a clear day. Yet there was none of that glistening, glimmery, tingly sensation you get when you feel snow coming on. Or that smell, like icy dishwater trapped in the clouds. She remembers reporting that to Mrs. Quinn when she came down for breakfast. "They say snow's coming, but I don't see it." And when the meal was done, at quarter to nine, for the clocks had chimed on the quarter-hour as always, she'd served Mrs. Quinn her second cup of coffee and waited for the smell of cigarette smoke before retreating up the back stairs to do her work. "Thank you, Annie," Mrs. Quinn had called out.

After more than an hour of waiting and pacing and dialing 911 and finally confirming that her first call was on record, that the police were responding, had responded, Annie calls her son Lester. It is almost 2 p.m. She cries into the phone, blathers the details. "I can come. It's not too bad out," he says. "I'm coming. Sit tight." She stays at the desk by the phone, diminutive against the high back of the leather chair, toying with a glass paperweight, a clear oval the size of an egg with red and black ribbons of color swirling like snakes at its center. She remembers—a gift from Emma to her grandfather that first Christmas after she'd gone away to school. He'd opened it in this very room beside a tree bigger than the one on the first floor at Wanamaker's. Mr. Quinn, beside himself that Emma was home. "It's hand blown," Emma had said, proud, grown up. He had never added it to his collection on the library bookshelves, the dozens of glass paperweights that had moved to Mrs. Quinn's desk, one at a time in the months and years that followed his death, each one a marker of her descent deeper into a kind of madness.

Annie knows she needs to call Emma. She knows that. But she is waiting for the police, for some word. And she doesn't know quite what to say—I've lost your grandmother? And what would Emma say to that?

Around 3 p.m., a flashing light appears beyond the front portico. Two men wearing yellow slickers and matching rubber trousers arrive at the front door. They are carrying the dog on a gurney, but the firemen don't bring Margaret Quinn. When Annie answers the bell, the short one speaks. "Is there somewhere we can put your dog?" It is baffling to her. She can't think what to do. Doesn't let them in. Can't give them an answer. "I called 911 four times," she says. "It's been more than two hours."

"It's rough out there, ma'am," one of them says. By then, she's tried to reach Emma at the university and left two messages on her answering machine at home.

The men are calm. But the situation is awkward. They are authorized to deliver a dog. They are not authorized to deliver any news.

"Where is Mrs. Quinn?" Annie says.

Specks of ice and snow sweep in through the front door, their rubber suits coated with the stuff. "Is there somewhere we can put the dog ma'am, so he'll be safe?"

Annie, unmoving, "Where is she?"

The men, patient, professional. "We need to bring the dog in, ma'am. The police will be here in just a minute."

Then it is over. The police car coming up the drive with Annie's son Lester behind them, his white pickup swallowed by the blurred landscape, and the steady scream of a siren, the ambulance carrying Mrs. Quinn rising, distant, from Miller's Lane. The men edge through the front door, all of them, in their rubber boots and oversized gloves, nearly knocking over the Imari umbrella stand in the front hall, rattling the antique walking stick with its ivory handle. "'Scuse us." Trampling the oriental runner beside the front stairs, swinging into the library, waiting quietly, taking in the rarefied air of the room, the wall of books, the tufted chairs, a Bakhtiari the size of Baltimore. Lester taking the stairs two at a time, grabbing a blanket from the foot of a bed, stepping into the library, helping them settle the dog on the hearth, gingerly, gently. Annie, ignored for a few moments. Then indignant. The firemen exiting. "Sorry about the mess ma'am." And Lester taking charge, ushering the two officers back through the house into the kitchen, guiding his mother, his arm around her waist, acknowledging the weight of it.

No. 4

It is late in the day when Lester finally reaches Emma, locked in her Manhattan apartment, snow still streaming in a dusky sky, silent and stunning. She doesn't grasp the news, doesn't understand. "Is she all right? Is she in the hospital?"

"No, no ma'am. No," Lester says. "She's gone, Miss Emma."

Standing against the wall in the long, windowless hallway that leads to her bedroom, closed in by its walls, Emma slides to the floor, squats there, her head bent down, one hand on her forehead, transporting herself to Delaware, trying to imagine the place. Annie and Lester. She hasn't seen them in more than two years. Her grandmother out walking the dog. Dead.

"How's your mom holding up?" Those are the words she chooses. "Is she okay?" she asks. Lester is reassuring, patient, explaining about the police, the weather, the turmoil. Emma listens, but does not hear. The questions come in waves. Logistical questions. How can I get down there in this storm? When do I need to go? What do I need to do? But not, how did this happen? That question doesn't occur to her, to any of them. It seems straightforward enough. Emma asks only if it's snowing there. Just getting the facts straight. "Yes, ma'am, we got a bit of a blizzard going," he says.

"And she went out in this snow?"

"Not exactly. We think she musta gone out before it started. Early today. Took Flip with her."

A dog that could barely move, she thinks. "It's bad here too, Lester. Take your mother home," Emma says. "Just take her home. No need for her to stay. I'll get there as soon as I can." After she hangs up, she calls back quickly to get Lester's phone number, knowing what lies ahead. A trip. Planning a funeral. Meetings with the lawyer, the bankers. Visitors.

Her mind calls up the scene at the Quinn estate after her grandfather's burial. A swarm of them ringing the front bell, filling the house, men and women she didn't want to see, cared nothing for—the Balfours and their followers, company people, politicians, aging socialites clutching highball glasses and canapés, grazing at the dining table, crowding into the library, peering around every corner. Picking at her with questions so they could take away a piece of her. "I understand you're at Holton." "Why do we never see you?" "And how is your grandmother doing, dear?" Bereft, all Emma had wanted at the time was to see her grandfather's face once more. Barely 16, she was old enough to have a go at entertaining, to serve as mistress of the house, to play-act with her puffy face and dark sunglasses. "And where was her grandmother then?" she thinks. "Locked up somewhere in the web of rooms she called her chambers."

Lester calls back, asks about Flip. "Of course, take him with you," she says. "Is that going to work? Yes, yes, please." She does not relish the role she will have to play in this drama. And she doesn't have a clue when she will get to Delaware in this blizzard.

No. 5

Margaret Quinn's body lies in the city morgue and the big house stands empty, snowdrifts lapping at its edges like an Arctic moat, snow falling still. They come in the night, six men, maybe eight, pull around back in a white van with a blue logo, Delmarva Power and Light. They lumber out of the van, slowed by the foot-high snows, and let themselves in through the mudroom leaving their boots in orderly rows. Then they slip up the back stairs in stocking feet, UPS cartons wrapped in plastic clutched under their arms, cumbersome, unassembled, the edges clawing at the stairwell walls. They find James Quinn's study at the top of the stairs, the room beyond the back bath, the one with the double sinks, and draw the curtains tight across the row of windows overlooking the frozen lawn, the black sky flecked with falling snow like a scene on some pointillist

Christmas card. Working in silence, searching the walls inch-by-inch with gloved hands, they look for hidden storage, for secrets, emptying the drawers of the antique mahogany desk, pulling binders from bookshelves, moving stealthily, communicating only with hand signals and gestures, although it's not necessary with the city frozen, the house set well off the road.

Two men wrestle with the boxes, struggling to slide them together. A third steps in with a punishing nod to the others. They pack up maybe a dozen, carry them down the darkened stairway and into the mudroom with remarkable agility and speed. Otherwise, they leave the office just as it was, as if untouched. The photo of the man himself, tall and handsome in a double-breasted suit and fedora with Mrs. Quinn, shot in black and white, probably in the 1930s or early '40s, left on his desk. A primitive clay pot, obviously pinched by the fingers of a child, painted purple like some artifact from another world still beside it. When they finish, one man, indistinguishable from the others, goes through the room, making sure everything is back in its place. Before he closes up, he pulls a photograph from the bookshelf, a 3 x 5 of the team at Oak Ridge, arms thrown around each other's shoulders as if they were a close fraternity of brothers engaged in some harmless fun. He shoves it in his pocket, then notices a small photo in a silver frame on a side table—a pretty young woman in a long white dress, a diploma rolled up in her hand. He takes that one as well and hurries down the back stairs.

Exiting through the mudroom, he looks up at the four-car garage, sees the team dismantling the 20-foot ladder perched at its edge, where they've installed a surveillance device. It's after midnight. When they depart, fresh snow covers their footprints, their tire tracks, their very existence. The van leaves the Quinn estate through the front gates unnoticed, heads slowly down Miller's Lane and left on the Old Mill Road along the ravine where Roy Howard lies buried under two feet of snow. Then makes its way up Interstate 95 toward Philadelphia, creeping along the empty highway as the storm subsides.

No. 6

Langley, VA

At first it seemed like nothing. "Bad timing," they said, clueless. "Old lady probably never showed," they said. They had all made it into headquarters on Tuesday morning from apartments in DC and Arlington and bungalows off MacArthur Boulevard, wound their way on streets slick with ice along the river, across the Chain Bridge, down George Washington Parkway, crawling through ice and snow. "Worse in Delaware," they told each other. They sipped black coffee from Styrofoam cups, checked the weather report, watching the snowfall through thick, square, bullet-proof windows, pulling off boots and scarves and hats and gloves. "He'll make contact," they said. But still they hadn't heard from Roy Howard. As the day progresses, they try again to reach him on the car phone between the seats of the black Bronco, now covered with a foot of snow behind the old Balfour Mill. Periodically throughout the day, they check for messages on the main switchboard. Bill Kidman, then his associates, stepping away from more important matters. "He's probably stranded at some motel off I-95 somewhere," they agree. But still no word.

Kidman had responded to the original call from Margaret Quinn that wound through the switchboard to his office the week before. He'd brought Roy Howard into it. Career CIA, lean and lanky, with a long face and uncharacteristically long hair that curls slightly over his collar at the nape of his neck, Kidman is approaching fifty. A man with two children in college—one at the Academy—and a reputation as a straight-up kind of guy, Kidman had been skeptical about the operation from the start. "Sounds like she's a bit of a crackpot," he told his boss from the beginning. But, because of her name, her late husband, his file, the connection with Balfour, they'd gone forward with it. Told Roy, "She might be unreliable, but she's hardly dangerous. Humor her. Go with her plan."

Finally, toward the end of the day, Kidman calls Margaret Quinn's house directly, but there's no answer. No machine. Nothing. Then he contacts the police in Delaware, fishing around for information. "Quinn woman's dead," he tells his boss, a man named Schmidt who looks like he walked off the set of a TV police procedural, crew cut, puffy jowls, flat affect.

"Dammit," Schmidt says, standing behind his desk, the two of them behind closed doors. He says it again, his voice rising, "God Dammit"—pounding his fist on the desk before turning his back on Kidman, looking out the window onto the fields beyond, the snowfall lighter now. "Go on up there," he says, his back still to Kidman. "Take whoever you need."

Kidman doesn't move. "What we're gonna need is a chopper."

"Of course you will," Schmidt says, turning then, facing Kidman, speaking firmly. "Who knew? Who the fuck knew?"

"Everybody knew," Kidman says. Looking down at Schmidt's desk, he sees the cover of *Time* magazine—a cartoony image of the new CIA director Stansfield Turner flanked by that of a spy hovering in outer space watching the earth through a pair of binoculars. The headline: "The CIA: Mission Impossible."

"Have you read this thing?" Schmidt says, following Kidman's eyes.

"Yeah. Nothing I didn't already know," he says. The story is a round-up of the changes underway at the agency, a backlash against the series of scandals—assassination plots, covert activities, bizarre experiments with hallucinogens and biological weapons, and general incompetence—all exposed in the press and at the Church Committee hearings in the U.S. Senate.

"So this op," Schmidt says, "keep it under your hat."

"Probably a bit late for that," says Kidman.

No. 7

Quinn Estate

It's after eight when Emma wakes in the darkness of an unfamiliar room, the half-moon visible beyond the open curtains, uncommonly bright, reflected off the frozen landscape. The window seems in the wrong place altogether, as if her bed has somehow turned itself around in the night. And the bed itself feels tiny, makeshift, like a cot, her feet crammed in so tight beneath the covers, the bedding so snug that she can't move them. Her forehead damp with sweat, as her mind begins to slip into gear she realizes she's wearing her socks and street clothes and that she's in her childhood bedroom. Confused, she hears a faint tapping, sees the line of light at the foot of the door, recognizes Lester's voice—"Emma." More tapping, so gentle she finds it comforting. And again, the voice, "Miss Emma."

Shortly after her arrival, Emma had wanted to lie down, needed to rest. Or maybe Annie had taken one look at her and insisted. Emma couldn't recall. But she knew she had chosen her old bedroom, the one off the back stairs near Annie's room, not the grown-up bedroom in the front of the house with its four-poster bed and the bizarre antique case clock bearing the portrait of a Victorian woman on its face. It was maybe four or five in the afternoon when her train had arrived. Lester had been waiting at the entrance to Wilmington station under the iron railway overpass, where sooty mounds of snow lined the curb. He's 20 years her senior, old enough to have a real job in town running a paint store and a daughter in college who never comes around, doesn't care for the Quinns. But Lester still comes by to help his mother out. He's probably more familiar to Emma than any other man alive.

She hears the tapping again. "Come in," she says dizzy from a deep sleep, raising herself up on an elbow, throwing off the covers, remembering that her grandmother is dead.

She is awakening from a dream in which she was riding a sleigh down Miller's Lane behind two black horses, with Lester at the helm clutching the bridle. He wore a top hat and spats, and black-face on top of his black skin as if he were a parody of himself. Snow falling. As they approached the fieldstone gates, the entry to the Quinn estate, Emma saw her grandmother standing by the side of the road, dressed in a full-length mink coat and her signature triangular mink hat, the one she wore to church and holiday parties on those rare occasions when she left the house, her hands stuffed into a fur muff like something out of *Little Women*, and a long red silk scarf streaming skyward from around her neck. In the dream, as they passed through the front gates, Emma's grandmother began to rise slowly in the air, Flip barking maniacally at her heels. And as they proceeded up the front drive,

Lester flinging a whip in the air, they quickened their pace. Emma saw then that the house was gone, nothing more than a ruin, a foundation, Annie sitting on steps leading nowhere, snow all around, her head in her hands, weeping.

Lester stands at her doorway, a tray balanced on one arm, the light pouring in from the outer hall. "There's someone here for you, in the library," he says. "I'll set this in your grandpa's study. You just take your time."

When Emma appears at the door of the first-floor library, wrinkled and groggy, her supper half-eaten, she finds a man perched awkwardly on the Victorian sofa under the front windows, a narrow piece that can barely carry his weight, long-legged, leaning forward with his elbows on his knees. He is dressed in an overstuffed down coat and a plaid wool cap, the flaps pulled down over his ears, so he looks rather like he's about to embark on a goose hunt. As Emma enters the room, she's startled to see a second man, younger, red-haired and ruddy-faced, leaning beside the door frame in a faux leather jacket that looks like it's made of plastic, a shoulder holster exposed against his chest.

"Bill Kidman," says the older man in a friendly casual way, brushing off his pant legs as he rises from the sofa, extending his hand. By now, he and his people have been to the Wilmington police station, put a hold on Margaret Quinn's body and searched her belongings. Kidman was the first to notice the missing house keys. "Did she have her keys on her? Her wallet? Did you return them to the family?" Then, "Call them. Tell them her keys were never recovered. Ask about the wallet. Suggest that they get their locks changed. Don't make a big deal about it."

They'd found the black Bronco at the old Balfour Mill, a half-eaten donut on the passenger seat, a half-cup of coffee, frozen, stashed on the floor. But there was no sign of Roy Howard. And they'd located Emma, tracked her Amtrak reservation and knew full well she'd be at home. Even so, Kidman asks if she's the lady of the house and listens patiently as she introduces herself and explains the circumstances that have brought her home. He lets her finish, then mumbles condolences, asks how it happened. "Sick? An accident?" When he gets his answer, he asks for more. "Out in that storm? On foot?" Feigning incredulity, he finally says, "Any idea where she was going?" Testing Emma, watching her, trying to determine what she knows.

"Just out walking the dog," Emma responds, "apparently." She draws the word out, speaking in tone that is so aloof, so damn Mid-Atlantic that it would endear her to no one but the most sycophantic among us. Then she gathers herself up and, wrinkling her brow, she asks, "How can I help you?"

The man with the holster shifts. Emma turns, sounding more like herself, her other self, what she considers to be her real self. "What's with the gun?" she asks.

Kidman takes his time, pulls out his badge, speaks slowly. "We're federal agents, ma'am," he says.

She examines the badge as if that will explain everything. Then turns to the other man, the redhead. "You too," she tells him.

"Wilson?" Kidman says, nodding his way as if he's reminding a child of his manners.

"We're just doing our job ma'am," Wilson says, flipping open his badge.

"And what job is that?" she asks, unaware of the other two agents waiting outside in a black SUV, beyond the front portico.

"We found an out-of-state vehicle down the road, abandoned in the storm. Apparently," he says. "The driver is missing. We're canvassing the neighborhood."

She stiffens. "We couldn't be farther from the road. Surely they would have gone to one of the cottages for help." Then her brow wrinkles as if she's thinking through the matter. "I've just arrived," she says. "And no one's been here…since…for a few days."

She turns as if to escort them to the door. But the redhead at the doorway with the gun doesn't move, and Kidman presses on. "I don't want to alarm you. But we're investigating a crime. We think the driver of the vehicle could be somewhere in the vicinity. Do you mind if we search the grounds?"

The question itself makes her uncomfortable. Gathering her thoughts, she moves toward the fireplace. "Sit, please." She's circumspect then, speaking quietly. "We had a call from the police today. Before I even got here. It seems my grandmother's keys are missing.

We've had to change all the locks."

"Would you feel more comfortable if we searched the house?"

Emma follows Bill Kidman up the front stairs to the second floor. He's dispatched the others, with their weapons and two-way radios, throughout the house. He heads first to her old bedroom, at the top of the stairs, with its four-poster bed and the case clock with the Victorian portrait, the chiming clock, silenced when she'd finally insisted in her early teens. Annie has obviously prepared this room for her arrival; the bedside lamps switched on, giving off a soft amber light, the bed turned down, its crisp, white sheets snapped tight, pillows fluffed. "See if it looks like anything's missing," Kidman says, checking the closet.

The second floor is labyrinthine, each room connected to the next through a series of landings, closets, chambers. They continue along the west side of the house to a small landing with its Jack and Jill bath, where Kidman flings the shower curtain open dramatically, then moves on to the guestroom beyond. There, nothing has changed since the 1950s—twin beds, chintz curtains, a pair of matching armchairs and, framed above the beds, an elaborate sketch of a man and woman seated at either end of a banquet table, a dark image that had frightened Emma as a young girl. Kidman shines his flashlight under the beds, play-acting, awkward on his hands and knees. As he stands, the light flashes around the room.

They proceed to the attached dressing room, unfurnished, with its faded wall-to-wall carpet. This was Emma's domain, her safe room, where she played in solitude as a child with paper dolls and Brio trains and Barbies, until she tired of them. It remained her refuge as an adolescent where she would listen to LPs of old Broadway musicals dancing without a partner, watching herself in the mirror that covers the north wall, imagining herself as a grown woman, not at all sure what to expect, and where she had daydreamed as a teenager on summer break, home from school. A pair of milk crates jammed with record albums sit on the floor. Her record player and a stack of old forty-fives lie warped in yellowing sleeves on the radiator cover. A poster of The Beatles is taped to a wall between two windows. "Yours?" Kidman asks.

Rows of built-in drawers line one wall. At its center is the door to a walk-in closet that opens up to the back hall at the other side, like a secret passage. This is where she'd hid on endless, empty afternoons a few feet from her grandfather's study. Kidman turns the knob, pulls the drawstring light. And after they've searched Annie's small apartment, and Emma's childhood bedroom with its baby dolls and stuffed toys, the covers thrown back from her recent nap—"Yours?" he asks again—they move back toward the front of the house and she grows increasingly uncomfortable, finding no evidence that anything has been disturbed, feeling that Kidman is showing a good deal more interest in the scenery than in ferreting out a criminal.

In her grandfather's study, when Kidman moves to pull open a drawer in the mahogany desk, she reaches past him, snaps it shut, nearly pinching his fingers. "I doubt that your man is hiding in there," she says. She's not sure why this seems surreal, aside from the obvious fact that a federal agent has appeared out of the blue to search the house. It seems a charade. Yet the man himself seems competent, steady, self-assured.

A call comes in on his two-way radio. "Nothing in the basement," a voice crackles, adding almost as an afterthought to keep up the sham of it. "And the lady here says nothing's been disturbed." Emma imagines Annie then as intimidated, scared, exhausted. She leads Kidman, finally, through the dark hallway to the front rooms where Margaret Quinn lived, where her grandmother spent her days in bed in her dressing gown and a bed jacket year after year, rising only to join them for dinner. "Drugged, probably," Emma had thought as she grew older. As a girl, she was permitted in this inner sanctum only when accompanied by her grandfather. And when he died, it was no longer an issue because it didn't take long for her to stop coming home altogether.

Entering it now, she recognizes the familiar smell—a combination of stale perfume and tobacco smoke, suffocating. She opens her grandmother's jewelry box, the drawers in her vanity, sees no evidence of a burglary, a theft, an intrusion of any kind. She sits on the edge of the bed, grounding herself, and motions toward her grandmother's closet, the long corridor of a closet that Annie had searched in vain a few days before. "You'll want to check that," she says, nodding. "It runs the length of the room. You'll come out on the other end." She speaks softly.

"Federal agents," Kidman calls out sharply, startling her, as he opens the closet door, pulling out his gun like a cop in a crime series. He spends a good five minutes rustling through the closet, finally emerging at the other end.

In the meantime, the ruddy-faced, red-haired boy of a man, Wilson, the one with the holster who is just doing his job, appears. "Attic's clear," he says, looking for Kidman. Together they walk the length of the room toward the foot of the closet, toward Margaret Quinn's sitting room. Kidman is already in there, flipping through the items on the long pine table set against one wall.

If the bedroom, dark and airless, reeked of illness and death and emptiness and loss, the sitting room reeks of insanity. Underneath the table are foot-high stacks of old magazines and newspapers, hundreds of them, its surface covered with clippings in fraying piles each topped with a glass paperweight. Emma freezes, taking it in. A faded flesh-colored manila folder on top of one pile is marked "1972–1974." Another marked simply MUNICH. Four news stories are stuck to the wall with rusty yellow thumbtacks. She scans the boldface headlines—"Terror in Mogadishu," "The Fate of Lufthansa Flight 181," "The Raid at Entebbe"— and leans in to get a closer look at the fourth, a glossy page ripped from *Time* magazine, mostly text, with a small black and white photo of an explosion in Beirut circled in magic marker.

"What's all this?" Kidman asks. He wants these papers, wants the entire contents of the room, but he doesn't let on, contains himself.

"No idea," she says, as if it's nothing.

He lets out a guttural sound, a "humph." The two stand facing each other, neither one speaking or moving, as if they can't imagine what to do next. There are no more rooms for him to explore, nothing else for him to see except the adjacent bath, the one with the double sinks and aging pink and green tiles, and a powder room that Mrs. Quinn called her own.

After the men have gone outside and Emma has reassured Annie, and they've shared a cup of tea in the kitchen—Emma, Lester and Annie—the three of them barely speaking, the soppy tea bags sitting on the edge of their plates as they watch the four intruders search the grounds, beams from government-issue flashlights shooting across the window for a good hour. And after Kidman has knocked on the back door and told them everything's quiet and left his card—*William J. Kidman, Director, Special Projects*—Emma ascends the front stairs. She opens the door to her grandmother's bedroom, compelled to revisit the bizarre collection of news clippings.

In the days that follow, she will take Annie up to the room, grill her on its contents. "After your grandfather died," Annie tells her, "that's when it started. And after they put her on that new medicine. The lithium." And Emma will sort through the files and stacks of folders and, later, pack them in boxes and send them on to New York, each paperweight carefully wrapped in tissue, each article preserved. She'll flip through the magazines and find pages torn out and turned down at the edges and finally read a handful of the clippings before they disappear.

But on this night, unnerved by her grandmother's death, by the men with their guns and this terrorist archive, she shuts off the light in her grandmother's study and moves through the big, old pink and green bathroom toward the back hall. She opens the door to the full-length closet, the one that leads to the dressing room, her childhood playroom, and leans against the closet wall and slides to the floor, closing herself in. She envisions herself hiding in this space so many years before, listening for her grandfather's footsteps, jumping out, surprising him as he left his office, being lifted in his arms, swinging in the air, laughing. "How's my little pumpkin?" he would say. And sometimes he would sneak in through the closet and surprise her at play. She hears someone in the hall beyond, coming up the back stairs. She sits, unmoving, barely breathing, until she realizes it is Lester bringing up her things. She listens as he moves toward the front of the house, to the big bedroom, the one with the disturbing clock with the face of the Victorian lady. She doesn't stop him, doesn't emerge, just sits for a time in stillness, breathing, waiting, listening.

No. 8

The Old Mill Road

It falls to Bill Kidman to notify the next of kin, after they find Roy Howard's body under the snowdrifts in the ravine. Roy was a new recruit, a young guy filling in for some of the more experienced personnel they'd lost in the purge. The Carter administration was cutting back on everything—people, weapons, covert ops. "He's going to dismantle the whole fucking company," Schmidt had said at some point when the cutbacks started.

Kidman is baffled. It had seemed like such a straightforward operation—a woman calls in with a crazy story about some conspiracy. "You let her pick the time and place," he remembers telling Roy.

"What the hell was I thinking? Maybe the whole thing was a set-up." That's what's going through his mind now as he walks back and forth between the Old Mill and the truss bridge with the recovery team. "Check inside the mill," he tells them, irritable, grasping at straws, still recovering from the sight of Roy's body, frozen, broken, lying in the melting snow in the mud with a hole in his head. They'd had to rappel down the ravine, seal him in a body bag, jury rig a set of cables from the old bridge to pull his body up, police cars cordoning off the whole area to keep traffic out, Kidman bowing his head as they brought him up.

Roy Howard had been destined for an assignment in Egypt or Cyprus, not at all happy about these options. He'd specialized in Eastern Europe and Russia, was eager to get over there. That's what he'd told Kidman—that he wanted a station overseas. London, he was hoping. Or Berlin. Maybe the Balkans. But the agency had been talking about sending him to the Middle East. "That's where things are happening," Schmidt had told him in the fall when he signed on. "We need a junior in Cairo." But Roy Howard knew nothing of the Middle East. He'd studied German and Russian. Grappled with the Russian. Failed at it, really. He was an ace shooter, good at getting people to talk, good at retaining information, analytical. His experience at West Point had served him well, beefed him up, allowed him to bypass Vietnam, drawn him in to field operations.

On the preceding Sunday, Roy had apparently done his reconnaissance. The odometer and the gas tank told them that. Then he'd spent Sunday night, his last night on earth, at a Howard Johnson's set among strip malls and service businesses—Firestone Tires, Carpet King, American Bath and Tile—a few miles away from the Quinn estate, although it could just as well have been another country. Based on their visit to the motel, they'd determined that he'd dined on a burger and fries. That he hadn't taken any calls or made any. That he'd retired early, apparently watched a TV movie. He was 28 years old, fully prepped for service to his country, dead in the woods in Delaware of all places. Kidman is angry, at himself mostly. "What a waste," he says to no one in particular.

When they're done, as he walks to the foot of Miller's Lane, he turns to a cop and asks, "Who the hell lives here anyway?"

The policeman takes him literally, surveying the row of cottages along Miller's Lane. "See those houses. They're all owned by Balfour Chemical. Homes for the young executives," the cop tells him. "I hear they're not allowed to live here until they've had their first kid."

Kidman scoffs at the idea.

"No, really," the policeman says.

Kidman tells his ruddy-faced sidekick to visit each one of the cottages, see if anybody saw anything. Then he climbs into an unmarked car. "Get me outta here," he tells the driver.

He knows if Margaret Quinn was delivering anything tangible—anything meaningful, anything real—it's gone. The killers have it, he's sure of that. He heads down to Virginia to meet with Roy Howard's parents, to deliver the news personally.

No. 9

For three days, oblivious to anything going on in the outside world, Emma has been culling through drawers, closets, entire rooms, opening cupboards, surveying bookshelves, sifting through boxes, stirring up memories. The last remaining Quinn, she had, of course, inherited just about everything—the estate overlooking Miller's Lane, the cabin in Saranac, and, with them, more china and silver and antique furniture and high-ball glasses and jewelry and cutlery than any one person could ever need. It falls to her to go through it all, to set the estate sale in motion, to let go of things. By Saturday afternoon, weary of it, she has made her way to the expansive attic, lit by a half-dozen clerestories and a handful of raw bulbs. In one trunk she finds all the dresses her mother had worn to all the parties during her run-up to adulthood. In another, nothing but riding gear and crops, jodhpurs and velveteen hats in every size imaginable, tracing her mother's development as measured by the size of her head. Late in the day, she sits in the grey light of the attic on the edge of an abandoned round, marble-topped coffee table, holding a single small black hunt cap, pondering her legacy.

Emma was five when her parents died after some sort of holiday ball downtown at the Balfour Hotel, but she knew, from Annie, from the recollections of others passed around in comments they thought she never heard, and most directly from her grandmother, that her father was a drinker. On the night of the accident, he had been drinking well into the early morning hours, long after the ball was over, at some tavern out in Centerville, a great distance from the Balfour Hotel. It had happened as they made their way home, finally, at three or four in the morning, on one of those narrow back roads that swung through the woods outside town, the hilly forested private preserve of the Balfours and their heirs and various cousins. There was no other vehicle involved, just the little silver sports car. "I knew when he got that damned toy that it would be the end of him," Emma had overheard her grandmother say. But he took their daughter with him, wrapped her around a tree in her grey-green ball gown two days before Christmas. And for that there would be no forgiveness.

For their funeral, Emma's grandfather had bought her a black wool coat with a matching hat and a new pair of Mary Janes, shiny patent leather, tight around her feet. Sitting in the attic, twirling the riding cap between her fingers, she recalls sitting in the front row of the church, her feet bound in those tiny shoes and how she yearned to take them off one at a time and throw them at the man up at the front, the one speaking in that gentle monster voice. And to run from them, all of them, in her stocking feet. But she sat frozen in the wooden pew between her grandfather and Annie, determined not to cry. Two monumental caskets stood at the foot of the aisle, so close she could have reached out and touched them.

She pictures the men in their white gloves, their fingers slipping through leather handles, lifting the caskets, their slow walk out of her line of vision. Her grandmother, wearing sunglasses in the winter, standing over her, speaking to Annie—"Just take her home"—raising her head as if her neck had been stretched in some preternatural way, settling that infernal mink hat around her head. Her grandfather holding his wife by the elbow, nodding toward Annie. "It's just too cold," he said. "Elvin will be out front. Take her home. After everyone's left the sanctuary." Then him scooping her up awkwardly from the pew, her skirt puffing out around her, crushed against the softness of his cashmere coat, as if she alone were holding him up, smothered by the weight of him. She recalls, quite clearly, the look on his face—a combination of grief and grace. Somehow, as he set her back down for the eternal wait with Annie, as the church spewed its contents out into the cold, he managed a wink.

Before the service, before they'd even left the house, when Annie had been buttoning her coat, she recalls her grandmother appearing at the foot of the front stairs, saying, "Now remember, we don't cry in public or make a display of our feelings." She was standing a good distance from Emma, pulling her long mink from the coat closet, looking down at her. "Exercise some self-control, dear," she'd said. Emma realized later when she was grown and grappling with the memory, that her grandmother was probably just steeling herself.

Afterwards, when all those people came to the house, Emma had hidden on the back stairs off the kitchen with the door shut tight in the half-darkness, protected within the stairwell walls, clutching whatever she had pulled out of the boxes scattered about in her new room, a bear, a rabbit, a baby doll. Annie peeking through the door to the stairwell now and then, to deliver a tea sandwich, a slice of cake, a champagne flute filled with ginger ale, saying, "Look what we have here," trying to make something good of it.

"No more," Emma says. She says it out loud, sitting in the attic on the marble-top table with the riding cap set on her lap, as if to the house itself. "No more." But she is not finished. When the day comes to an end, she retires early to the four-poster bedroom and begins to thread her way through the news clippings from her grandmother's sitting room, a bourbon by her bed, rising occasionally to stand at her window, cracking it open, smoking a cigarette, her grief reflected in the glass.

Upright against a pair of goose down pillows, sitting cross-legged on the bed, she sets down the manila folder, "1972–1974" scrawled across the front. She unfolds whole pages from *The New York Times* and spreads them out around her. She stacks the news stories clipped carefully from *The Times* and *Time* magazine, some of them with multiple pages, stapled together, fraying at the edges. She scans the headlines: "Terror at School." "The Bitter Road from Bloody Sunday." "Arab Guerrillas Kill 31 in Rome." "Grenades Hurled." "Belfast Bombings." Then she reads the stories, one by one. In Ireland, "bombs," it says, "carefully calculated to kill as many people as possible…more casualties than any other attack since the fighting over Northern Ireland began five years ago." In Dublin, during rush hour, set by Protestant militants. Shoppers, babies. Two girls "window-shopping…blown through a window…their bodies fused together by the blast." An abundance of disturbing details. Graphic photographs. She tries to imagine her grandmother in her bathrobe on a Sunday morning, clipping away with her sewing scissors. "Like some *tricoteuse* in revolutionary France," she thinks, "her knitting." And the irony of the analogy does not escape her.

On the front page of *The Times,* dated May 15, 1974, marked with the thick black scrawl of an X, she reads this story, these words: "A day of terror ended in this northern town this evening with a savage, 10-minute burst of gunfire and grenade explosions that killed three Arab terrorists and 16 of the high-school students they were holding hostage." She pauses periodically, sipping her bourbon, staring at the face in the case clock across from her bed, the woman in her feathery hat and brocade shawl, absorbing the details: 1974. An attack in Ma'alot. Israeli students sleeping in the school, on an outing, a holiday, the remembrance of the founding of the state. Three Arabs demanding the release of 20 prisoners. Seventy students wounded. Sixteen dead. A guerrilla, wounded by

Israeli soldiers, half-dead himself, "turned his automatic weapon on the students, spraying the second-story classroom indiscriminately," it says. She reads on. "The screams of the terrified teenagers could be heard a hundred yards away as the shooting erupted."

But there is more to this rampage, more to the story, as if that weren't enough, spread across another page deeper in the newspaper. En route to one massacre, there had been others. The marauders had stopped a van full of Arab women on the road to Ma'alot headed home from their night shift. Two women shot dead. And the men had gone door-to-door in the small town, masquerading as Israeli security forces, and been admitted to the home of a young family. The parents and two of their children—a boy, a girl, four and five—gunned down in their nightclothes before the sun had risen. A toddler, a baby really, a boy, discovered later, alive, hidden under a bed. From there, they had moved on to the school, "greeting the janitor with a cheerful good morning," the story says, asking if there were students in the school, coming upon them. All the details laid out in black and white on the inner pages of the paper. As if this had never happened before. As if it would never happen again. There are pictures, photos of students being carried from the scene. A young woman, bloodied, crying out, in the arms of Israeli soldiers.

The same photo—of the young woman—appears on a magazine cover in the file. *Mid-East Massacres*, it screams. Bright red splotches dot the slick cover, as if the page itself is bleeding. And her grandmother had carefully cut the edges of the story, stapled it to the cover. She reads it through to its end. "The next day Israeli jets retaliated with deliberate strikes against Palestinian refugee camps and commando bases in Lebanon. Their bombs and rockets left 50 people dead and more than 200 wounded." Rising from her bed, she lights another cigarette, moves to the window.

These images, these stories, now spread across the Florentine matelassé on Emma's bed, meticulously gathered up and filed away by Margaret Quinn, chronicle a change that has been under way in the world for some time now. Emma is struck by the fact that, in its mass, its completeness, it is a stunning documentation of a new reality. She realizes, too, that she has only the vaguest recollection of some of these events. Of course, she remembers Munich. And certain hijackings stand out in her memory more than others. In Ireland, there had been so much terror that the bombings blur together. But she remembers Ma'alot, including the details—or perhaps because of the details. She checks the date. The end of May. 1974. Nearly four years earlier. She would have been at Columbia at the time, working on her thesis, teaching, the school year winding down. In May, she would have been heading off to Saranac for the summer, carrying her research with her. She tries to place it in the context of her own life and her grandmother's, standing at the window, blowing smoke into the cold night. Was this the start of the summer that she'd sat in front of the television set, lakeside, fans whirring, absorbed in the Watergate hearings?

She's not sure. No, no, she tells herself. That was 1973. In 1974, she would have been pressed to finish her thesis, to get her Ph.D., to secure her position in the History Department, just as she is pressed now to finish her book, to get tenure. In '72, she would have been distracted by Vietnam, the escalation of the war in Cambodia. In the spring of that year, Columbia had shut down, however briefly. There had been marches, protests. She tries to remember whether she'd been back to Delaware in 1972 or '73 or '74, whether she'd even seen her grandmother during those years. She tries to imagine Margaret Quinn amassing this vast library and what exactly she was up to. Was it just another aspect of her insanity or was it something else altogether? "It began after your grandfather died," Annie had said, "after she started taking the lithium."

No. 10

Langley, VA

It is a small meeting, private, held in the department chief's office on Sunday morning. Three men—Bill Kidman, Kidman's boss, Carl Schmidt, and Schmidt's boss, the chief of the department, who sits behind a formidable desk in front of his office window facing the others, a white-haired white man, grandfatherly, dressed in a grey, cable-stitched wool sweater vest as if he's come directly from a fireside chat. Kidman is in need of rest. Schmidt seems uncomfortable, shifting around in his chair, overdressed in a black suit.

"So, we've got a dead agent and a dead woman," Kidman says, laying things out. "Roy Howard took a bullet in the head. Found him buried in the snow at the bottom of a ravine. The Quinn woman took a nasty fall. Obvious hit. Police have been very cooperative. Looks like a scooter, motorcycle, maybe even a bike."

"You gotta be kidding," the Chief says, swiveling in his chair to face Kidman.

"Autopsy results aren't in yet. Might be more to it. We don't have much to work with at this point. Shoes. Street clothes. They left the poor woman's coat on, but the pockets were empty. Took her keys, if she had them." Kidman hesitates for an instant. "So let's hope she was smarter than we thought."

"Well, tear everything apart and put it all under a microscope," the Chief says. "Maybe we'll get lucky. Jewelry? Watch? Search everything for microdots."

Schmidt looks up skeptically.

"Why not?" the Chief says. "Tools of the time."

"She hardly seems like a pro, sir," Schmidt says.

"Well, she seems a lot more like it now that she's dead, doesn't she?"

"Right," Schmidt says, although he sounds unconvinced.

"So, what else you got?" the Chief says, turning back to Bill Kidman.

"We went through the house. Met the granddaughter. Quinn woman had a pretty extensive collection of news stories, recent stuff—uprisings, hijackings, bombings, that sort of thing—spread out all over her study. I got some images. Couldn't go through the man's office... study...whatever...on the second floor. But Wilson's still up there, getting a search warrant."

"Good." The Chief leans back in his chair, throws his hands behind his head, speaking into the air. "So, who made this mess?"

Kidman defers to Schmidt, who clears his throat before he speaks. "We're going through the old files, putting together a short list. Doing a full workup on her late husband. It crosses agency lines, so it could take a little time."

"What about the leak?" the Chief asks.

Kidman jumps in. "What leak? Everyone on the floor knew about this. It was a nothing. A distraction."

"We totally misread the situation, sir," Schmidt says, but the Chief ignores him. "Let's talk about the girl," he says.

Kidman pulls out a file, refers to his notes. "Hard to get a read on her. Obviously to the manner born. But she's no dummy. Teaches at Columbia University. History, of all things. And she was raised by her grandparents. The parents died in a car wreck when she was a kid. So she's the last of them, and that means something." He stops for a minute, shuffles through some papers, goes on. "She's headed back to New York today on the Metroliner. First time she's left the place since she arrived. The housekeeper and her son were in and out. He drove off with a truckload of boxes on Saturday. They're shipping to her apartment. She had two visitors in four days. Lawyer, a man named George Treadwell. And someone named Martin Simon. Old guy. We followed him back to his place. Looked like a friggin' chateaux in the South of France. Anyway, we're working on them."

"Good. Keep me posted," the Chief says. "And stay on the girl."

No. 11

Upper West Side, Manhattan

No milk. No coffee. That's what rolls through Emma's head when she wakes in her apartment on Monday morning. She left Delaware with much unresolved—the police still holding Mrs. Quinn's body to confirm the cause of death; the funeral postponed altogether in favor of some sort of memorial service. "Perhaps down the road," George Treadwell had said, much to her relief. She knows she has to go back on Friday to finish up with the estate, the packing, matters at the bank. For now, she's grateful to be back in New York, in her apartment, the place she considers home.

Her suitcase sits open on her bedroom floor, overflowing with clothes, her standbys—jeans, cords, turtleneck sweaters, black, brown and more black—wrinkled, unwashed, unwearable. She digs deep in her closet for something, anything that's clean. Chooses a long black skirt, a cashmere sweater, never worn, sent by her grandmother one Christmas past, knots her hair behind her head, clips on a pair of silver earrings. Looking in the mirror, she sees a woman she doesn't recognize, uncharacteristically polished, like the socialite she might have been had she grown up in another time, before Germaine Greer and marijuana and Woodstock, and before Vietnam and Selma and Attica, all of which even Holton-Arms and Bryn Mawr couldn't fully insulate her from.

On her way out, she checks the answer machine, set on a small table between her bedroom and the bath at the foot of her hallway. Now, for the first time, she hears the message Annie left for her a week earlier. The automated voice speaks first. "Monday, February 6, 1:35 p.m." Then, "Miss Emma. I can't find your grandmother. She seems to have wandered off. I called the police." Then a pause. "This is Annie Daniels speaking." Then the second message, voice-stamped 2:46 p.m. on the same day, Annie sounding frantic. Emma can make out only random phrases. The message is long. "It's me again. She must have left…Flip is not here." Then a jumble of words. "She didn't tell me. I don't know… Where would she go?" Then something about the police and "they haven't come yet." Finally, she seems to collect herself and slow down a bit. "It's snowing bad, Miss Emma. Please call me. I'm afraid something terrible has happened." Emma stops the recorder, struck by the turmoil expressed in Annie's voice. When it kicks back in, she hears a brief message from her department head, obviously from the week before: "Emma, it's Donald. I'm sorry to hear about your grandmother. Take the week if you need to. I imagine we'll be closed most of it anyway." Then another message, this one from yesterday, Sunday, that consists of nothing more than a long stretch of silence followed by a dial tone.

She erases all of them then throws on a down jacket, tosses her backpack over her shoulder and heads out into a clear, brisk morning.

As she makes her way up West End Avenue toward the intersection with Broadway, a man follows twenty yards behind her. He stays with her for nearly 20 blocks, until she slips into the Chock Full o'Nuts at 114th Street. Then he picks her up again across Broadway, inside the gates that mark the entry to Columbia. He fits easily into the scene, lean and angular, dressed in a pair of faded jeans, a heavy sweater, a navy blue pea coat. In the days following what is now being called The Great Blizzard, the snow has dissolved save a few gritty piles here and there, and he wears shiny black loafers. His dark hair is slicked back, held in place by a Yankees ball cap, his sunglasses expensive—all of which gives him the oddly mismatched look of a Middle Easterner dressed like an American and accessorized by a European fashion house, which is to say he could easily be in International Studies, Economics, the business school. His name is Serge. He is unobtrusive, keeping his distance, tracking her as she heads across the campus to Fayerweather, to her department, to classes.

Toward the end of the day, at close to five o'clock, he reappears at the top of the Low Library steps overlooking the quad. He waits for nearly an hour as the sky darkens, until Emma emerges from Fayerweather and descends the steps, merging into a swell of people. Hands jammed in pockets, necks wrapped in scarves, they're heading for dormitories and dinners, or beyond the university's main gate to apartments on side streets up and down Broadway, over to Riverside Drive or Barnard or out into the city. Crossing Broadway, he loses her for a moment, stranded on the median when the light changes, traffic surging in both directions, crushed by the crowd. Emma is oblivious, unaware that he's watching as she brushes past a bottleneck at the subway entrance at 114th and turns left, weaving along the crowded sidewalk in the dark, her backpack bouncing on her shoulder. Breathless, he catches up beyond 114th and watches as she turns into a bar midway down the next block. The West End, it's called. A neighborhood place.

No. 12

Chevy Chase, MD

Two cars are parked in the driveway of an oversized, shingle-style bungalow in this cushy DC suburb on this Monday evening—a cream-colored Volvo wagon and a silver BMW, which is very nearly jutting out into the street. In the first floor study, Hugh Grenville is leaning against the edge of his desk. He wears running shorts, a U.S. Naval Academy sweatshirt, flip-flops. A distinguished-looking man, Grenville is tall and thin, greying at the temples with an aristocratic nose and a long face—made imperfect by a large reddish-purple birthmark that runs down the bridge of his nose and across his right cheek.

He is sitting sideways at his desk, a habit he's taken on to minimize the impact of the birthmark. Behind him, the plantation shutters are closed tight. A woman sits across from him, her brownish hair in a pixie cut flecked with silvery streaks, her legs crossed at the knee. She wears a Chanel jacket, a navy skirt, heels. She could be his wife, but she's not. She's a mid-career bureaucrat. And it's late, well after cocktail hour. The speakerphone is on and Grenville is doing the talking. "So, was it worth it?"

A man's voice comes through the speaker: "I believe so." To an American's ear, the accent sounds like a mix of German and French, and the tone is soft, mild-mannered, almost gracious. "We did stop her," he says.

Grenville is obviously irritated. "Seems to me you stirred things up pretty good in the process." The woman is listening, silent, her eyes darting from the phone back to Grenville's profile. He continues, "And you found nothing, am I right?"

"No," the voice comes back.

"Meaning, yes, you found nothing. Correct? What about the hat? The mink hat?"

"Nothing," the caller replies. The calm and the patience in his voice are audible.

"And your people went through her pockets. Everything. Right?"

"Yes," and, after a brief silence, from the speakerphone, "Perhaps she was carrying it all in her head."

The woman puts up her fist, flicks her wrist back and forth. Grenville ignores her. "You better hope it was all in her head," he says.

The woman signals Grenville again, pulling at each of her fingertips. Grenville rolls his eyes. "Okay," he says. "We want the keys, the hat, the gloves, everything, so we can scan it all. Now, what about those files?"

"They arrived in our Philadelphia office. Perhaps you want them destroyed?"

"We'll see," Grenville says, but he's shaking his head, indicating to the woman that he has no intention of destroying any of James Quinn's files. She jots something on a piece of paper. Passes it to Grenville. "One thing," he says into the speakerphone. "Turns out there was another office. The woman had an office, a study or something in the house, filled with information. We think the girl has it. In New York."

"We can take care of that."

"Good," Grenville says, rising from his chair to take a turn around the room. He looks up at a painting over his mantle, an oil of geese in flight. The woman is fluffing her hair, a gesture that has no meaning, but throws Grenville off, distracts him. The voice comes back over the speakerphone. "Okay. We will take care of the girl."

Grenville turns back toward the desk, visibly irritated, his face reddening around his birthmark, very nearly throwing himself at the speakerphone. "For God's sake, don't hurt the girl. We've got problems enough," he says. "Just get the documents."

"I understand," the caller says. He sounds unphased, almost cordial.

But Grenville doesn't let up. "You know—they're not happy they lost a man. That was a major fuck-up. In fact, the whole thing is looking like a major fuck-up."

There is only silence on the other end of the line.

"We'll talk in a few days," Grenville says. "See where we are." Then he holds down the receiver, disconnecting the line.

No. 13

The West End is dark, as always, loud and full of students. Emma moves toward the back, past the bar. This is where they congregate, a random mix of historians and scholars—usually on Mondays, always on Thursdays. To drink, share war stories, compare notes, kvetch. There are nine at the table sharing two pitchers of beer when she arrives, obviously engaged in a heated discussion. "This is going to be big," someone is saying. "A lot of people are going to be very disappointed." Emma spots a friend and colleague—Will Short—at the head of the table. They've known each other since graduate school. Lean and gawky with wire-rimmed glasses and floppy blond hair, he has an unassuming charm about him. He rises when he sees her. "Everyone's all worked up tonight, I'm afraid," he says. "How are you?" He offers her his seat, pulls another chair up to the table. Emma's glad to see Jean Buchman, in American History, from Barnard. As she settles in between the two of them, Professor Buchman squeezes Emma's left hand and stops for an instant, whispers, "So sorry to hear about your grandmother."

The three men sitting opposite are deeply engaged in a discussion. Emma recognizes two of them—an English historian, Oxford-educated and somewhat distinguished-looking, with a hearty appetite for Scotch. The Oxford Don, they call him. And Jim Stanton, stout and white-haired, a lefty and a notoriously passionate soul. He too teaches American history. Stanton and the Oxford Don are regulars. Sitting between the two of them is a man Emma doesn't know, has never seen before. Jim Stanton is talking. "Shouldn't be a surprise to anyone. He basically laid the whole thing out in that *New York Review* piece a few years ago. Debunked the idea that Hiss was framed."

"He did a damn good job of pissing everybody off, as I recall," the Don says.

"Well, he couldn't manage to send the manuscript around for any kind of vetting," Stanton says. "That didn't help."

"Ah, but now we have something to work with," the third man says, the man Emma doesn't recognize. Then he hesitates a moment. He's quite obviously the focus of all the attention. "An advance copy," he announces.

Stanton looks mystified. "Impossible."

"*Perjury,*" the new fellow says, smiling, nodding his head up and down. "All 700-plus pages of it."

The Oxford Don lets out a howl. "You rascal. You fox," he cries, and he and this fellow—this man Emma has never seen before—throw back their heads, laughing. Their beer mugs clacking, they toast one another.

Jean Buchman leans into Emma. "They're talking about Allen Weinstein's new book on the Hiss case. Coming out in April."

Emma nods. "I figured as much," she says. It's not Emma's specialty, but she knows the basics of the case—that Alger Hiss was accused of spying for the Soviets back in the day and that he's maintained his innocence for 30 years. She knows that quite a few of her colleagues at Columbia believe him and that this new book purports to prove his guilt.

"I don't imagine it's that difficult to get an advance copy at this point," Buchman whispers. And as the men lower their steins and the brouhaha subsides, this new fellow reaches his hand across the table toward Emma. "Mac McLearan," he says. Given the noise level, what she hears is very little—a deep voice and an accent—Scottish? Welsh? Irish? she wonders. What she sees, on the other hand, is someone uncommonly self-assured, a compelling alpha male with a rugged, of-the-people look to him and a broad, genuine smile.

"This is Emma," the Don says. "Emma Quinn. Columbia. European History."

The man stands to shake her hand. "Of course. I know your work," he says. "I read your piece on Rosa Luxembourg in *The Russian Review*."

"Mac's here from Edinburgh for the semester," the Don offers by way of an introduction.

"At Columbia?" Emma asks, intrigued. He seems not to hear. Back in his seat, he leans forward, across the table, toward her. "At Columbia?" she says, louder this time. And he shakes his head no. "In the States. Doing some research."

"He's looking at the Hiss case from a new angle," the Don tells Emma, then raising his voice, "And now we learn he has a copy of Weinstein's book. Very hard to get your hands on that, I hear."

Jean Buchman can't resist jumping in. "Not anymore apparently," she says. "Did anyone see the story in this week's *Time*? They gave it a nice piece of real estate. And a big headline." She pauses to make sure she has everyone's attention. "Hiss," she says. "Guilty as charged."

"Well, I don't believe a word of it," says Stanton. "I mean really. Nixon? Hoover? McCarthy? The whole damn thing was a sham. You know it was."

Then Emma's friend Will leaps into the fray. "Don't be so sure," he says. "The fact that his accusers were squirrely hardly exonerates him." Mac sits in silence, but the rest of them erupt into a chorus of boos and Will all but recants, saying facetiously, "Well, we all know there was plenty of evidence that Hiss fraternized with known communists." He puts a stress on the words "fraternized" and "known," with a hint of irony.

"Known communists," Stanton exclaims, drawing the word out to great effect as if he's describing the boogeyman, raising his hands in the air and wiggling his fingers, comically. And they all laugh.

"Well, we wish you the best of luck in this great endeavor, my friend," the Don says, turning to this new fellow. And they all clink their glasses and the conversation begins to break down as they turn their attention to other subjects and the prospect of having a few more beers. By their deference, it's become clear to Emma that this man, this Mac, is someone important. And for the next hour or so, until Emma departs, she's conscious of every move he makes, as he seems to be conscious of her as well.

No. 14

The next morning, when Emma arrives at Fayerweather, she finds the historian from Edinburgh, a man she knows only as Mac, leaning up against her office door. He has a pair of bifocals perched on the edge of his nose, his legs crossed at the ankle, and is absorbed in a thin, hardcover book. As she draws closer she can see the shadow of a day-old beard. He doesn't look up, and there is no way around him. She fumbles for her keys, rustling through her backpack. He ignores her, as if caught up in his reading.

"Morning," she says finally, jangling her keys in the air. "My office," she nods, signaling toward the door. He's tall, taller than she'd realized, and looks a bit older in the light of day but no less compelling. She guesses he's in his mid-forties, maybe a bit older.

"Ah. Yes. I know. Nice to see you," he says with a certain warmth, a nod of his head as if they're friends.

She steers the key into the lock, feeling the force of his weight on the door. Together, they fairly tumble into the room, a space so small that, as the door swings open, it jams against the edge of her desk trapping the two of them in a triangle of space. Their bodies almost touching, they jockey awkwardly as she drops her bag on the desktop and squirms around the edge of it to accommodate him. He towers over her. "Won't you come in?" she says. If he detects her sarcasm, he doesn't show it. He looks around the cramped space, surveying the books that line its walls. The three volumes of Karl Marx's *Capital* in hardcover. Kropotkin's *In French and Russian Prisons.* Solzhenitsyn's *Gulag Archipelago,* in Russian. The poster of Rosie the Riveter hanging beside her desk. "Looks like you and I have a lot in common," he says. Then, shifting gears, softening, "I'm sorry to hear of your grandmother's death." He bends forward slightly as he talks.

"Yes. Well, I appreciate that."

He ducks out into the hallway, grabs a plastic chair and pulls it into the office. "Please have a seat," she says, smiling. He flips the thing around and sets his elbows on the chair back as he sits. She remains standing.

"Well, this may be a bit awkward," he says. Emma raises an eyebrow, wondering where on earth he's going. "But I'm hoping you'll be able to help me with my research."

She hesitates, taken aback. "If you mean your research on this Hiss business, I think it falls outside my wheelhouse." But she's curious now, because there's a palpable energy between them.

"Well, your grandfather worked for Balfour Chemical. Am I right?" he says, and she stiffens. "He worked on the Project—with Balfour— didn't he?"

Still standing, she averts her eyes downward to a yellow legal pad on her desk and, in a noncommittal sort of way, begins to leaf through the pages, feigning distraction, waiting silently for an explanation. She knows full well her grandfather was involved in the Manhattan Project. "Peripherally," he'd told her, when she'd raised questions about the atomic bomb, about his involvement, as a schoolgirl. He'd explained matter-of-factly, that the company had been asked to join the effort. And he'd expressed a certain pride in the role he'd played in ending the war, using phrases she understood and remembered and repeated as a young girl about defending our country, defeating our enemies, saving thousands maybe millions of lives. She's having difficulty imagining why that's relevant. But then he says, "There seems to be some evidence that Balfour was involved in the Hiss case."

She is brusque when she looks up and finally speaks. "Have you talked with them?"

"With Balfour?" he says, smiling, raising his eyebrows. "And how do you think that would go?" She gives him a shrug, a grin, an opening. "Listen," he says, "I'd been planning to interview your grandmother as part of my research. I didn't realize you were related until last night."

Emma looks confused. "I think you're…"

"I called her some weeks ago—and she agreed to see me," he says, digging in deeper.

"That's hard to believe. The woman never left the house."

"Except to walk her dog?" he says.

Frozen for an instant, she takes a deep breath. "I'm sorry if her death was inconvenient for you, but I think you're on the wrong track here."

"Perhaps she knew more about your grandfather's relationship with Alger Hiss than…"

"That's enough Mr.…."

"Please call me Mac."

"I think you'd better go."

He pulls a card from his wallet. "This is my number in New York," he says, jotting it down on the back of the card. "I'm staying at the International House on 101st."

"I really don't think…" She moves to hand it back to him, but he steps out through the door.

"I hope you change your mind," he says, bowing slightly before he turns to go.

After he's been gone a few minutes and she's closed her door behind him and taken a seat at her desk and gathered herself up, she lifts the business card. "Angus McLearan," it says. She stares at it, unmoving. McLearan. She knows exactly who he is. His latest book, *The End of Communism as We Imagined It* —researched in part in the Kremlin of all places and full of revelations about the machinations of the Stalin regime—was a bestseller. She knows full well its author has a colorful reputation as independent-minded, irreverent, ingenious. She remembers describing him as brilliant in a lecture the preceding spring. She ruminates on it, disappointed that she failed to recognize him, pegged him as an interloper, turned him away.

Now, she revisits the conversation. On the face of it, the idea that her grandfather could have been connected with Alger Hiss seems absurd. But, running back over the conversation in her head, shifting her perspective, she realizes she knows very little about what he actually did at Balfour and surprisingly little about the company itself. She was a child when he retired and a teenager when she left Delaware. She thinks of Balfour Chemical as a maker of fertilizer, household products, synthetics—and the holder of the patents that go with them. She knows its slogan *Bringing Chemistry to Life* and its public image—philanthropic, benevolent, civic-minded. She's well aware that any corporation that large, that entrenched, that powerful, has committed its share of sins. But the idea of a connection with Alger Hiss? And her grandfather? "What on earth?" she is thinking.

No. 15

Langley, VA

When Bill Kidman is called into his boss's office for a noon meeting, there's a young woman standing beside his desk holding a single manila folder. Schmidt is uncharacteristically warm, as if welcoming him into his home. "Meet Miriam Frankel," he says, with a shit-eating grin on his face. "She's yours." The introduction feels odd, awkward, but Bill reaches out his hand and she shakes it vigorously—looks fresh out of college, well-scrubbed, dressed in a maroon pant suit, a pair of heavy black boots poking out from beneath her bell bottom pants. Schmidt seems to visibly puff up as he speaks: "Miriam is Max Frankel's granddaughter. A graduate of Radcliffe. She's working in research, and I've put her on the Quinn project." Noting Kidman's look of concern, he plows ahead. "Don't worry. I've known this one since she was a baby."

Kidman nods, recognizing the woman's look of embarrassment, responds deferentially. "Well, that's reassuring, Sir."

"She's your go-to girl from here on. Right, Miriam?"

She looks a bit irritated about being referred to as a girl, but she comes back with a hearty "Yes, sir."

A thin, manila file passes from Miriam's hands to Schmidt's, then on to Kidman, and Miriam says her goodbyes and clomps out of the office in her heavy black boots. "Let's have a look," Schmidt says to Kidman as she closes the door behind her.

"Well it looks like Miriam Frankel has her work cut out for her," Kidman says, leafing through it. "Not much here."

"We've got to assume multiple files," Schmidt says. "And some of it's probably going to be classified."

Kidman is already absorbed in his reading. "If it hasn't been destroyed," he says without looking up. Then, after a few minutes, he asks, "Have you read this?" And he starts reading aloud—

"James Percival Quinn, born in 1900, would have been 17 years old when the United States entered World War I. He joined Balfour Chemical as a young adult in 1925. Four years into his first job, the stock market crashed, marking the beginning of the Great Depression. During those years, Stalin came to power in Russia and capitalism was under fire. By 1933, when National Socialism was on the rise in Germany and Adolf Hitler on his way to office, James Quinn had come to play a leadership role in one of the largest chemical companies in the world.

In 1942, he toured Oak Ridge on behalf of Balfour Chemical and was involved with the Manhattan Project. So he played a role in the development of the atomic bomb that ended the war in the Pacific theater in 1945. Subsequently, he handled government affairs for the company, and served as a liaison with the federal government and the U.S. intelligence community on a range of issues, including the establishment of the Atomic Energy Commission and Soviet activities in the nuclear arena.

A true patriot, he lived out his entire life in the town of Wilmington, Delaware, a company town where social rank was considered one of life's great blessings. He believed in the system that granted him such blessings, married well and dedicated himself to protecting his own. He was very much the product of his generation and his own achievements."

Kidman pauses. "Who the hell writes this shit?" he says, then goes on—

"Too young for military service in the first Great War and too old to serve in the second, his war was The Cold War and the great battle of his life would have been the battle against Communism. He retired from Balfour in 1954 and withdrew from government service."

He stops again. "Withdrew from government service. What the fuck does that mean?"

"Not sure. Either it's a poor choice of words or he was an operative of some kind," Schmidt says, suggesting that Kidman calm down, that it's just the public file in the main system and that they'll obviously have to dig around a bit. "It's just a start."

"I get it," Kidman says. "But this is it? The whole profile? Ridiculous. Oh, then there's an addendum—

"James Quinn died in 1964. He was survived by his wife, Margaret Rothenberg Quinn, also born in 1900, whose father, Jacob Rothenberg, was a financier associated with Balfour Chemical. The Quinns' daughter Catherine was killed in a car accident with her husband in 1953. (See also Robert Wellford Gardner). The couple had one child, born Emma Gardner in 1949. Name legally changed to Emma Quinn in 1954."

He tosses the paper toward Schmidt's desktop, but it falls to the floor, weightless. "Not much else here," Kidman says, shuffling through the file. "Some sort of commendation for his work on the bomb. A copy of the contract between Balfour and the U.S. government. Pretty standard. The company accepted a token fee of $1 for the work, agreed that the patents went to the government, consented not to start reproducing anything, selling bombs. All very above board."

"Right," Schmidt says. "Sounds like there's a file on the son-in-law. I'm assuming there's also going to be an FBI file, maybe Defense. So, you can get with Miriam on that."

"And what makes you think they're going to release those files?"

"They're cleaning house too. You never know. Or we can request it through the Freedom of Information Act."

"Very funny."

Schmidt ignores him. Kidman is examining the inside of the manila folder. Written in pencil, barely legible, he sees the word "Skilling." He points it out to Schmidt, but doesn't read it aloud, doesn't say the word, the name.

Nothing registers on Schmidt's face, nothing obvious anyway. But he scribbles something on a legal pad, shows it to Kidman.

"Fletcher Skilling," it says. And, below that: "Talk to Max Frankel."

"Me?" Kidman asks aloud.

"No," Schmidt says. "I'll handle it."

No. 16

It's late in the day when Emma leaves Fayerweather for the library determined to set things right with Angus McLearan. This man, this

Serge, follows at a distance, but she's unaware of his presence. She heads first to Ta-Kome, the deli on Broadway across from the university. The place is empty, the space tight, the lights on full-beam. "Hey, it's the turkey lady," the deli man calls out from behind the counter. "I know. No mayo, no mayo." She grins. "Perfect," she says, adding a meatball sub to her order for Manny, knowing he will still be at the research desk.

"So, you got a sweetheart," Tony says, seeing Serge outside, leaning up against the low concrete wall that marks the entrance to the subway.

The other guy behind the counter, the older one, the father, winks at her. "That's a good thing," he says. "It's cold out there." By the time she turns to go, Serge has disappeared around the corner of the building, invisible again.

"Happy Valentine's Day," she tells Manny, presenting the sub wrapped in paper, as a gift, an incentive. It is late, nearly closing time. She has maybe an hour.

"Cool," Manny says, accepting the sub with uncharacteristic grace. "And you need…?"

"Background on the Alger Hiss case."

"Of course you do." Manny unwraps the sandwich, unleashing the smell of onions and garlic and grease and overcooked meat. "What happened to Ms. Luxembourg and Mr. Bebel?" He speaks through a mouthful, turning his attention to the computer screen.

"I got sidetracked."

Manny looks at this watch. "Okay. Go," he says. She wants the story from the *New York Review of Books,* the one that was mentioned by her colleagues at the West End. "Sometime in 1976," she tells him. "By Allen Weinstein."

He starts typing. "Okay. That's easy," he says, but he begins to wriggle in his seat as she continues.

"I need all the rebuttals. And I know there was some coverage in the mainstream press when that piece came out. He was unveiling his thesis, if you will—that Hiss was guilty. That he'd proven Hiss guilty. It was a big deal."

"Ah, yes. His thesis…if you will," Manny chides, mimicking her, as he continues to type.

Emma's fairly certain they're going on a wild goose chase. Standing over Manny's desk, waiting silently, she's thinking about Angus McLearan contacting her grandmother, unaware that she lived in a general state of confusion, an alternate universe. She pictures him asking questions about Balfour, about Alger Hiss, and scheduling a meeting that would go on Margaret Quinn's imaginary calendar. Then wishes she'd told him the truth—that her grandmother was reclusive and perhaps a bit mad, that she never saw anyone and would probably have agreed to meet with David Berkowitz if he gave her a call. Still unaware that her grandmother was killed, Emma is now preoccupied with clearing her grandfather's name. She wants to be prepared when she meets with McLearan. She wants to do her homework.

Manny tears off a printed sheet. "So, you'll have to use microfilm. But we should have hard copies of some of this stuff. From 1976 at least."

"Perfect," she says, grabbing the sheet. "Thank you." And without skipping a beat, adds, "And can you print me out a list of articles on the case since maybe, I don't know, since 1970?" Now he's rolling his eyes and bobbing his head and chewing all at the same time, like some mechanical toy, which finally makes her laugh and slows her down. "Just journal articles. And maybe *The Times*."

"Okay. Okay," he says, studying the database.

"I'm going to Newsreels," she says.

He's waving her off. "Okay. Okay."

"Whatever you do, don't leave until I get back," she says. He crosses his heart. And, walking backward away from the research desk, she blows him three kisses and calls out "thank you" three times in a loud whisper and then, in a kind of panic, mouths these words: "Just don't leave." And as she turns and runs off toward the elevator, he waves half a sub at her and says, under his breath, "She's gotta be on speed."

The third floor of Butler is quiet, very nearly empty. An archivist, a kid barely out of college, steers her to a small screening room and tells her to wait, then delivers a stack of metal canisters, newsreels. She's looking for an overview, basic background, a refresher. "This one's the best," he says. "The Red Scare. Real kitsch. 1949."

Once she settles in, she's hyper focused. It's a cumbersome process—threading the film through the projector, clicking everything into place, lining it all up. As she tilts her chair back slightly to reach for the light switch on the wall behind her, the door opens, startling her. "You got about 30 minutes," the kid says. "We close at 8:30."

In the dark, a large, grainy photograph of Joseph Stalin fills the screen. "Never has the threat of Communism been so great." The voice-over is loud, crackling above the whir of the projector. "Under the leadership of Joseph Stalin, the Soviet Union has spread its tentacles throughout the Eastern Bloc." A map of Eastern Europe, the Eastern Bloc countries—Czechoslovakia, Yugoslavia, Romania—appear in red. Then the image morphs into a map of the entire continent, a wave of color sweeping across the land. "Communist parties throughout the continent threaten the survival of democracy as we know it." Suddenly, the entire continent is awash in red. "Mao Zedong has taken over China." An image of the fall of Peiping, people running through the streets in mass panic. "Are we headed for a world dominated by the communist menace? Here on the home front, eleven communist spies have been brought to trial, accused of a conspiracy to overthrow the U.S. government." A photograph of the leadership of the U.S. Communist Party. She recognizes Gus Hall, muses that he's still alive, that he ran for president in 1976. And she thinks about her grandfather. He was born in 1900, so he would have been 49 at the time. Well established. Still working for Balfour.

"But one red spy has recanted and stepped forward," the narrator continues. "His message is a frightening one. Communist spies have infiltrated our government." Emma recognizes Whittaker Chambers, knows him as Alger Hiss's accuser. The image is in black and white. He's a bulky man, rough-looking, round-headed and slightly overweight, dressed in an ill-fitted suit. He's leaving the U.S. Capitol, stepping into a black DeSoto under guard. As it drives off, the camera follows. "Ex-spy Whittaker Chambers has named names…a circle of highly placed government officials in league with the Communists."

Next a grainy headshot of Alger Hiss dominates the room. He is a distinguished-looking man with a patrician demeanor. But she knew that, she has seen this image before. "The jury is still out in the case of Alger Hiss, former assistant to the Assistant Secretary of State. Once a clerk to Supreme Court Justice Oliver Wendell Holmes. A Harvard grad, and a man who helped draft the United Nations Charter. Is this man a Communist agent? Did he pass government documents to Whittaker Chambers in the 1930s when Chambers was a Soviet spy?"

She watches the footage of the House Un-American Activities Committee (HUAC) hearings. Sees Alger Hiss and Whittaker Chambers sitting at the dais in the U.S. House of Representatives. She is reminded of the Watergate hearings, set in the Senate, broadcast on television five years earlier to a rapt nation, hearings that led to President Nixon's resignation. The camera scans the HUAC panel. She recognizes a much younger Nixon. She knows that the Hiss case was the first Congressional hearing ever broadcast on television. She imagines that the public must have been riveted by the probe as it unfolded and that this aggressive young senator, this young Nixon must have gained a good deal of political capital. Nixon the schemer, now exposed as a scoundrel, a liar, a man without honor.

The narrator continues. "On August 25, 1948, the House Un-American Activities Committee forced Alger Hiss to admit that he had indeed known Communist spy Whittaker Chambers." She stops the projector, freezes the frame on an image of the hearing room, walks toward the screen trying to stay clear of the light from the projector. She can only get so close. She is looking for anyone else she might recognize, perhaps even her grandfather. Save Hiss and Chambers and Richard Nixon, the faces are unfamiliar. "What am I thinking?" she says to herself.

When the projector kicks back in, the scene shifts to the hallway outside a civil courtroom, Alger Hiss surrounded by a swell of spectators, reporters, attorneys. "Is Alger Hiss guilty or innocent? Was he funneling U.S. secrets to the Soviets or is he the unwitting dupe of a sinister plot by Whittaker Chambers? The jury is still out. After 14 hours and 44 minutes of deliberation, a hung jury emerged in the Alger Hiss trial—unable to decide who was lying and who was telling the truth." She knows Hiss was ultimately convicted of perjury and sent to prison. She knows enough, she thinks.

The sound of a marching band fills the small, dark room. Footage of an anti-communist rally appears on the screen. "Where," she wonders, "where would this have been?" Then the overhead lights flash on and off, a signal that the library is closing, but she catches the final fragment of the newsreel. "The fight against communism at home continues. Three professors at the University of Washington have been dismissed as Communist Party members. More evidence that the reds are infiltrating our institutions. When will America be safe?" Then the music rises to full tilt, a black and white bull's eye appears and then the screen turns white with flecks of black and the film begins to flap against the projector.

Emma sits, trying to imagine how audiences would have reacted to such a newsreel before catching some Hitchcock movie or Katherine Hepburn and Spencer Tracy bantering with one another. "Fear-mongering," she thinks. "And so soon after the horrors of the Nazi regime were exposed, and the bombings of Nagasaki and Hiroshima changed everything. People had reason to be afraid and this is where they put it all, on communism." She does not find it kitschy. She finds it disturbing. The archivist appears at the door, telling her they're shutting down for the night. "Was I right?" he says, smiling. She just stares up at him.

It's dark when Emma emerges from the library. She notices the young man sitting on the front steps with a stack of books in his lap, the couple up ahead with their arms locked, their matching backpacks, and another man beyond. The collar of his pea coat is turned up against the wind and he's smoking a cigarette, moving toward College Walk at the center of campus. She outpaces all three of them. As she passes Serge, the cigarette registers, like the smell of a small brushfire, but not his face or the navy pea coat or the slippery black hair. She turns left on College Walk, merging into the safety of the crowd, heading out through the gates and across Broadway as she does every evening.

In the subway station, Serge hides in the crowd, then slips into the car behind her and rides it to 96th Street, watching her through the door between the trains. But she's oblivious, stuck in her own head, trying to remember the details of her meeting with McLearan. She's almost relieved that she didn't know who he was. She imagines she might have been intimidated, knows she would have responded differently. The relentless thumping of the subway car distracts her. Two teenage boys hang from the arm rails above her, laughing, jabbing at one another playfully. She can't see beyond them to the man who is watching her through the door at the other end of the car. She can't think. And after the subway lurches to a stop, lights flashing, graffiti flying by, visible through the windows like some cryptic message from another time, she stands awkwardly, shoves her way out through the crowd, the turnstile, up the stairs to the street.

She is still mulling over her meeting with McLearan. Her mind lands on her own comment: "The woman never goes out." And his response, "Except to walk her dog?" She finds that particularly troubling. How would he know such a thing? It felt almost like a taunt, a dare of some kind. It might be proof of the truth of his story. He could have called the estate to confirm their meeting, she reasons. Or done so when her grandmother failed to show up at the appointed time. He might have spoken with Annie, heard the news of her grandmother's death, asked for details. Or it could be something else altogether.

This is what's running through her head as she turns off Broadway and down 98th Street, from the bright lights into the shadows. From here, the route is quiet, dark, empty. It's all residential—stairways leading to townhouses and basement apartments, alleyways that slip around corners, pre-war buildings with locked doors and covered entries and not a doorman in sight. As she makes her way down 98th, Serge watches from Broadway, then catches up when she turns up West End toward home, observing her from the shadows then following behind. He crosses to the opposite side of the street, keeping his distance, tracking her. Watches as she unlocks the door to her building, retrieves her mail in the lobby and disappears into the elevator. Then waits on the street below to see if he can detect a light go on, but her apartment is toward the back of the building, hard to spot from below.

Arriving home, she drops her backpack by the front door. It's loaded with articles and lists of resources amassed with Manny's help. She's eager to climb into bed and review them, get a handle on the Hiss case. She pours herself a bourbon, draws a bath, presses the button on her answer machine. There are only two messages. The first from Angus McLearan, voice-stamped 3:55 p.m. "I think we got off on the wrong foot. I hope you'll give me a call." She resolves to call him, to set up a meeting so she can exit the situation gracefully, only half-listening as the message comes in from United Parcel Service reporting that her shipment from Delaware will arrive on Thursday, the 16th.

No. 17

Langley, VA

"I know. I'm sorry." Bill Kidman is leaning back with his feet up on his desk, a file opened on his lap, cradling the phone on his shoulder. "Afraid so—if I get home at all," he says. It's late, close to ten. A box of red roses sits on the sofa in his office. "I know," he says, gazing up at the ceiling, his head resting on the back of his chair. He takes a deep breath. "I love you too," he says when he hangs up.

There's a call coming in on the other line. It's Wilson, young red-headed, slope-shouldered Wilson, calling from Delaware. "You ready?" he asks without saying hello. "Well, Happy Valentine's to you too, pal," Kidman replies.

Wilson is sitting upright at a small desk in his hotel room, referring to his notes. "One," he says. "The autopsy. They found an injection site at the nape of her neck. Cyanide. So, it's a definite hit."

"No surprise there," Kidman says. "Old school."

"Two. The lab. They tore the woman's clothes apart. No paperwork sewn into the lining. No microdots. And if Schmidt asks, we put her wedding ring under a microscope before they even took her off the slab. So nothing there."

"Okay."

"Three. We got the warrant. We'll go through the place tomorrow."

"What about the two visitors?"

"Tomorrow," Wilson says.

No. 18

The International House bills itself as an intimate European-style hotel. It's set on a side street between Broadway and West End Avenue, a few blocks from Emma's apartment in an unassuming pre-war townhouse. Small, minimally staffed, slightly worn, but it has an elegance to it—in the lobby, marble floors, a mission-style check-in desk with cubbies for the keys and an old-fashioned elevator with a wrought iron door that exposes its passengers going up and down. A chubby little man wearing a toupee welcomes her at the front desk. He seems to be looking down his nose at her, but it may well be the angle, the geometry of his face, his gaze fixed upward, his head slightly askew beneath the toupee. He sends her to McLearan's suite on the third floor. The wrought iron door clangs shut, and she watches the lobby disappear as she ascends.

McLearan is all grace and charm when she arrives. He is wearing jeans and an Irish sweater that exaggerates the breadth of his shoulders, his hair mussed a bit, as if he's just rolled out of bed. There's a twinkle to his eyes that makes him seem as if he's laughing from the inside, or perhaps smiling, something light and impish about him. This time, there are no reading glasses perched on his nose and there's a bagel balanced on the fingers of his right hand. She's struck by his ease, his magnetism. "I'm glad to see you. And glad you changed your mind," he says.

She offers an apology, something about "just getting back from Delaware and crazy week," but she skips the fawning and settles in on the sofa accepting his offer of a coffee. He sits opposite her across the big glass coffee table. She feels at a disadvantage—like his junior, diminished somehow, and is glad that she did her research, is buttressed by it.

"Anyway, I'm glad you're here," he says. "I could really use your help on this Hiss thing. There's some urgency to it."

"Urgency?"

"Well," he stops, takes a bite of his bagel, chewing before he speaks, taking a sip of coffee. "As I think you heard, Weinstein's book will be out in a few months." He licks some cream cheese off his thumb and gets up to grab a napkin from the kitchenette, speaking into the air as he moves across the room. "I'm trying to see if I can poke some holes in it before it hits the shelves. Weinstein maintains that Hiss is guilty. I have some questions about his…his scholarship."

"So, what does this have to do with my grandmother?"

"Your grandfather," he says, correcting her, and sits again, looking down as he wipes his hands on the napkin.

"You contacted my grandmother."

He nods, takes the last bite of the bagel, wipes his hands again.

"Right. She agreed to see me."

"Look, I need to explain about my grandmother. She was pretty out of touch with reality. I don't know what she told you."

He's matter-of-fact, straightforward. "She didn't tell me anything," he says. "I told her I was working on the Hiss case and she agreed to see me, to give me access to your grandfather's private papers."

"But I'm trying to tell you that doesn't mean anything. She was… she was eccentric…completely isolated in an imaginary world. She was a lonely woman. And not a terribly healthy one. If she encouraged you in any way, I assure you, it meant nothing."

"Well, okay, let me ask you this: Are you aware that your grandfather and Alger Hiss crossed paths back in the 1930s? Around the same time Hiss was allegedly spying for the Soviets."

She sits very still for a moment, confused. That's not at all what she expected. She's been focusing on the case itself and the investigation. Hiss was accused in 1948, at the onset of the Cold War. Now, McLearan is suggesting something else—that James Quinn knew Alger Hiss in the 1930s when Hiss would have committed the acts of which he was accused. She's not sure how to proceed. When she speaks, her voice rings with skepticism, her brow wrinkles. "Are you suggesting that my grandfather was a spy?"

"What do you mean?"

"That he was a Communist spy?"

"No, no, no." He is shaking his head, but being slow about it, speaking softly. "Nothing of the sort. I'm just suggesting that your grandfather's files may have some relevant information in them. Because of his work, his connection with Balfour, the company's activities."

They both sit in stillness for a moment. Emma speaks first, trying to sound detached, picking up on his tone despite a sense of unreality. "What kind of information? What exactly are you looking for?"

"My plan is to prove that Alger Hiss was framed." He lets it sink in, watching her as she absorbs it.

"I thought you were looking at the case from a new angle," Emma says. "If I'm not mistaken, the idea that Alger Hiss was framed has been amply explored."

"You'd think so, wouldn't you?" He's genial now and there's that twinkle again.

"So, what's the new angle? What makes you think my grandfather's papers would even be relevant?"

"It seems Balfour was engaged in helping the FBI make their case against Hiss."

Her face flushes. "Is that right?"

"It's a known fact."

"Now, I am confused. Are you suggesting that my grandfather was connected somehow with Alger Hiss in the 1930s—or in the '40s, during the McCarthy hearings?"

He holds his hands out of front of him, palms out, facing her and speaks softly, earnestly. "I'm not suggesting your grandfather was involved in any kind of wrongdoing," he says. "Just that his papers may be of some value."

"That sounds a bit like double-speak to me," she says, turning to reach for her coat, clutching it to her chest.

"Do you have any idea why he retired so young?"

"What?"

"In the fifties, he suddenly left the company."

"I believe that was because of me," she says. "Because of my parents. Because my parents died. And there was no one else to take care of me. I can't imagine how that's relevant to anything." The preceding evening, she'd spent hours reviewing the current thinking on this case. She speaks firmly, confidently, but not in anger. "It's my understanding that there are already six theories explaining how Alger Hiss could have been framed. The most likely seem to be that the incriminating documents were forged, that the typewriter was a fake. Or that the microfilm was somehow fabricated."

"Is that right?" he says. "Six? It sounds like you've been reading Allen Weinstein himself."

"I have no reason to question his research. After all, he's the first historian to have access to all the FBI documents."

"Do you really think J. Edgar Hoover would have let incriminating documents lie around? And that the public suddenly has access to them? You're aware, I assume, that he had separate file systems for secret operations and that he destroyed many of them."

"And you're imagining what? That my grandfather would have copies?" She now feels not only ill-prepared but also as if she sounded like a prig. "Six theories. What am I thinking?" she says to herself. But out loud, recovering, she says, "Again, if you think Balfour was involved, I suggest you turn your attention to the company itself."

"I don't think Balfour was involved," he says. "I know Balfour was involved."

"Then, feel free to send me whatever proof you have," Emma says, standing. She makes her way around the coffee table, reaching her hand out to him, acknowledging his reputation, his prominence, for the first time—"It's been an honor to meet you"—although it comes out a bit canned. Then, hesitating for an instant, she adds, "I don't think I can help you. But you're welcome to write a formal request to the estate to gain access to my grandfather's records." He's standing now. And she gives him no time to respond or react. "Just send it to my office."

Then she's out the door, moving briskly, bypassing the elevator, finding the exit stairs, the fire stair, moving through the lobby and back out to 101st Street. After a few blocks, breathing deeply, recovering her composure, she runs through the conversation in her mind. "Are you aware that your grandfather and Alger Hiss crossed paths back in the 1930s?" That's the remark that sticks. And this: The idea that Balfour was engaged in helping the FBI make their case against Hiss and his words—"It's a known fact."

No. 19

Langley, VA

"Put that thing out," Kidman says as he walks through his office door. Todd Wilson is sprawled across the sofa, smoking a cigarette. It's late afternoon and he's just arrived from Delaware. "You're gonna kill the flowers." A vase of roses, half dead, obviously forgotten the night before, stands on his desk. Kidman sits, attentive, ready for the run-through. "Ok. So. How did it go?"

Wilson reads from his notes. "Went through the place today. A couple of things," he says. "Mr. Quinn's office was empty, clean, nothing there. No files. Not a single slip of paper. No address book. No records of any kind. The three-ring notebooks on his bookshelves, a whole row of them, all empty. Nothing in the desk drawers, not even a checkbook. I asked the housekeeper about it. She said the girl didn't touch the office."

Kidman, his elbow resting on the arm of his chair, moves his hand to his forehead, looks down at the floor, rubbing his temple, absorbing that last detail. Shaking his head. Wilson holds off, lets him be, until, finally Kidman looks up at him. "They used the damn key. They walked right through the door and into an empty house. Of course.

Before we even got there." Wilson just listens as Kidman goes on. "If they haven't got the evidence at this point, they're totally incompetent."

"Well, could be the FBI," Wilson says. Kidman lets out what sounds like the beginning of a laugh that goes nowhere, and Wilson picks up where he left off. "Mrs. Quinn's study was cleared out—those magazines and everything. Went into boxes and off to New York, according to the housekeeper. I checked UPS. Shipment arrives on Thursday."

"Shit. Well get with our contact on that."

"Lastly, the visitors. This guy Treadwell is for real. A lawyer. Mainstream. Lots of rich clients."

"And?"

"I kinda fished around to see if he knew anything. Made him nervous. He handled the will, said it was a matter of public record, gave me a copy."

"And?"

"Not much of interest," Wilson reads from his notes. "Small bequests to the housekeeper and her son. Otherwise, the entire estate goes to the granddaughter—house, its contents, investments. According to this attorney, the girl already had a sizeable trust. Mr. Quinn left the limit to the housekeeper as well. Also, some cabin in upstate New York. Saranac. To the girl, that is."

"Okay. What about the other visitor—this Martin Simon?"

"Nothing yet."

"Any good news?"

"Think so. We may not have a leak. Phones at the Quinn estate were tapped. Old device, must have been on there for years."

Kidman perks up. "No kidding," he says. "Well, this is getting interesting."

No. 20

Emma is obsessing. She is focused on Balfour Chemical, on her grand-father and on Alger Hiss, although she's still skeptical of any connection. When she arrives at the library on Thursday, Manny is AWOL. Another fellow is sitting behind the research desk, someone she barely knows. She files her request—cross-referencing Balfour Chemical and Alger Hiss—and is told to check back end of day tomorrow. She has no hope of ingratiating herself to this other fellow and no intention of wait-ing, which is problematic, because she's not sure precisely what she's looking for and needs the database to find out. She spends a good four hours grinding through microfilm, reviewing news stories related to the Hiss trial. She does a search on Balfour in the late '40s and comes up with nothing of substance. Balfour seems to have stayed out of the limelight. In the 1930s, she finds a few brief business stories in *The Times* and one long piece profiling the Balfours and their company, mentioning an appearance before the Nye Committee, a Senate com-mittee investigating the munitions industry. The story talks a good bit about how vast, how powerful, how rooted in Delaware the company is, and very little about munitions or the purpose of the inquiry itself.

Before she leaves the library, she leafs through the card catalog for books that might be relevant. It feels futile, like a dead end. "If I can find it in a book, what on earth is McLearan up to?" she thinks. But she's curious now. And relentless. She hovers over the "B"s. Under Balfour Chemical, she finds a jumble of call numbers and heads for the stacks. Leafing through books, pulling them from the shelves, one after another, hours after she should have stopped for lunch, well into the afternoon, tiring, she finds something recent, something weighty, promising, footnoted, published in the late '60s—*The Balfour Legacy: Dynasty and Disaster.* Seems credible enough.

Then she finds a place in the stacks, a carrel against the wall, barely lit. Snug in a fiberglass chair, she checks the book's index. Her grandfather is not listed, as if he'd never existed. Nor is Hiss. She thumbs through its 500-plus pages. She has imagined a standard corporate history, but it is something else, more critical, more thoroughly researched than she would have expected. She finds a dozen black and white photos in the back of the book—one of the company's first powder mills, the old mill that stands abandoned less than a mile from her home, dating from Balfour's earliest days, a mill that supplied explosives for war after war, according to the caption, a reality she has always known but never acknowledged, accepted, absorbed. That, interspersed with elegant photos of the scions of the family, ladies in mid-length suits and frumpy hats posed for a garden club portrait; the family at a society wedding; past heads of the company, Balfours all, with high-ranking politicians and friends with names like Mellon and DuPont and Roosevelt.

Across the floor, beyond a dozen shelves, the elevator door opens and Serge emerges, making his way through the stacks, quietly, unobtrusively. He passes two students on the opposite side of the library, against the far wall, talking quietly. Walks along the row of books, pulls one out and pretends to examine it.

A few rows away, Emma remains immersed in the photographs. Her eye settles on a picture taken in the chamber of the U.S. Senate. The caption: "Balfour comes under scrutiny by the U.S. Senate during the Munitions Hearings (1934)." There behind Thomas Balfour and his brothers sits James P. Quinn as a young man, bespectacled, a pipe in his mouth, his hands folded across his lap. He is not identified, like a shadow figure, a ghost, irrelevant. Feeling as if she may have found something, she searches for Munitions Hearings in the index. She reads quickly, scanning the eight pages on the hearings. Here it's all laid out in detail—accusations against Balfour of war profiteering and evidence of millions of dollars in increased earnings during World War I. That, along with the fact that before the war, munitions made up fewer than two percent of the company's business. There are laundry lists of weapons supplied by Balfour to European nations, including Germany, in the years leading up to the First World War and continuing as the world propelled toward the Second. Agreements with German companies, shared patents, partnerships in an era when Hitler had already consolidated his power, ghettoized the Jews and was assembling the Nazi war machine. She reads snarky comments made by the Balfours and quoted in the press—charges that the Senate committee itself was controlled by Communists, calling it a witch hunt. She finds that things turned nasty when a reporter published the salaries of all Balfour's top executives in the Washington paper. Her grandfather was not listed among them. This is new to her, all of it—the hearings, the weapons trade, the partnerships with German companies. How, she wonders, could I have been so oblivious?

Then she comes upon it—Alger Hiss—right in front of her. Alger Hiss was working with the Nye Committee, the Senate Committee conducting the probe. He was involved in the investigation, the accusations, which appear to be true. Her grandfather was on one side, Hiss on the other. And it seems that Whittaker Chambers, his accuser 15 years later during the McCarthy hearings, was at the hearings as well, as an observer, as a journalist covering the proceedings.

This episode and her grandfather's role in it are disturbing. She's torn between pride that she's found something and dismay that McLearan might be onto something—bad blood between Balfour and Hiss; the possibility that, if given the chance, Balfour could have tampered with evidence. And it could implicate her grandfather. What had seemed ridiculous a day earlier, now seems possible, however remotely. She closes the book, tosses it in her backpack, rides the elevator to one and, unaccustomed to breaking the rules, hesitates before bypassing the checkout desk.

Serge lags behind, taking the stairs. When he exits the building, he watches Emma make her way toward College Walk and turn left toward the main gate. "As always," he thinks. He makes no effort to conceal himself, moving fast along a parallel route, leaving the campus through the south gate. It's dusk. And it's frosty cold. He can make her out crossing Broadway, blending in and out of the crowd. But she doesn't enter the subway. Instead, she turns left, down Broadway, toward home. It's Thursday. She's headed to The West End. He follows with his eyes from the opposite side of the avenue.

No. 21

Quinn Estate

Annie is in uniform—grey cotton dress, white Peter Pan collar, sensible shoes. "Nurse shoes," she calls them. Or "ugly old things." Sometimes she'd call Mrs. Quinn "Miss Crackpot" but only to Lester or her granddaughter. And they'd all laugh. She'd arrived as expected early this morning, before 7 a.m., as always. Just as she had the preceding day, before the CIA agent and well before Mr. Treadwell, the family's attorney. She'd asked the young man to wait outside until Treadwell arrived, wasn't at all sure why she even answered the door. "Just habit," she thinks, recalling the events of the previous day. Todd Wilson in his faux leather jacket, his gun secured safely in its shoulder holster, had stayed in his car with the motor running, smoke steaming from the tailpipe, Annie watching from the library window.

The house is quiet now. Empty. Something about the stillness, the way the late morning sun casts a shadow across the library, the half-darkness/half-light, that reminds her of the day she spent across the street packing up the cottage after the accident. This will take a lot longer, she's thinking. "This ain't no cottage," she says aloud, laughing at herself. The process of folding things away has already begun but the dismantling hasn't yet. "That's when it gets creepy," she thinks. "When everybody's gone, and everything's gone." She's worked here for nearly 40 years, spent the better part of her life here. She knows full well this will take some getting over. Annie has no time for mourning, but she feels a heaviness in the air, as if the building itself is grieving.

The CIA has been here twice. Yesterday, they had largely ignored Annie as they moved about the house, concentrating on the work spaces—the library, Mr. Quinn's study, Margaret Quinn's sitting room. She had been given little advance notice and no time to prepare. Now, concerned that they will return, she intends to look everywhere, everywhere except the attic. She'll save the attic. "Too cold. Too dark," she thinks. On Wednesday, before anyone had arrived, she'd searched all the drawers in Mrs. Quinn's bedroom and the sitting room. She'd checked Mr. Quinn's office, but everything was gone from there. The kitchen is already almost empty. And there is nothing to speak of in the dining room. Today, her plan is to scour the closet in Mrs. Quinn's room, to cull through her clothes and shoe boxes and purses and pockets in the hope of finding anything that seems too personal, too private for the government's eyes. Correspondence, private papers, personal notes, financial documents. She knows there's a diary somewhere. She thinks maybe Emma knows what it is they want, or Mr. Treadwell, that one of them has secured things. But she's not at all sure. She's afraid to ask. And she's afraid the agents will return.

Yesterday, when the young agent had gone, Mr. Treadwell had explained to her the circumstances surrounding Mrs. Quinn's death. That it wasn't a fall. It had been an accident, and someone had driven off without claiming responsibility. "Who would do such a thing?" she'd asked him. When he left, she sat on the sofa in the library beneath the front windows and sobbed in great quivers of sound until the tissue in her hand was soppy and frayed and torn. She had to work her way through a dozen more of them before she was finished. She feels as if the whole thing was her fault, so there's the guilt. And then the letting go. Now she's wondering—Why have they not returned her things? Why are they not letting her body go? Why does the CIA keep coming back? And what are they looking for? She has her suspicions, but she's not at all sure. And, whatever it is, she wants to find it before they do, for Emma's sake, for the family's sake and maybe for her own.

No. 22

It's early yet. Emma knows full well that students will be storming The West End shortly. There will be heavy drinking, slippery floors, all manner of antics, the air clouded with smoke. She moves toward the back, toward their regular table—sees the Oxford Don sitting at one end holding court with a handful of professors, Jim Stanton among them. Her old friend Will appears to be absent tonight, and she sees no sign of their newest companion, this Angus McLearan. She spots her pal Jean Buchman at the far end of the long rectangular table conferring with a student, a young woman in a rather dramatic full-length leather coat, a sheet of long black hair flowing down her back. Buchman grabs Emma's arm as she approaches and holds onto it until the student departs. Then looks up at her. "I got your message. Sit...I wish I had more time." She leans in toward Emma. "You're going to work with McLearan?"

"I think so," Emma says.

"That should be interesting," Buchman says. "So, you want my thoughts on whether Alger Hiss was framed."

Emma nods. "I've been doing a little research," she says. "Seems there are a number of theories—that Nixon planted evidence or

Hoover manufactured the Woodstock typewriter on which Hiss allegedly typed the documents."

"Yes. There's been much ado about the typewriter. And what was it Hiss said? 'Guilt by forgery.' Something like that."

"Right," Emma says. Pausing, she waves the waiter away, turns back to Buchman. "And then there's the business of the microfilm— the Pumpkin Papers. Those may well have been forged."

"That always seemed more likely to me."

"So you think it's worth pursuing?"

"Don't know," Buchman says, a casual tone to her voice. "I'll be interested in seeing what Weinstein has to say, when *Perjury* comes out. But I'm not sure it will change anything."

"Because both sides are so dug in, you mean?"

"That. And because it's easy to miss the forest for the trees on this one," Buchman says. "Fact is, Whittaker Chambers was a government witness. Nixon and Hoover went to great lengths to validate his testimony—chasing down evidence, searching for the typewriter itself, holding private hearings in secret locations, manipulating the press, manipulating public sentiment. The whole thing was a circus. Did they literally manufacture evidence against Hiss? I don't know the answer. Still, I doubt it will change anything. The truth is, the committee was out to get Hiss. The transcripts from the Senate hearings already tell us that."

"So whether or not Hiss was framed is irrelevant?" Emma says.

"In a larger sense, yes. McCarthy's demagoguery—and the very existence of such a thing as a House Un-American Activities Committee and the zealousness with which the committee pursued its mission— that was the set-up." Buchman stops for an instant, finishing off her beer. "If you look at it that way, the idea of a literal framing becomes almost superfluous. "

"To your point," Emma says. "I read an op-ed piece today that was written a few years ago. The author argued that the documents them- selves were insignificant. That the microfilm included meaningless Navy memos that were available to the public."

"Exactly. I remember that piece. Everyone was stirred up about the sudden—and rather dramatic—appearance of these incriminating documents, but nobody really paid much attention to their content." Buchman is standing now, tossing some bills on the table. "And why was that? Because McCarthy needed the win. The Hiss business came after the Hollywood Ten—at a time when Joe McCarthy was losing his credibility. It put McCarthy back in the game. And put Nixon on the map." She throws on her coat. "C'mon, I'll give you a lift home."

Outside, walking against the wind as they exit the bar, the two make their way up Broadway. It's dark and below freezing. A rowdy bunch of college kids sweeps past them heading for the West End. Buchman slips her arm through Emma's, draws her toward the curb and Emma picks up where they left off. "So you think Hiss was innocent," she says.

"I'm not sure I'd go that far," Buchman says. They're still walking arm-in-arm, hands jammed in pockets, leaning in close to one another. Shouting against the wind, Buchman goes on, "But McCarthy and Nixon had a vested interest in his guilt. And, in my opinion, that tarnished the entire process."

They hop into the freezing car, Buchman revving up the engine and Emma rubbing her hands together in an effort to get warm. Once they settle in, Buchman says, "You know, Hiss was a New Dealer, a liberal. There's a pretty good chance he was hanging out with a bunch of Communists back then. He may well have been a member of the party."

"Good God," Emma says, "Given the sorry state of capitalism, what thinking person wouldn't have leaned to the left in the 1930s?" She pauses for an instant. "And I imagine back then, in the minds of most Americans, the leap from New Dealer to Communist sympathizer to Communist spy wasn't that great."

"Right," Buchman says. "But he may well have been guilty of treason. You'd be wise to keep that in mind."

They're on West End Avenue now. She slows the car down, squinting out the window, searching for Emma's place. "You know, I'm surprised McLearan's trying to prove someone took liberties with the evidence," she says. "Seems like he's getting caught up in the weeds. Unless he has someone specific in mind, and a pretty strong case."

As Buchman pulls over and puts on her flashers, Emma is digesting that last comment. She hasn't mentioned McLearan's suspicions related to her grandfather and the idea inspires her to ask one last question. "If Hiss was guilty, how could he lie about it all those years? How could he hide it? His whole life would have been a lie."

"Pretty crazy," Buchman says. "But how could he not? He'd become a hero to the left. Something of a martyr really." The two sit in silence for an instant, before Buchman puts the car back in drive. "I suspect if anyone can prove he's innocent, it's probably McLearan," she says, speaking into the air as Emma climbs out of the car. "Kind of admirable."

No. 23

There's a message from George Treadwell when Emma arrives home, very nearly tripping over the boxes stacked helter skelter all over the living room, each one labeled in her own script. "MQ Sitting Room." "Paperweights." "Photographs." "Treasures." There were things she still hadn't found, hadn't packed, although she'd searched for them—the photo of her grandfather at Oak Ridge, a small pendant that he'd given her on her 18th birthday, her grandmother's mink hat and that ubiquitous diary of hers. Treadwell's message is from the night before. And it is brief: "Hello Emma. George Treadwell here. I have some news—some difficult news—to share with you. Please give me a call."

Then there's one from Annie, from today: "Miss Emma, one of those government men came back. He had papers and he looked all over. You need to come home." Emma stops the machine, concerned. She tries to reach Annie, but there is no answer at the estate, at Annie's home, anywhere. Then she turns the machine back on, half-expecting a message from Angus McLearan, as if he were courting her, as if she was counting on it. But there is none. A kind of emptiness, a numbness, maybe a feeling most of us would recognize as loneliness—or rather aloneness—takes hold.

She rings Treadwell at home. "I have bad news," he tells her. "Upsetting news. It was apparently a hit and run," he says. And when she asks for more information, he tells her only that it's under investigation, that the FBI seems to be involved. "They don't seem to know anything yet, except that she was struck by a vehicle of some kind. I'm sorry to have to be the one to tell you," he says. "Just get back here as soon as you can."

Still wearing her coat, her keys jangling in her pocket, Emma circles the apartment, going from room to room, cursing into the air, angry and upset—Dammit. Goddammit. Her unfinished manuscript sits abandoned on her coffee table in a room filled with boxes. Her grandmother's death has opened doors to places she did not want to visit, secrets she doesn't want to know, or that she always knew but never fully faced. And now there's this—her grandmother cut down on a morning walk, this Hiss business, the FBI searching the house for

God-knows-what. And this—investigators contacting Treadwell. She looks for her backpack, her wallet, wants to find Bill Kidman's card. Wants to call him like now. But it's nowhere, and she can't remember when she last had it. She retraces the day in her mind—knows she had her backpack in the library, believes she took it to the West End. She fumbles through the Manhattan phone book, finds the number and dials the bar, starting a process that takes an interminable amount of time: getting the bartender's attention, telling him where her colleagues are sitting, asking him to check for her backpack, yelling into the receiver, losing him. Trying him back, getting no answer. She hangs up the phone, agitated, exhausted, tossing her coat on her bed, wandering from room to room, switching on all the lights, switching them off again, searching for a cigarette. But she has none.

She finds herself finally in the tiny railroad kitchen, a space that can barely accommodate more than one person, flipping open cabinets, drawers, the refrigerator, as if maybe she's stashed a pack of Camels in the freezer. Nothing. It's a small, aging Frigidaire, greyish, rounded at the corners, empty save a few eggs, a loaf of bread, a pint of milk. She doesn't have the energy to go out for smokes, realizes she doesn't have her wallet. "Can't even call for Chinese," she thinks. Not sure she can muster the inspiration to scramble an egg, she opens the fridge again and pulls out a grey cardboard carton, reads the sell-by date and tosses the entire thing in the trash, abandoning the idea of dinner. Then she rustles through the cabinets for a tin of peanuts, flips off the kitchen light and heads for the bedroom, a bourbon in one hand, the tin of peanuts in the other, switching off the living room light with her elbow. Bathed in darkness now, she nibbles on the peanuts, sips the bourbon, moves slowly back and forth between her bedroom and bath, half-naked, turning on the tub, stripping off her clothes.

Serge stands at the corner of 97th and Broadway at a payphone, dropping in another dime, dialing her number. He had left her at The West End less than an hour ago, made his way toward her place, assuming she'd spend a few hours at the bar then pick up the subway home. He thinks he knows her patterns.

She closes the bathroom door just as the phone begins to ring. "No," she tells herself. "No," she says again as she climbs into the tub. The machine picks up on the third ring and she hears her own voice. "This is Emma Quinn. I'm sorry I'm not here to take your call. Please leave a message." Then the sound of a dial tone, the caller hanging up. Emma closes her eyes. She is thinking about her grandmother, picturing her lying in the snow on Miller's Lane, wondering how much she suffered, as if she hadn't suffered enough. And her grandfather. It's becoming clear that he may not have been the man she imagined he was. Then she settles on her mother. She wonders if her mother knew about her grandfather's life. What she might have known about his work. What she knew, if she knew, about the Munitions Hearings or the Manhattan Project or what Balfour did and where the money came from for all her party dresses and riding lessons. Unlikely, she decides, her mind set adrift by the bourbon and the bathwater and the deep sense of aloneness.

Her eyes closed, her spinning brain settles on her parents. Emma remembers her mother as child-like, playful, slight. She pictures her in their old living room in the cottage on Miller's Lane, lying on the floor in her stocking feet, her head resting on her hand, Brio trains stretched across the oriental rug. "I am in play position," her mother would say. And she remembers her father as a busy, busy man, always in a hurry and her mother's words—"Ah, the white rabbit is here"— when he came home in the evenings. Dressed always in a suit, that is how Emma recalls him, with an array of entertaining bow ties. He had a yellow one with little pink fishes on it and she has always imagined that he was wearing it that night with his tuxedo. The night they died, although she knows it's implausible. She has a clear vision of her mother dressed in that soft grey-green gown, the last one she ever wore, drawn in at the waist like a corset with a skirt of silky filament, baubles on its bodice that twinkled as she walked, emitting tiny sparkling flashes of light. Emma remembers her leaning over for a kiss that night. The subtle smell of roses. And touching the top of the dress, the nubby feel of the tiny pearls, the shiny little baubles beneath her fingers.

She can't remember her mother's face, except of course from still photographs and from black and white home movies she watched, incessantly for a time, with her grandfather in the years that followed. Her mother's sweet smell and the feeling of those baubles, that's what lingers still. And Emma always recalled Annie being there that night, the night they died, although she's never been clear on the logistics, the details of how she got from her home to that of her grandparents. Perhaps the driver came or maybe they walked across Miller's Lane from their little cottage and up the formidable drive in the middle of the night. Doubtless, she was carried. But she slept at the big house, deposited in the bedroom closest to her grandparents. That memory couldn't be clearer. She slept in the massive four-poster bed, encased between its sheets, the antique clock with the austere woman painted on its face striking interminably through the night, chiming, waking her in the darkness, not a thread of light creeping into the room, her fear bottomless. And, in the morning, she had awakened to the sound of her grandmother's wails and her grandmother's words, nasty words that spun through the upper halls. Emma never went home again, to her real home, to her real bedroom, to their cottage on Miller's Lane. "You are responsible for your own things," her grandmother had said when those things were delivered in boxes and suitcases to the little room toward the back of the house, near Annie's room, off the back stairs.

This is what Emma is thinking about when she hears the first of the sounds, lying in the tub in her darkened bathroom. About her mother, the ball gown, the country road, the case clock and her grandmother's anger, her inability to let it go for all those years. She hears the sound of a door opening. Hears someone moving about in the living room. Knowing full well she didn't flip the damn dead bolt when she got home, she doesn't move, just listens. It's as if someone is going through the boxes. There is a stripping-away sound, as if a box is being cut.

She lies frozen in the hot bathwater, until, finally, after who knows how long, when she can bring herself to set her elbows against the rim of the tub, she does so with great care so as not to move the water, lifts herself, eases her leg over the side onto the bath mat, careful not to slip. She holds the edge of the tub, reaching for the towel on the opposite wall, her eyes adjusting to the darkness. Then she stands still listening, wide-eyed. She imagines that the intruder must think the apartment is empty. She doesn't think he's come for her, thinks he's come for something else. And he is still at work or they are still at work. She stands in silence, patting her body with the towel against the sound of her own breath.

She is half-dry now, grasping in the darkness for the cashmere robe that hangs on the back of the bathroom door. She takes care not to jostle the door, lowering her robe as if it were as breakable as glass, wrapping herself in it in slow motion. She knows she can climb out the fire escape through her bathroom window, that she will have to move carefully and be quick about it once she gets the window open, for the noise. And her snow boots. She knows her boots are on the floor, left to dry by the radiator. She can see them now.

Holding the edge of the tub, she moves toward the boots, toward the window. Her ankles still wet, she grips the edge of the sink, putting on a boot, jerky, awkward, fearful that she might lose her balance and draw the intruder toward the back of the apartment. When she is finished and standing there in a single black leather boot and her robe, she hears nothing. "Where have they gone?" she asks herself, still in the darkness. Then the drop of a box, the scrape of the knife. Cardboard tearing and angry, clear as day, the voice of a man. "*Sheeps.*" One word uttered in exasperation, the hint of a foreign accent. "*Sheeps.*"

The phone rings then, sudden, shrill, accelerating her panic. Wrapped in her robe now, with one boot in her hand, one on her foot, she steps between the thick, floor-length curtains in front of the bathroom window and grasps the lock, turning it on the second ring. On the third, she slips her foot into her other boot, catching it, sticky and wet against the leather. Bends down to zip it up. Hears the machine pick up: "This is Emma Quinn. I'm sorry I'm not here to take your call. Please leave a message." On the beep, she opens the window, the flesh of her hands against the splintered paint of the wooden sill, climbing out into the cold, scrunched up, exposed, pulling her long robe out behind her, naked against the wind. "Hey, Emma. Pick up. I know you're there." She hears the footsteps moving down the hall, from the living room toward the bathroom. "Hey. I've got your backpack…" Then a fragment of the message as she reaches up to close the window behind her. She can see someone turning the nob on the bathroom door, then hear a body slamming against it as she slams the window shut, sweeping down the fire escape into the cold night, not stopping to breathe.

She had practiced on this fire escape. In the summer. Climbed out the window, running down the three flights, sliding the moveable ladder down to the floor of the airshaft with a jolt, the super at the ready to catch her if she fell. The building required it. She cooperated without protest. "Makes sense," she told Rodriguez. "I think it's stupid," he said. "If there's a fire, you'll figure it out." But the landlord had insisted. She is grateful now as she jumps off the bottom rung, her boots striking the ground, her palms landing in the gravelly pit below. She rises, running, moving past a dumpster, trash bins, a stack of old paint cans, to an alley that leads to 98th Street, half-wet, freezing in the darkness, her robe flying out behind her. Not thinking now, just running.

At 98th, she cuts up toward Broadway, to hide in the crowds in case the intruder follows. She tells herself he won't, that surely he thought the apartment was empty. This is what she tells herself as she runs up 98th to Broadway. It's a short block, and in an instant, she is there. Taxis, busses, lights, people. Couples, leaving restaurants, strolling arm in arm. A crowd lined up outside the movie house across Broadway. She imagines she looks like a crazy person, that someone will stop her or call the police. Then she tries to look like a crazy person, so no one will approach her, talking to herself, using whatever words pop into her mind. "Goddamn Alger Hiss. Goddamn Margaret Quinn. Goddamn Angus McLearan." She repeats these words again and again, under her breath, slowing to a brisk walk, heading uptown, suddenly cold, holding her robe against the wind, hoping it resembles a coat, grateful that her hair is not wet. Terrified.

The journey feels unreal, interminable, like a dream where she will fall through space at the end and awaken in her own bed. When she arrives at 101st, the coffee shop on the corner is dark, empty. She looks to the left, down 101st toward West End Avenue, sees the International House awning, knows she can gain entry. She is trembling when she presses the bell and the man with the toupee buzzes her in. "Good evening, madam," he says and watches her open the wrought iron door and ascend to three, as if he sees women arrive in their bathrobes with some regularity. Halfway up in the wrought iron cage she is thinking, "Could it have been McLearan? Could he be that desperate for information?"

No. 24

Emma awakens on Angus McLearan's sofa in her cashmere robe, crumpled, in the fetal position, wrapped in a blanket, staring at two empty snifters. There had been brandy. And she remembers the confrontation. "Did you send them?" she'd said when he opened the door to his hotel room. Half-naked, lips blue, trembling and out of breath, she had not screamed it but had spoken in a tone that carried weight.

"Come in. Shut the door." He spoke brusquely and left her standing, moved to the adjacent room returning with towels from the bath, a blanket, wrapping it around her in a fatherly sort of way, asking what happened, ushering her to the sofa as she explained in rushed sentences, then, as she sat and faced him head-on. "How did you know she was walking the dog?" she said.

"We better get you dry," was his answer. He put the towel around her neck, dried her face as you would dry an injured child or wounded pet, gently, sweetly. She had a glazed-over look to her, as if she were in shock. "It's you, isn't it?" she said. "You sent them. Because I wouldn't help you. You sent them."

"Sit down," he said, leading her to the sofa as she pulled her arm away, saying, "You did this, didn't you?" He shook his head, knelt at her feet, unzipped her right boot, wrapped her foot in a towel, rubbed it fiercely. "What the hell is going on?" She said.

"Good question," he said. There was an odd calm to the scene.

"What on earth have I got that you want so much?" She was looking down at the crown of his head, his shoulders, his strong hands massaging her feet.

He'd answered with a question. "What have you got that someone wants so much?"

"Did you kill her?" she said.

"You're not making any sense," he'd responded. Waking now, she's not quite sure how it happened. She remembers him holding her. Tears and a sense of exhaustion, his comforting her with brandy, with his arms, with his words, with the calm of his voice. At some point in the night, she felt safe with him, felt reassured. She'd fallen asleep on the sofa, and he'd retreated to the other room.

Now an old Mercedes-Benz is double-parked on Riverside Drive, lights flashing, Emma's car, inherited from her grandfather after his death. Angus McLearan sits behind the wheel. It is a hulky box of a sedan, charcoal 300SE made in the early '60s, one of its maker's finest. He'd been enthusiastic when Emma took him to the garage on 43rd Street to pick it up. "That's a beauty. Where on earth…" Then he stopped himself, the answer being obvious. "Drives like a charm," he said as the two rode up Broadway toward Columbia in the early morning hours.

They'd been to her apartment, surveyed the damage—someone had gone through all the boxes from Delaware, rifled through her dresser, her closet, her kitchen cabinets. A half-dozen of the boxes were gone—the paperweights, a box of family photographs and all the news clippings from her grandmother's study save a few files that she'd stashed in her knapsack. "Who would do this?" she'd asked. He had stood by her as a brother might, or a father. "Take deep breaths," he'd said when they first entered the apartment, the living room in shambles. After they'd climbed around the shipping boxes, shredded with the blade of a knife, and after she'd gone through the bedroom and he'd asked the extent of the losses—"papers, my grandmother's papers, mostly"—after that, he'd turned his attention to the apartment itself: the Soviet posters, the evidence of Emma's obsessive writing habits, the bare kitchen. Then, standing at the piano, he'd leafed through her sheet music—Gershwin, Beethoven's *Appassionata*, a good bit of Chopin. "I hadn't figured you for a romantic," he'd said. That morning, when they'd left the hotel, he'd grabbed a handgun from his night table and made no effort to conceal it. She had looked on in astonishment. "What, you don't have one?" he'd said. "Seriously, if you'd spent three years in Moscow researching a book about Stalin and the KGB, you'd carry a gun too." Then he'd paused for an instant, adding, "And I'm concerned."

Somewhere between that moment and their appraisal of the

damage at her apartment, she withdrew to her bedroom and put on some clothes of her own, got herself cleaned up, packed a small suitcase. Sitting on the edge of her bed, she began to put things together: The hit and run, the appearance of federal agents at the Delaware estate, their return and now this, this break-in—they were all part of the same puzzle, one that she could not assemble. But she knew they were all connected.

She felt safe with Angus McLearan, but she remained wary, uncertain of how he fit into all this. His sudden appearance, his questions about the family, his eagerness to see James Quinn's papers, the presence of a gun—it all compounded her uncertainty. After she emerged from her room, the two spoke very little. Emma was perfunctory. She told him she needed to get her car. He'd stayed with her as if it was expected somehow, as if they had a tacit agreement: They would do this together. Then they'd headed to Riverside Drive in the Mercedes in virtual silence, McLearan at the wheel, to Jean Buchman's. But Emma didn't tell McLearan where they were going—about Jean Buchman or the backpack or her plan to head to Delaware. She wasn't at all sure she could trust him.

She is watching him now from Buchman's apartment, from vast windows overlooking the Hudson, watching the top of the Mercedes from six stories up. "Thank goodness you got my message," Buchman calls from another room. Emma turns to the wall of books, runs her hands along the titles, slowly, glancing up as Buchman comes into the living room, the backpack dangling from her fingers.

"What do you think of Angus McLearan?" Emma says.

"The man or the historian?" Buchman laughs. Emma doesn't answer. "Well, I don't begrudge him his bestseller, if that's what you're asking. I think he's good. Thorough. Imaginative. I have a lot of respect for his work."

Emma likes Jean Buchman. She doesn't ask any questions, doesn't pry, gets right to the point, just follows along. But Emma wants to know more. "Had you ever met him before?"

Buchman shakes her head no.

"Me neither."

"Ah," Buchman says. "I understand he's a bit of a ladies' man." And she grins.

"You don't happen to have his book, do you?" Emma asks. Don't assume anything, she reminds her inner historian—never assume anything.

"I do have it. In fact, I got it out the other night. After we met him." She eases across the room to a stack of books on a long wooden sofa table. It's a hardcover with a sharp black and red book jacket, the title written in a blocky font across the front in all caps—THE END OF COMMUNISM AS WE IMAGINED IT. She flips open the back cover, examines the flyleaf, and is reassured, relieved really, to find his face staring back at her. A little younger maybe, but it's the Angus McLearan she knows, although in this particular incarnation, he sports a full beard and has less grey around the edges.

Emma turns back to the window, monitoring him. He's found a parking space up the block a bit and is easing the monster of a car into it. She knows then precisely what she needs to do. "Mind if I use your phone?" she asks. Buchman ushers her into a small study off the living room, windowless, lined with another crop of books. When she switches on a small Tiffany lamp, Emma sees the half-cup of coffee, old milk curdling on its surface in a circle, a white lifesaver stuck to one of the file folders on the desk, a dirty sock rolled up on the floor. "Forgive us the mess," Buchman says, grabbing the cup. "My husband."

Emma rustles through her backpack, looking for the other book, the Balfour book from the library, wants to be certain it's there. Then searches her wallet for Bill Kidman's card, sits for a moment looking down at the rotary phone, trying to gather her thoughts, rising before she dials, opening the office door, calling out across the apartment for permission to make a long-distance call. And she checks on the Mercedes again before sequestering herself back in the dim closet of a study. She's not sure what to ask or what to expect, but when she gets through to Kidman, it's clear that he recognizes her name immediately. "Where are you?" he asks.

"New York," she says. "I want to report a break-in."

"Where are you exactly? Are you calling from your apartment?"

"No. I'm at a friend's place. On my way down to Delaware. What difference does it make?"

"I just want to be sure you're safe. Are you alone?"

"Yes. Well, no. She's here. My friend. In the other room."

"Ok. Where was the break-in? In Delaware?"

"New York. My apartment. They've stolen some of my grandmother's things."

"Did you call the police?"

"I thought…It seemed like maybe I should call you. Since your people paid a visit to the estate yesterday. Since the boxes were transported from Delaware. Since no one has bothered to call me about any of this—including the fact that my grandmother was killed."

"I tried to reach you yesterday, Miss Quinn, at your office."

"You're with the FBI, am I correct?"

"Central Intelligence Agency. What exactly was stolen, Miss Quinn?"

Without realizing it, she is toying with the white lifesaver stuck to the file folder, picking at it with her fingers. "For one thing, the old newspapers and magazines, those files that were in my grandmother's study. The ones you saw…you know, that night when you were searching the house…if you recall." By now her voice is rising, and Jean Buchman raps on the door, opens it—"You okay in there, Emma?"— and Emma holds up her hand, nods. But she's not okay.

"Well, I'll do whatever I can to help you," Bill Kidman says. "You say you're headed to Delaware?"

She freezes up, reading the card in the dim light. "Director, Special Projects," she says flatly. "What are Special Projects, Mr. Kidman?"

"Is your friend coming with you to Delaware?" he says. There is a studied calm to his voice, as if he's talking to a child, or someone who is confused or unstable. On the other end of the line, he's jotting everything down as she speaks. When she doesn't answer, he speaks again. "I want you to stay where you are. I can send someone for you."

"No," she says. "No. I'm driving down with a colleague. We'll talk again."

No. 25

There are those who do not hug, not comfortably, not routinely. It's not in their nature, not part of their culture or vocabulary. It's no surprise that Emma is such a person. In Emma's neighborhood, if you can call it that, for no one really interacted with their neighbors, people didn't hug one another. That, despite the fact that all the men on Miller's Lane worked for Balfour and all the wives saw each other socially. They didn't cook out in their respective backyards or call across the fence or share a glass of wine on their back steps. And they certainly didn't hug. Of course, once Emma passed the age of five and lost her parents, she in effect had no neighborhood. Oh, she embraced her grandfather on occasion. But she didn't hug Annie, old sweet spindly woman that she was, or Margaret Quinn or anyone else for that matter. "Good to see you"—definitely not, "Nice to see you," which has a pedestrian ring to it—that's how her people, her tribe, say hello and goodbye. One and the same—"Good to see you." Clean, simple, never effusive, and without any sort of physical contact—and whether it's good to see you or not. As an adult, even if the impulse struck her to reach out her hand or wrap her arms around a friend, she resisted unconsciously. Keeping her distance, holding back a piece of herself, as if that were part of the social contract.

So, when Emma picked up her backpack and swung it over her shoulder and prepared to leave Jean Buchman's apartment to reconnect with Angus McLearan who had spent a good 30 minutes sitting by the curb in her Mercedes, the last thing she expected was a hug. But Buchman reached out to her. "Take care of yourself," she said and wrapped her arms around Emma and pulled her close. Maybe it was the note of sympathy in her voice, the motherly nature of the embrace, the sheer warmth of it, but Emma teared up. It was not unlike the feeling one experiences when a marching band goes by playing Sousa or the national anthem kicks in at a ball game—an irrepressible swell of emotion.

"Shall we go to Delaware?" she asks McLearan as she throws herself into the car, dropping her backpack at her feet, leaning in, half smiling at him.

"Why not?" he says turning the key in the ignition.

"I have a theory," she says, as he's easing his way out of the parking space, his arm over her seat, his neck stretching to get a fix on how to navigate, caught in a tight spot.

"What's that?" He stops then, looking at her straight on, his hand on her headrest.

"About who broke into my apartment. Just a theory."

"Well, are you going to share it with me?"

With that her tone grows more serious. "I'm not sure. I can't help but wonder if there's some correlation between your appearance— your research project—and the theft of those boxes. I just don't know what it is."

He's trying to get out of the tight spot he's in, focused on not crunching the rear fender of Emma's Mercedes against the blue van behind them. "Well, let's see," he says. Then, checking the side mirror, pulling out onto Riverside, stepping on the gas, he proceeds. "Well, did you have anything about Alger Hiss in those boxes? Anything about Balfour Chemical's activities in the 1930s and 1940s? Anything about," he hesitates, raises his voice and takes his eyes off the road to look straight at her before he continues, "the subject of my research?"

"Hmmmm. Let's see," she says, teasing him back then.

"I didn't think so. And you said they were your grandmother's papers, not your grandfather's?"

Then she throws it out there, just to get a reaction. "Do you think anyone at the CIA or the FBI still has a vested interest in the Alger Hiss case? I mean, it happened almost 30 years ago."

"Well, Frank Church and his committee seemed to have a great deal of interest in illegalities that go back 30 years or more. Hoover's activities. The CIA's activities. They're all under scrutiny. There's no statute of limitations on any of it."

"But Hoover's dead now, isn't he?"

"Yes, but Alger Hiss is still very much alive. And there are plenty of people who want to see him vindicated while he's still alive—want to see the slate wiped clean."

"Maybe so," Emma says. "But I doubt they work for the CIA or the FBI."

They are on the West End Highway now, making their way toward the George Washington Bridge. It's a narrow, high-speed, pothole-ridden four-lane road suspended between the river and the city with a low, cement Jersey wall at its edge. He's concentrating on maneuvering the massive car between a produce truck, a merging motorcyclist and the cement barrier. So he pauses before he answers, as if he can't do both things at once.

When he speaks again, his tone shifts, turning soft and serious. "What's going on Emma?"

"My grandmother didn't fall down walking her dog. It was an accident. A hit and run. And, afterwards, the CIA came around, looking for something." She stops herself, doesn't want to implicate her grandfather, omitting the information about the warrant and the most recent search of the estate. "And now someone has broken into my apartment and taken my grandmother's personal papers."

He's focused on the road, not answering, just listening. And she goes on. "So, you tell me. I'm thinking—where do you come in? You arrive out of nowhere asking about Balfour and Alger Hiss and my grandfather. Where do you come in?"

"Let me just think on this a minute," he says. "About this CIA business."

Emma removes her boots, perches one foot on the glove compartment with its burled walnut finish and black lacquer trim, leans back against the leather seat, her right leg bent at the knee, shaking her head, waiting.

"What exactly was in those boxes?" he asks. They're crossing the bridge now to Jersey and she's looking out the window over the water as she speaks. "Papers. My grandmother's papers. News stories. A crazy batch of news stories that the CIA just happened to see in my grandmother's sitting room." They're both quiet for a time. As they pull up to a tollbooth at the entrance to the turnpike, he rolls down the window to grab a ticket and cold air sweeps through the car. She wraps her arms across her chest, around herself. "So what about you?" she says. "Why are you so intent on my grandfather?"

He takes his time, chooses his words carefully. "Emma, I'm not just looking at Balfour. I'm looking at other companies. Quite a few, in fact. I have a theory. That if the FBI fabricated evidence in the Hiss case, they didn't do it by themselves, internally. They tapped one of their corporate friends—someone with the technical capabilities to build a fake typewriter or manufacture documents and produce them on microfilm or whatever it was they did. I don't know what they did. It's just a theory."

"You know you're not the first to try. You know that don't you?"

"Of course."

"So why Balfour? Why my grandfather?"

"Some of the companies I'm looking at had a particular grudge against Hiss. And Balfour's one of them."

"Because of the Munitions Hearings?"

"Yes." He's impressed by her question and noticeably so. "Yes."

"So, you're convinced Hiss is innocent?"

"Honestly, it's not about whether Hiss is innocent or guilty. He could just as well be guilty. But that doesn't mean he wasn't framed."

"Then what's the difference?"

"You don't really mean that, do you?"

He relaxes then, as if he's made his point, made his case. As if now it should all make sense. Emma rolls it around in her mind. She has turned in her seat to face him, her left leg bent, her whole body swiveled toward McLearan, her knee grazing his leg. "So," she says. "You're saying maybe my grandfather didn't do anything wrong."

"Not exactly." He almost winces, lets it go, sees no point in arguing further, feels the weight of her leg on his. Feels the connection between them, the physical attraction. He wants her to shut up, to stop talking before the conversation gets out of hand, goes any further, further than he wants it to go anyway.

But she won't let it go, because it's falling into place in her mind for the first time. All of this is new and there's nothing theoretical about the discussion. It feels real and threatening and damning, although now, again, she feels she can trust him, having seen the flyleaf of his book, knowing he's who he says he is. She goes on. "Well, let's see if I can get it exactly," she says, turning her body back to the front of the car, shifting her leg, pulling away from him. "So maybe the CIA's looking for some kind of evidence related to Balfour and the government because they have something to hide? To cover up? And you're looking for the same thing because you want to expose it? Is that possible?"

He nods slowly as she's speaking. "Anything's possible," he says, exiting at Rahway. "You hungry?"

No. 26

Washington, DC 11 a.m.

Hugh Grenville is wearing safety glasses, which both distort and magnify the purplish birthmark that shadows his right cheek. His squash racquet set on a bench outside the courts, he is pulling a tiny paper cup from the water cooler. Although he's in his sixties, he has the body of someone 20 years his junior, to all appearances. But his Izod shirt is soaked with sweat and beads of it are running down his face. A navy sports bag stands by the water cooler. It contains Margaret Quinn's gloves, her triangular mink hat, her house keys stuffed in a small brown manila envelope. His squash partner is gone, the hall empty.

He sees Tina Dowd approaching in one of her signature Chanel jackets, her heels clip-clopping on the tile floor. Without acknowledging her, he turns away, heading for the locker room. She picks up the bag and is gone in a flash. En route to a meeting out at Langley, she stashes the bag in the trunk of her silver BMW. Later in the day, the lab at the Defense Intelligence Agency will find nothing of interest among Margaret Quinn's things. The keys, two of them, on a small brass ring, will yield no new information. In fact, they have yet to find anything anywhere. Grenville is beginning to think that it was all a wild goose chase, that Margaret Quinn had nothing with her, knew nothing, that the entire thing is a fiasco. But Tina Dowd has decided that the agency—Kidman and his people—may have the evidence. And she's determined to find out.

No. 27

Rahway, NJ

Angus McLearan pulls the Mercedes Benz into a parking lot on a gritty four-lane highway off the Rahway exit of the New Jersey Turnpike.

Next door, there's a car wash and an unmarked, prefab building, another empty parking lot. Across the highway, a furniture outlet festooned with a blue plastic banner that screams "Winter Sale" and a rough-looking Chinese restaurant with an oversized wooden canopy of an entrance. The car sits in the shadow of a diner. "Fucking cold," McLearan says to himself as he gets out.

It's mid-morning and the place is empty. "Ladies room?" Emma calls over to the guy behind the counter as she enters.

"You gotta eat," he says, and she falters.

"She's with me," McLearan calls out, heading for a booth.

"I'll have a juice and a muffin," she tells him.

The bathroom is clean enough, some kind of fake marble everywhere, three or four stalls. Before sitting, she wipes down the toilet with a pile of wet towels from the dispenser near the vanity, then dries it meticulously with toilet paper. When she's finished, she stands in front of the mirror for a few minutes, messing with her hair, examining her skin. The events of the past 14 hours have taken a toll. She looks ragged, unkempt, splotchy. She washes her hands, splashes her face with cold water, grabs an elastic band from the pocket of her backpack, pulls her hair into a ponytail, applies some Chapstick. Then washes her hands again and hangs onto the paper towel so she doesn't have to touch the doorknob with her bare hands as she exits, maneuvering herself so that she can hold the door open with one foot and toss the paper towel back into the trash, an awkward and elaborate move.

She finds the payphone adjacent to the restrooms, dials the operator who puts her through to the police in Wilmington. There's a wait before she reaches anyone who can help her. Finally, she gets the investigative unit, asks about the hit-and-run case, her grandmother, whether there's been any progress. "It's not being handled here," they tell her. And, when she pushes back, they make it clear: If she wants more information, she'll need to come down to the station and bring her ID.

In the meantime, McLearan has ordered Emma's muffin and the coffees have arrived in thick, white cups. "I like what you did with your hair in there," he says, without lifting his eyes from the menu.

"I look terrible," she responds.

"That's what I meant," he shoots back. They both smile, then sit in silence until the waitress sets down Emma's muffin.

"Don't you think you ought to eat more than that?" Angus says, and, when Emma shrugs, the waitress jumps in with—"Honey, listen to your father."

"Not funny," he says, later, after he's placed his order and the waitress has departed. And once the food arrives, Emma ventures into the simple, the safe. "Where are you from anyway?"

"Scotland," he says.

She picks at the muffin. "And you have a family…" She lets it trail off, wondering if there is a wife, children, but her pride keeps her from the specifics.

"A rather large one," he says. "I grew up in the country. On a pig farm. One of seven children. Hence, my left-leaning tendencies." He slows down a minute. "Life involved a great deal of sharing."

And later, after he's started in on a hefty plate of bacon and eggs, and requested another coffee. And she's leafed through the table-top juke box and picked a few selections—soul, mostly. Temptations. Marvin Gaye. And after the music has ended, he asks why she decided to study history and why contemporary and finally, why Europe? Why Russia?

She starts with her experience at Bryn Mawr, something about taking a few history classes in her sophomore year and being "struck by all the things I didn't know," mentions her interest in "the political and social upheavals of 19th and 20th century Europe—anarchism, socialism, communism, fascism." She's had this conversation before, but here, with McLearan, she doesn't know how much she wants to reveal about herself. And she's not at all sure which he's doing more intently—listening or eating. Eating, she thinks. "I originally planned to study economics. But I took a course in European history my sophomore year," she says, still picking at the muffin. "That was the first time I'd heard anything about the Holocaust. My second year of college."

"Only in America," he says.

"Right," she goes on. "But my great-grandparents were Jewish, so you would have thought someone…"

"Ah, now it's starting to make sense," he says.

She looks at him, perplexed.

"I've just been trying to figure out why someone like you would be specializing in…"

"Someone like me?"

"Forgive me. Someone from your background."

"You don't know anything about my background."

"Well, I assume your grandfather was a certified capitalist. Although I probably shouldn't assume anything about his politics."

"Or mine. And the fact that my great-grandparents were Jewish tells you what exactly?"

"Fair enough," he says, sheepish then, hands in the air, surrendering.

"Apology accepted," Emma says, calling for the check. "Anyway, originally, I planned to study economics. But it didn't make sense to me. Too many charts and graphs and a lot of theoretical nonsense based on assumptions that seemed questionable, at best. Criminal, at worst."

"Ha!" he says. "The one that got me was the concept of scarcity. It made me think of a sparrow."

"What?" Her confusion registers on her face.

"Well, the way I see it, any sparrow knows where to find what it needs. It's all out there. I ask my students—Where is this scarcity they're talking about?"

"Right," she says, coming to life then. "This boundless desire for scarce resources. That's not what drives the economy."

"Exactly. Forget these imaginary motivations."

"It's the system. How resources are being dispersed, shared, not shared, allocated, distributed."

"And how it does and doesn't work."

"That's what economists should be…" They're both raising their voices and waving their hands around, and, when the waitress interrupts to deliver the check, she's laughing at them, which stops Emma mid-sentence.

Once she departs, Angus leans over toward Emma. "I tell my students," he says, speaking softly. "In attempting to make economics a science, they made it science fiction."

"Alas," she says, grabbing the check. "A failure of the academy."

Later, as they make their way back to the New Jersey Turnpike, past the car dealerships and the diners and strip malls and the five and dimes, as Emma watches the New Jersey landscape pass them by, she says, "Not the most scenic drive, is it?"

And he nods out the window. "Every place has a seamy side," he says. "A messy side. We all do. Don't you think?"

"Well, I think New Jersey certainly does," she says, giving him nothing. Then—"Actually, I'm wondering why you're here instead of Edinburgh at the moment, or Moscow. Why the sudden interest in American history?"

"I'm attracted to your country's idealism, the foundational principle of liberty and justice for all. It's a lofty notion. "

"But you're drawn to the seamy side of our history."

"I'm interested in the ways in which your history conflicts with those principles." He's distracted by a passing truck, focused on the rearview mirror. "The McCarthy era was certainly a low point," he says. "And that's where my studies of the Soviets tend to take me."

"And to the Hiss case in particular."

"Yes. Well, that's one of your great unsolved mysteries, isn't it? And I suspect, these days, quite a few of your historians approach it with a political bias given recent revelations about J. Edgar Hoover and Richard M. Nixon."

"Probably so," she concedes, then shifts the conversation. "Tell me this. What exactly are you hoping to find among my grandfather's papers?"

"Not sure. A communication with the FBI maybe. A record of some transaction. A calendar. A handwritten note. Anything that might be relevant. It's quite possible that Balfour had the ability to forge some of the documents used against Hiss—or plant them. Even more likely that they doctored the microfilm."

"But how likely do you think that is?"

"I was encouraged by your grandmother's reaction."

"I think that's where you made your mistake."

After that, they drive in silence for nearly an hour before Emma picks up the conversation again. "Look," she says and starts to call him by his first name but hesitates. "I can get you access to my grandfather's papers. But I'm going to want to go through all of them first."

"So you want to screen everything."

"That shouldn't surprise you. It's my family—they're my papers."

They are within minutes of Emma's home, approaching the Delaware Memorial Bridge, a twin-span that carries the rest of the world through this tiny state as they make their way to points of greater interest. "Is that a deal?" she says. He nods, and she tells him she'll have her lawyer draft up a contract. "But you'll have to wait until this whole business is over."

No. 28

Arlington, VA

When Tina Dowd arrives at the Pentagon, there are more than a dozen people at the conference table, mid-level people from the various intelligence services—Army, Navy, Defense, CIA. The subject is staffing—vulnerabilities, gaps in foreign intelligence and where the assets are needed most. It's an information-sharing session involving people who don't like to share information.

A map of the world is projected on the wall, with each agency's assets highlighted in a different color. And there are numbers indicating who has what where. The higher-level people and area specialists are at the table, other staff lined up in chairs set against the wall, all of them bathed in dim artificial light. Tina Dowd recognizes Carl

Schmidt from CIA, who has a seat at the table, and sees Bill Kidman sitting behind him against the wall. It's an unusually diverse crowd. Often, she's the only woman in the room, but there are a handful of other women present today, a few at the conference table—Human Resources being one of the top spots for filling quotas, particularly in the military. Navy's got a woman at the table. Army's got the blacks. The area specialists—intelligence analysts, a bunch of white guys— are doing most of the talking. Nobody else wants to reveal too much, to put their weaknesses on display, and nobody's making any final decisions today.

As Tina Dowd takes her seat against the wall, someone from CIA is up front doing a briefing on the staff cuts, referred to in the press as the Halloween Massacre. In-house, they call it Carter's humanitarian bullshit, and it's widely acknowledged that there's more to come. The press is all over it. "We're still under the microscope," the Chief had told Schmidt in advance of the meeting. "So keep it tight." Tina Dowd is there as an observer, on Grenville's behalf, for Defense Intelligence— DIA. One of his directors is at the table. The CIA guy up front refers to the profound impact the cuts have had on covert operations, which was clearly Jimmy Carter's intention.

Kidman's trying hard not to let his mind drift, but the conversation quickly grows tedious. This is a rare opportunity to mix with a multi-agency crowd, so he wants to stay alert. He thinks Roy Howard's name might come up, knows there are maybe six or seven agents available for overseas posts, that there's a shortage of manpower, and Roy's name hasn't been edited from the official list. They've kept a tight lid on what they're now calling OpState1—which stands for Delaware—because of a shared suspicion that someone in U.S. intelligence has to be involved. "You think Mossad came over to hit this Margaret Quinn? Or maybe MI6?" the Chief had said. "It's gotta be someone on the inside. If not here, DIA, FBI, somebody." The notation in Quinn's file—the name Skilling, Fletcher Skilling, had sealed that suspicion. But they don't have any hard facts yet. "Haven't been able to catch up with Max Frankel," Schmidt has told Kidman, adding, "Apparently, once you retire from the intelligence service you get unlimited vacations."

Late in the day, after a buffet of fruit salad and mushy sandwiches, multiple heavy refills of coffee and too much time spent in a closed-up, windowless room, everyone's a bit jumpy. And as they dig deeper into a discussion about the Middle East, lips are loosening. Given the escalating tensions in the region, PLO activity, and the shadowy prospect of peace between Egypt and Israel, the consensus, among the analysts at least, is that the top priorities are Beirut, Cairo and Tel Aviv. But that's a subject they've already covered in the morning session. Everyone in this meeting knows full well that the region's stability relies on three countries—three friends in the region: Israel, Saudi Arabia and Iran. The United States continues to funnel huge sums of money and piles of weapons into all three to keep things that way. That's where the conversation heats up. All the analysts seem to agree that the regimes in Saudi Arabia and Iran are rock solid.

"Stable" is how one analyst describes Iran. "Well, relatively. Russia can't touch Iran," he says.

"Better be stable," a guy from Defense pipes up. "We've given them about 20 billion dollars in military aid over the past decade." He pauses for effect. "And I mean billion."

"Well that's about to end," an analyst volunteers. It's no secret that the administration is pushing for cuts in weapon sales across the board.

"Not necessarily," says another. "If you read *The Times* a few days ago, you'd know the president is having a tough time saying no to the Shah."

"Since when do we get our intel from *The Times*?" a director from Armed Forces pipes up, giving Carl Schmidt an opportunity to draw the conversation back to its center.

"Well, unfortunately," he says, "we're relying on *The Times* for a lot of our information these days. As you can see, we're down to two agents in Iran—bare bones. Anyone else?"

"We've got a hole there too," a DIA director says. "But under the circumstances it might be hard to justify beefing up coverage. What we need is more intel on Iraq. As I assume everyone knows, they're about to go on the terrorism watch list. It's ugly over there."

"Agreed," Schmidt says. "What's the consensus?" he asks the analysts.

"Iran has a pretty sophisticated military at this point—one of the strongest in the region," one analyst volunteers. "The Brits have been supplying them with arms as well." He passes out a sheet of paper detailing the state of Iran's military strength and buttresses it with some PR-speak about the U.S. commitment to backing the regime. Everyone looks at one another, knowing full well the CIA put the Shah in power in 1953, ousting a parliamentary government that was threatening to cozy up with the Russians.

They seem to gloss over any possibility that the Shah could be deposed. "The internal threat is viewed as minimal," says another analyst. "Primarily religious fanatics trying to get a toehold in a place that is now highly westernized."

"The Shah's done good things for his country," says a third.

Kidman locks eyes with a CIA analyst who has yet to speak. They both know the Shah's record on human rights abuses is abysmal, that President Carter's threatened to pull military support if it doesn't improve. They know there's a lot of bullshit flying around the room, but neither of them speaks up. There's a new sense of vulnerability, inspired in part by the confusion surrounding Roy Howard's death and their suspicion that there's an internal threat, but more than that, to administration policies—the staff cuts, the military cutbacks, the changing strategy. And the agency itself is haunted by a laundry list of failures.

After the meeting draws to a close, an Army officer approaches Schmidt. He's from the Deputy Chief of Staff's office on the intelligence side—Mahmoud Hariri, a man of Lebanese descent wearing a slew of decorations on his uniform. Kidman has never met him before, and he lingers on the edge of the conversation. Tina Dowd is perched on the edge of her seat, watching from across the room.

"I understand you lost a man. Sorry to hear it," Hariri says quietly. "He was one of ours—West Point. We need to work together on this."

Noticing Dowd, Schmidt raises his voice, shuffles some papers around in his briefcase. "Well, I'd be a lot happier if we had more people on the ground over there."

Hariri picks up on it. "What we're hearing from our sources inside Mossad is that Iran's not so stable. They're getting ready to tell all the Jews there to get the hell out of Dodge. And if the Shah's government topples, it's going to be a shit storm." He lowers his voice slightly. "It may be worthwhile for us to meet." He touches Schmidt on the sleeve of his jacket as he turns to go, a gesture that's uncommon in this particular group. Kidman makes a mental note of it.

No. 29

Wilmington, DE

"Well, I'm happy to see you. So stop apologizing," Annie says, pouring coffee from a stainless steel pot, unplugged from an outlet on her kitchen counter. The room is tidy, homey, with a single window that overlooks a concrete cubicle of a yard. It's well past noon. Annie is flustered, fussing about. "We already ate. I swear it," Emma says, then, "Sit. Please sit. How are you holding up?" she asks and Annie just shakes her head.

They had driven straight from the diner in Rahway to Annie's home, a brick row house in downtown Wilmington just blocks from the expressway exit. When they'd arrived, Flip was rolled up in a ball in one corner of the front room on an old dog bed. Seeing Emma, he'd struggled to rise, crouched there, wagging his hindquarters, bowing his head, pleading with his eyes, squealing. She'd gone directly to him. "My sweet boy," she said, getting down on her hands and knees, stroking him until he settled down. Distracted, she had neglected to introduce Angus to Annie.

"Call me Mac," he'd said, taking it upon himself.

"Well, Mac, welcome," Annie had said, shooting Emma a look of pleasure. And then, "Come on," leading him into the kitchen.

By the time Emma leaves Flip's side and joins them, Annie is pouring three coffees and setting down a small pitcher of cream. "Tell me—have you talked to Mr. Treadwell?" she asks. Emma nods. "So you know, then?" Emma nods again. "Who would do such a thing? Run over an old woman and leave her to die in the snow."

"I don't know," Emma says. "But we'll find out. I promise."

All three of them sit in silence then, Flip whimpering in the outer room. "Is he all right?" Emma asks. Her concern registers on her face and in the tone of her voice.

"Been this way since it happened," Annie says. "Can't move so well."

"Remarkable that he survived," McLearan says. And Annie gives him a good, long stare.

"Mac is a historian," Emma says, "He's interested in doing some research on Grandfather's work."

"Is that right?"

"I wonder if you remember Grandmother mentioning his name— Angus McLearan. Apparently, she had agreed to meet with him before the accident."

"Is that so?"

"You don't recall that?"

"I can't say that I do," Annie says, eyeing McLearan up and down.

In the stillness that follows, the dog's pitiful cries worsen, growing into a full-blown wail, and Emma rises. "Hey," she says softly. "Hey there," as she moves through the kitchen door and out into the living room, the front room.

She half hears McLearan speaking to Annie. "I imagine you've been with the Quinns a long time," he is saying. "This must be hard for you."

"Well of course it is," Annie snaps back at him. But Emma doesn't catch it, doesn't hear, focused on the dog, a good distance from the kitchen now. As she kneels by Flip and begins to stroke his side, she doesn't see the look of dismay that crosses Annie's face or hear the anger rising in Annie's voice as McLearan plows ahead.

Lying on the floor in the outer room, Emma can make out only snippets of their conversation. She hears the persistence in McLearan's voice, hears Annie telling him that she doesn't know anything about Mr. Quinn's work, her voice rising as she says, "What on earth are you talking about?"

And now Annie too has risen and turned her back on McLearan. Shaken, she's pulling a small tray from the cupboard, preparing to carry the coffees into the living room. Emma hears McLearan offering to help. But she doesn't see Annie rejecting the offer in a flash of rage. By the time they enter the front room, Annie has regained her composure, but Emma, unaware, unthinking, eager for answers to questions of her own, plows ahead, crawling on all fours to her backpack and pulling out the book, the one she found at the library about the Balfour family, *Dynasty and Disaster*.

She flips through the photos at the back of the book as Annie and McLearan settle in on the couch, then lays it out on the coffee table before turning back to the dog, stroking him as she speaks. "Do you remember this?" she asks Annie. "Do you remember these hearings? These Munitions Hearings in the U.S. Senate?" she says.

By now, it's mid-afternoon and the row house faces east. With only two windows in the room and a few small table lamps for light, Annie has to strain to see the photo clearly. Sitting as far from McLearan as she possibly can, she examines the page, zeroes in on the photograph. "This one?" she asks Emma, who is sitting cross-legged on the floor now, with one hand on Flip's side. "My, my," Annie says almost to herself, arching her back, stiffening. "He looks so young." And then, "Oh dear."

"What?" Emma asks, turning away from the dog to get a closer look at the photograph.

All three of them lean in as Annie sets the book down on the table. "That woman there," she says. She is pointing to a woman seated beside Emma's grandfather. Her face is pale and thin, her dark hair swept up behind her head. She wears a dark suit with the padded shoulders that would have been the style. It's hard to make out her features, but the image reminds Emma of photos she has seen of Wallis Simpson, the Baltimore divorcee that drove the king of England to abdicate the throne in the 1930s—fashionable, but not pretty in the traditional sense and somewhat austere. "Your grandmother did not like that woman. Nooooo she did not," Annie says, glancing over at McLearan, back at Emma, growing uncomfortable, having second thoughts. "But you two don't need to know anything about that." Then, to Emma, "When was this?"

"Nineteen…" Emma checks the date again. "1934."

"Why, that was before my time," Annie says, but she seems to be searching her memory or calculating something in her head. "I had no idea the…the association went back that far."

"The association. Who is she?" Emma asks.

"She was Mr. Balfour's secretary. Or Mr. Simon's. I'm not sure," Annie says, turning to McLearan, speaking in a patronizing tone.

"Mr. Balfour was Mr. Quinn's boss. And Mr. Simon—Martin Simon—worked for Balfour way back when." Then she turns to Emma. "She traveled with Mr. Quinn. For many years," she says and draws the book back up to her face, examining it one last time. "Anyways, she was a tramp. That's all I have to say on the subject." Then she drops the book on the table and snaps the cover closed.

"What was her name, Annie?"

"Why on earth would you need to know her name?" and, then, "What are you two up to?"

McLearan volunteers an answer. "As I said, I'm doing some research on Balfour's involvement with the Alger Hiss case."

"Do you have any recollection of that case?" Emma says.

"I already told him no," Annie says and her voice begins to rise as she turns to Emma. "Your grandmother is not even in her grave. Lord have mercy." Then, emboldened, "And who are you anyway, Mister… Mac?" As Annie's voice rises, Flip reacts by growling, but he can barely muster the energy, and the sound he emits is odd, feeble, guttural. He's unable to lift his head, drooling, his jowl flopping against the dog bed.

As Emma turns to comfort him, she sees that he is lurching through a full-blown seizure. "Oh no oh no oh no," she mumbles. "Sweet thing," she says, trying to calm him, Annie and Angus standing over her by then, all eyes on the animal. And the adrenaline that has been pumping through Emma since she escaped from her apartment the night before is now concentrated on Flip, who continues to tremble and twitch and shudder beside her. "We've got to get him to the vet," she says, looking up at them.

She watches as Angus gets down on one knee, leaning over, examining his eyes, then reaching out and lifting the dog in his arms and rising to his feet in a single, smooth motion. "Now, now," he says. "I've got you, fella," Flip's limbs dangling in the air. "I'll drive," he says, Annie still visibly upset, opening the front door. "I'm sorry," Emma says as she turns to go. "I'm sorry we upset you."

Grabbing her backpack, the book, their coats, and running out behind Angus, Emma turns, calls out —"We'll meet you back at the house." And as this scene unfolds, Emma's heart is still racing but the ground is beginning to shift. Her reticence, her skepticism, her distrust of Angus McLearan is beginning to dissipate.

No. 30

Langley, VA 4 p.m.
Bill Kidman has Miriam Frankel and Todd Wilson in his office for an afternoon meeting. He's got a lot on his plate and, at the moment, this Quinn business is a low priority. He's circling the room popping peanut M&Ms. Every time he passes the bowl on his desk, he grabs another handful.

"Here's what we know about James Quinn," Kidman says as he paces, juggling the M&Ms in his right hand. "He was one of the guys that went down to Oak Ridge in 1942. He also made some trips with a couple of engineers looking at other sites. So, he was involved with the Manhattan Project through Balfour."

"Right. Here's the report on that, sir," Miriam says. "Not even classified. From the archives."

"But if you go further back—before the war, the company came under fire. Miriam?"

"In the '30s, Balfour Chemical was accused of war profiteering," she says. "And records show a trail of sales to Germany and Belgium between the World Wars. Some bad publicity. So, with the Manhattan Project— and after World War II—there seemed to be a desire to clean up their record, their relationship with the government. Apparently after the war, Quinn served as a kind of liaison between Balfour and Washington.

"What was his job exactly?" Kidman asks.

"His title was Director of Government Affairs. Sort of anomalous really," she hesitates, adding, "Sir."

And Todd jumps in. "So he was a bag man?" Miriam looks confused. Todd explains. "Somebody who took care of the company's dirty business."

"Potentially, yeah," Kidman says. "But I don't think we know that. If Balfour was trying to rebuild their relationship with government, rebuild their image, Quinn could have been more of a fixer.

Miriam, tell him what else you found."

"Yes sir," she says crisply, and Kidman grabs another fistful of candy. He winces every time she calls him sir. He wants to remind her this isn't the military. But she's a good kid and he holds off. Says lightly, "At ease, Miriam." And she goes on.

"Defense Intelligence has a file on Balfour. I had to requisition it. Just about everything was blacked out, classified. But there was a copy of the contract for the development of Agent Orange." She sets a slip of paper on Kidman's desk. "Dated 1958. Only thing is, according to the records, James Quinn was no longer with Balfour at that point. So, I'm not sure it's relevant."

Kidman stops pacing, pushes the bowl of M&Ms aside and sits behind his desk. "Okay folks," he says, leaning against the back of his chair, his hands behind his head, his elbows splayed out. "Here's the slippery slope we're headed down. After the war, Balfour was involved with some of the projects that surfaced in the '50s and '60s—including BCWs." He hesitates. "Biological and chemical weapons," he says, translating for Miriam, then goes on. "So, if Margaret Quinn had some sort of information—proof, as she called it—it could be anything. It could be classified. It could be something that incriminates Balfour. It also could be something that incriminates the U.S. government—the CIA, DIA, NSA, any one of us. Maybe it relates to a foreign government. Whatever it is, it looks like somebody still cares about it. What else?"

Miriam leans forward. "We also know that in the late '40s James

Quinn had some kind of relationship with the FBI, with Hoover's people.

"Oh right," says Kidman. "That business with the microfilm."

"Microfilm?" Todd says.

"He was called in to authenticate some of the evidence against Alger Hiss," Miriam explains.

"James Quinn?"

"Well, on behalf of Balfour," she says. "It was Balfour's film. Some of it anyway."

Kidman's ready to wrap this up. "Miriam," he says. "See if we have access to some of those Hiss records." He sits up straight, closes the file on his desk. "Nice work," he says, looking at Miriam, who comes back with a sharp "Thank you, sir," and Kidman stands. "I'm pulled in about 20 directions right now, so just keep at it."

No. 31

It's a good, long drive from Annie's downtown row house to the animal hospital, a straight shot from the center of town, through the traffic light at the top of Miller's Lane, past the entrance to the Quinn estate, out the Kennett Pike and deep into the surrounding countryside. "Just stay on this road until we hit the Pennsylvania border," Emma tells McLearan, sitting in the back with Flip's head in her lap.

They've been together since Emma arrived frantic and half-dressed at his hotel room the night before, and they've not much talking left in them. But somewhere between the town of Centerville, where her parents had shared their final toast the night they died, and the animal hospital not far from the Pennsylvania state line, Emma speaks this story into the air, gazing out her window, unconsciously stroking the dog: "My grandfather drove me out here one night." She goes on in a kind of ramble as McLearan watches her in the rearview mirror. "I'll never forget it. I was nine or ten years old and he woke me in the middle of the night. Seems the Russian circus had just arrived. It must have been around midnight. And he woke me by whispering in my ear—the circus is in town."

She leans forward slightly in the seat, cushioning Flip's head, lowering her voice a tad. "Come quietly or I'm certain they'll try to stop us." Then she raises it again and looks up at McLearan in the rearview mirror. "So, we snuck down the back stairs and out through the mudroom. And we drove and drove," she continues, stroking Flip, looking out at the pasture. A few horses graze near the roadside. "Imagine how exciting that was—stealing off into the night, 'Come quietly or I'm certain they'll try to stop us.'" She says it again, then is silent for a moment looking out at the open pastures bordered by forest. They pass an old white stucco house that must be 200 years old surrounded by a low fieldstone wall.

"I'm not even sure where we went exactly. But it was somewhere around here—just an open field in the middle of nowhere. Must be a train track around here somewhere." He's watching her, thinking that she seems finally to have let her guard down. "That was really something. The black sky. The stars. There was some kind of light on the ground—spotlights maybe. But it was like another world." She can see it in her mind's eye and is trying to paint a picture for him—or for herself. "They were setting up the tents and some of the animals were just roaming about—elephants and some kind of monkeys. And the bears. I'll never forget the bears." He doesn't respond, just watches her in the rearview mirror. "My grandfather and I walked right out into that field as if we belonged. There was a man walking around on stilts in some sort of robe, like an apparition." They sit in silence for a moment, then she adds, "Sometimes I wonder if it was a dream. My grandfather. He was really something."

By the time they arrive at the Quinn estate, she's so accustomed to McLearan that she forgets he's never seen the place. "Well, this is a monster, isn't it?" he says as it comes into view. The domed roof, the red brick façade, the massive white portico, like something in the Virginia countryside.

They park in the back, oblivious to the surveillance device above the garage. And Emma ushers her guest in through the mudroom and the dim, windowless back hall to the dining room, where Annie is setting the table—putting out silver, crystal, linens. She asks about Flip, but there's no warmth to her greeting. She barely looks up when Emma explains that they've left the dog overnight for observation.

"I've prepared the guest room over the garage," Annie tells Emma. "And I've made up your small room toward the back."

"Good," Emma says, trying to catch her eye. But Annie continues, all business, looking down at the table, laying out the utensils. "I'm afraid the pantry's as good as empty, but I picked up some fresh salmon and a few vegetables. I'll put dinner out shortly. And I plan on spending the night." When she finally looks up, she offers to serve cocktails in the library, but Emma says no and leads McLearan directly to the kitchen.

She has decided that there will be no more prodding of Annie, no more grilling, no more information gathering, in Mac's presence. And McLearan takes her lead. As they putter about the kitchen, their chatter is limited to which whisky he wants—"Dewar's"—and how he wants it—"straight up, no chaser"—and, once Annie joins them, whether they can maybe dig up a nice white in the cellar. Although there are no more questions about Munitions Hearings or the woman in the photograph or the accident, it hangs there between Annie and Emma —the facts as they know them: that the CIA is investigating Mrs. Quinn's death or Mr. Quinn's life and that something is awry. "You two go on in the other room and let me cook," Annie says. But Emma settles McLearan and his Scotch in the living room and returns, leaning over Annie, whispering—"The men who came to search the house, what did they say to you?"

"It was one man. He didn't say anything. I made him wait outside until Mr. Treadwell came. Then they hardly spoke to one another the whole time," Annie hesitates a minute, closing the kitchen door. "I asked him if it was because of that car." Emma tilts her head slightly. "You know. That car they found down by the mill. I suspect that's the one that killed her." Annie seems jarred by the word she herself has chosen and begins to tear up, leaning her back up against the kitchen counter, steadying herself. Emma reaches out, squeezes her hand. "We'll talk in the morning."

"You don't trust him, do you?" Annie says.

"I don't know who to trust right now."

While Emma is in the kitchen, Angus McLearan has time to decompress, to mull over the events of the day. It has occurred to him that Emma is as uncomfortable in her hometown as she was at the diner in Rahway. It's as if she doesn't really belong anywhere. But he sees now that she is absolutely at home within the boundaries of this estate. As she entered the house, the change had been physical. She seemed to grow taller, more confident, to take on a new persona. And it struck him that she was much the same as she'd been that first day he met with her, in her office at the university. Regal, aloof. He decides that it's the outside world she finds threatening in some way. But, he's thinking, no matter where she is, she carries with her a transparency, an earnestness and lack of guile that he finds appealing.

He is sitting at the center of the house in a large, square room that is oddly furnished with four leather chairs set in a circle on a worn oriental rug. With multiple entryways, it feels more like a waiting room than a living room, or maybe a traditional parlor, a holding room. In truth, the Quinns rarely used it, except to wait for one another before leaving the house or to receive guests. Over the mantle in a heavy gilt frame, is an oil painting of a ship at sea—the black ocean teeming with whitecaps, the ship's dark hull and towering masts lurching into the air, and ominous clouds gathering at the painting's edge. "Cheers," he says, raising his glass to the painting and turning his attention to his Scotch. Seeing the house and all it holds has put James and Margaret Quinn in a new perspective for him. Theirs was clearly old money, established, rooted, dug-in, plentiful, he is thinking. Like the landed gentry of his home country or British royalty, they enjoyed the kind of wealth that draws respect and prestige in a community that itself reeks of privilege.

Angus has a sense of this town now. Like vast swaths of the English countryside, the entire area is pristine, untouched, undeveloped precisely because it is all privately owned. Even the animal hospital had an air of luxury to it—with its yellow stucco knee-wall, its stables, the interior rooms all clean and fresh with none of the suffocating sick-animal smell of your average country kennel or the cheap cleaning solutions typically used to cover it up. No, this is a very fancy place, he is thinking. The little shop where they'd stopped to pick up a soda on the way home was as upper crusty as it gets—spotless, small-scale, friendly. On their way in, they'd passed a handful of ladies in camel hair coats and boiled wool jackets hustling to the specialty grocery next door to pick up a few last-minute items for Friday evening—doubtless, cheeses and crackers, frozen appetizers. They seemed to be practical, wealthy, waspy sorts, everything about them grounded in tradition. This is where the Quinns lived out their lives, he is thinking, which means this was not the kind of family that would risk its position easily, carelessly—unless their position was threatened in some way. He is curious and confused, unclear on what has happened here. It is clear to him, however, that Annie Daniels has taken on the ways of this family, and somehow, in their absence, she has appointed herself the matriarch, the monitor, the protector of the family name.

After dinner, Annie escorts McLearan out through the back to the guest quarters above the garage. Before she says goodnight, she asks him straight up, "Who are you really? And what are you doing here?" He reiterates that he's a historian, that Emma invited him to come along. Again, he insists that he contacted Mrs. Quinn shortly before her death. "By phone," he says. "Over the holidays." Annie emits a series of sounds—a humph-humph-humph under her breath that's audible, but barely, making it clear that she doesn't believe him. And before departing, she shows him the intercom next to his bedroom door. "I'm going to go lie down and take the word, Mr. McLearan," she says in her imitation dowager voice, authoritative and condescending. As a Scot, he finds her manner unexpected in a black American. "I trust you'll buzz me if you need anything," she says, adding. "It would be a shame for you to find yourself wandering around the place."

When Annie retires, Emma is downstairs, smoking a cigarette by the fire, thinking about what is afoot and how much she knows, which is very little. As a historian, she is trained in reconstructing events, in recovering some semblance of truth from whatever's available—letters, memoirs, interviews, speeches, radio broadcasts, anything—and digging out what's never been found before. But she's at a disadvantage here. Still unaware that her grandmother's death was anything more than a cruel accident and guided by McLearan's interest in the Hiss case, she feels as if she's on the wrong track altogether.

Sitting by the fire, she remembers a visit by Martin Simon in the wake of her grandmother's death. A man she'd always called Uncle Martin, although he wasn't, he'd arrived at the front door unannounced offering condolences on the first Friday evening following the accident, a few days after Emma herself had arrived. He hadn't stayed long, but he'd sat in this very chair while they'd shared a drink in the library. She hadn't seen him since her grandfather's funeral 15 years before. But she knew they were close and wasn't surprised when he appeared.

Emma remembers feeling almost relieved to have someone to talk to other than Annie, who was perennially on the edge of tears at that point. And they'd sat by the fire as he nursed a rye on the rocks. She'd told him that she rarely spoke to her grandmother, hadn't been down in several years and, flatly, that she didn't know her very well. "We weren't close," Emma said, as she always did when asked, sipping on a brandy. "I suspect I reminded her too much of my mother."

"Ah, yes," he said. "That pushed her over the edge a bit." He's still for a minute. "She was rather a misanthrope, you know. And a bit off-kilter. But she always had an eye for the truth."

Uncle Martin, as she called him, was not a good-natured man and not at all like her grandfather, who had a charm and levity to him. Their friendship seemed unlikely to her. Martin was all sharp edges. As he spoke, his eyes darted around the room. At one point, he got up. Holding the rye in one hand, the ice melting away, he walked around behind the mahogany desk where bookshelves stretched from floor to ceiling. "He had a brilliant mind, your grandfather." Surveying her grandfather's books, Martin was talking into the air, his back to Emma. "He told me the next great war would be in the Middle East. He was always thinking ahead of his time. He read all these books, you know," turning back toward Emma then. "Had he lived to see the 1967 war, he wouldn't have been stunned like everyone else—by the brevity of it, the command of the Israeli army." Then he began to walk back toward his chair, slowly, with a slight bend to his back, as if it was a great effort simply to move his legs. "Wonder if that's where you got your interest in history," he said, as if he was putting two and two together for the first time. "In a way," she said.

When he was ready to leave, he set his rye on the table between them and spoke brusquely, as if he'd had enough of this sentimentality. "I trust you'll be going back to your teaching in New York," he said. "Yes," she said as she rose. He moved forward to give her a hug, but it was awkward, his crooked body reaching toward her. It wasn't an embrace of any kind, for he barely touched her. To Emma, it felt as if two stiff, bony branches were trying to encircle her and failing, just brushing her arms ever so lightly. "Good to see you," he said before he left, without a trace of feeling, putting on a fedora, and as he turned to go out the door added, "Be safe."

Now, ruminating on it, she reaches for another cigarette. But she's smoked her last and decides to hunt one down, heading first to the kitchen, searching for a carton in the pantry. Annie was true to her word. Save a few boxes of crackers and a six-pack of soda, it's empty. So she slips up the back stairs, tip-toeing into the back hall, through the massive bath with its double sinks and into her grandmother's sitting room. Stalking cigarettes is something she's good at, something she'd practiced here on trips home from boarding school and college, and part of her routine at home. She neglects to buy them with any regularity, leaves opened packs lying about or stashed in pockets and drawers, and she takes a certain pleasure in the search. But this is not going to be easy. The house has been turned inside out. The drawers in her grandmother's sitting room, the most likely spot for a fresh pack of Camels, are clean. The closet that runs like a hallway alongside her grandmother's bedroom, once home to a host of promising purses and pockets, holds little hope. Everything is gone, she thinks. Annie has been busy.

Moving through the bedroom—the bedside tables, the dressing table, the dresser itself—Emma's search begins to morph into something else altogether. She tries to imagine what the CIA was looking for and where they would have begun, heads for her grandfather's study. She goes through the desk and finds the drawers empty—no files, no records, no papers, no pens. Combing the shelves, she leafs through empty binders tossing them aside, then slams open the file drawers in the credenza and the cabinets. She finds nothing, no remnant of his work or record of his life aside from books and magazines, still photographs and the degree hanging on his wall. She opens some of the books, looking for notes or hidden secrets, then abandons that process for now. Resolving to call Treadwell in the morning to ask about her grandfather's private papers and about the CIA's visit, she moves on to her grandmother's study. There, behind an overstuffed chair, she discovers a promising metal box. Inside—old passports and birth certificates, including her mother's and her own, the deed to the house and what seems to be a copy of her grandfather's will. She carries it downstairs, sets it on the floor in the front hall closet. As she leans over, the edge of her grandmother's long mink coat rubs against her neck like a living thing. She jumps back, grabs the damn thing and tosses it into the hallway, standing over it, unmoving, until she gathers her senses, shaking her head, laughing at herself, to herself.

Setting it back on the hanger, musing at the iconic monster of a coat, Emma rummages through its pockets and finds a near-full pack of Camels, a small black cigarette holder, a silver lighter and, beneath them all, a handwritten note, folded carefully at the corners. She sits down by the fire that is very nearly out and smokes two cigarettes, to dizzying effect, unfolding the note to read these words: MURIEL MARKHAM, 652-8074, Pinehurst 21 Wood Hollow 2/2/2pm.

No. 32

It's after midnight when Emma gets into bed. Agitated, over-stimulated by all the nicotine, by McLearan's presence, by the cryptic note she found in her grandmother's pocket, Emma sleeps poorly. She stays awake making a mental list of people she needs to see, people she needs to talk to—George Treadwell, Martin Simon, Mr. Kidman from the CIA, the Wilmington Police and this Muriel Markham. And Annie, of course. She still hasn't had a chance to sit down with Annie. Then there's this business with Angus McLearan. She resolves to check with Treadwell about her grandfather's papers. But it occurs to her that she might have to send McLearan on his way. Caught up in the logistics of it, she sleeps fitfully, tossing her covers off, rolling from side to side in the tiny bed.

After a few hours, she finds herself downstairs wearing night-clothes that she doesn't recognize and standing in the kitchen near the bay window that faces the backyard, the boxwood garden, the four-car garage. The room is unlit. She is surrounded by darkness, looking through the window into more darkness when she spots a glint of something outside. It draws her closer to the window. There, lights flash across the yard—just as they did the night Bill Kidman and his men searched the grounds. Leaning in until she is only a few inches from the glass, she peers out, pressing her face against the windowpane. As she does, she is stunned to see someone, something on the other side, approaching the glass. Then right in front of her, coming in so close she can feel it, a face pressing against the glass, a pair of eyes a hair's breadth from her own. Terrified, she awakens, wailing a muted moan of a wail that spills through the house and brings Annie to her side.

"They were lying," Emma says. "When they came and searched the house, they were lying."

"Of course they were," Annie says. "They had no business here."

In the morning, Emma awakens, groggy, only half-rested. Annie is waiting for her in the kitchen, walking in circles, wound up, pacing, ready to pop. "Where is he?" Emma asks, speaking slowly, pouring herself a cup of coffee. "Out walking," Annie says. "He has a gun. I saw it. Why would he have a gun?"

"He carries it with him" is all Emma can muster, seating herself at the kitchen table. She's rumpled, disoriented. Annie sets down a plate—two pieces of wheat toast, a dollop of strawberry preserves, a sliced apple. She's hovering. "Eat," she mutters. Emma looks up at her. "Who's Muriel Markham?" she asks.

Annie doesn't hesitate. "It's that woman," she answers. "The one in the photograph in that book of yours. That secretary," Annie says, and

Emma just shakes her head, saying, "Was she Uncle Martin's assistant? Or Mr. Balfour's?"

"I don't know. Why?"

"Because it seems Grandmother met with her last month. Right before she died. Is that possible?"

"Where did you get that idea?"

"She wrote it down. It was very explicit."

"Of course it was," Annie says.

Emma pulls the note out of the pocket her jeans, handing it to Annie. "On the 2nd of February. It would have been the Thursday before she died. At two in the afternoon."

"Good Lord," Annie says, looking up at Emma. "Lester takes her out on Thursdays."

"Where?"

"Beauty shop. Drug store. Doctor. Wherever she wants to go."

Emma spends the hour that follows in her grandfather's second-floor office with the door closed. She calls Lester first, then George Treadwell. Asks about the visit from the CIA. "Or was it the FBI? Your message said the FBI." He speaks slowly, laboriously, and Emma grows impatient. It's as if she has to pull the sentences from him like taffy. And in the end, he tells her only that it was the CIA, that they suspected foul play of some kind and that someone else was killed that morning near the old Balfour Mill. "Who?" she asks.

But he has no good answer. "They said that it was a federal matter. Apparently, that's why they're involved. Because of that incident, not because of your grandmother's death." He offers this explanation for why they came to search the Quinn estate: "They think she was just in the wrong place at the wrong time. But they said they just needed to make sure she wasn't involved in some way. I told them, I said, Good Lord the woman was an 80-year-old recluse. And I mentioned her mental health history to drive the point home." He reports that the CIA requested a copy of the will.

"They're lying." That is what Emma wants to say, but she doesn't. She holds back, unsure whether she can even trust Treadwell. Instead, she says, "Why would they need a copy of the will—unless they believe that she was murdered?"

"They said, and I quote, just to cover all the bases," he explains.

"Precisely," she says.

He tells her that James Quinn's papers were never archived. "They'd be in his office at the house, as far as I know." And reports that the CIA—not the Wilmington Police—are handling the investigation.

Her next call is to Martin Simon—Uncle Martin—who seems glad to hear from her and immediately invites her over. "I had a visit from the Central Intelligence Agency," he says. "Most disturbing." Emma is convinced that Bill Kidman and his friends at the CIA have stolen all her grandfather's papers, everything. And that they probably broke into her apartment to collect those news clippings. She has tried to reach Bill Kidman three times, to no avail. After the third try, she dials Muriel Markham's number, lets it ring ten, maybe 15 times before hanging up. Then she heads out before Angus McLearan returns.

No. 33

For reasons unknown to anyone in the surrounding community, Martin Simon has given his home a name. Emma has been there only once before, for a Christmas party some years ago when she was a student at boarding school and home for the holidays. She recalls her grandparents talking about it on the way over—the naming of Uncle Martin's house. Her grandfather had called it a contrivance. Her grandmother had said simply, "Well, it's absurd." Emma can still picture the tops of their heads, visible to her from the back seat of her grandfather's Cadillac—her grandmother in that boxy mink hat of hers, her grandfather at the wheel. Martin's is not a small home. It's set back off the road in the countryside near the Balfour estates and has the look of a small castle, crafted of stone with a turret at its corner and a long circular drive. She remembers the bronze plate at the front entrance. Crestmere, it said. "What on earth does that stand for?" her grandmother had remarked when they arrived at the door that Christmas Eve. And she recalls her grandfather leaning over, whispering in Margaret Quinn's ear, silencing her.

On that festive night, Uncle Martin had decorated a large ever-green in the front yard with colored lights and there was a valet stand-ing at the top of the drive, taking keys and bringing the cars round. Emma remembers the exact dress she wore and recalls feeling special and grown up and conscious of their place in the scheme of things. The feeling was not one of superiority but rather a self-conscious appreciation of the aesthetics of wealth. Even after she got older and wise enough to feel a shame in it, she still on occasion experienced that sense of elegance and grandeur, of privilege, but always as if, in experiencing it, she was removed from reality somehow, playing out someone else's fantasy, living in a make-believe world.

She recalls the Christmas party—holiday music flowing through rooms decorated with bayberry candles and fresh garlands, a massive crystal punchbowl filled with eggnog, champagne. Early in the eve-ning, she'd met a young man, someone's son, a local boy who was, like Emma, away at school. She can't recall his name anymore, but she has a clear image of him in her mind. He wore his ash-colored hair in bangs, swept over to one side of his forehead like someone in a surfer movie, and had a round, handsome, suntanned face and an athletic build. He was arrogant, and she remembers him trying to get her to sneak upstairs with him. Although she rebuffed his advances, she recalls his relentless determination and being flattered by it, feel-ing attractive and not in the least threatened. She remembers, even as a young girl, feeling uncomfortable about the world in which she was raised, but at the same time, feeling safe and protected. This is what drifts through her mind as she makes her way up the driveway to Crestmere, the surfer boy from Choate with his tweed jacket and his persistence, and her own conflicted feelings about the boy and the party and the place where she grew up.

Martin never married, so there was no Mrs. Simon to greet them the night of the Christmas party or today as Emma arrives with all her questions. He answers the doorbell himself dressed in athletic apparel—grey sweat pants, a hooded sweatshirt, bright white sneakers. He seems mildly agitated. "I didn't know what to think when the CIA contacted me," he says, ushering her back to the kitchen. It's a large, unrefurbished room with linoleum countertops and a tin top table off to one side. The kitchen walls are a minty green, a color popular in the 1950s and distinctly unappetizing from Emma's perspective. The refrigerator is massive, obviously a restaurant unit, as if the house was built for entertaining. "I was just fixing myself a sundae," he says puttering over to the counter. "Join me?" Surprised by the idea of it, she assents. Here, at home, he seems a bit softer, rather like a playful scarecrow with his small frame and craggy features. A box of fresh raspberries sits on the counter beside a can of whipped cream, a jar of cherries. She pulls a chair up to the tin top as he proceeds to disembowel a tub of swirly vanilla fudge. Then, presenting the sundaes, he leans in conspiratorially as they sit. "Soooo," he says, drawing it out until it becomes a question.

"So, I was hoping you could tell me about their visit. The CIA people," she says. "What was it about?" She tastes the whipped cream and feigns a swoon.

He's oblivious, perfunctory. "Well, it was a young man, and he didn't say much. Just asked a lot of questions about Balfour. About what your grandfather did. About his job. His activities in Washington—that sort of thing." Even as he speaks, he's attacking his sundae as if it's the first meal of the day, which it may well be. "I suppose they were fishing around to see if I knew anything about why she called them."

Emma looks up. "Excuse me," she says, bewildered.

He nudges her, speaking through a mouthful. "Eat up. It'll melt before you know it."

She asks him to repeat himself and he says, "Your grandmother apparently called the Central Intelligence Agency and told them she had some kind of proof of wrongdoing, some kind of documentation of God-knows-what."

It's the first Emma has heard of this, which of course changes everything. He goes on, sinking his spoon deeper into the sundae, swirling it around as he speaks. "I explained about her mental condition," he says. "And I suggested that, whatever she had told them, it was probably not reliable." Emma is leaning in, listening intently. "That she was prone to imagining things, to a certain amount of paranoia." He pauses, staring out the window, heaves a small sigh. "What a tragedy," he says.

Emma has lost interest in the ice cream, trying to digest this new information, to make sense of something that doesn't make any sense. "But if she was making something up—why would this have happened?"

"In the world of espionage, I imagine anything can happen my dear."

She's taken aback by his use of the word espionage and presses him. "Well, can you imagine anything my grandfather might have been involved in that would interest the CIA?"

"My dear, I can imagine a dozen things he could have been involved in, but I'm inclined to think your grandmother knew nothing of them." She sits still, waiting, listening, letting him talk. "The company was involved in quite a few projects that might raise eyebrows. All legal, mind you. The bomb, of course. And once Russia got hold of it, the administration confronted us with a new challenge—to find something that would scare the hell out of the Russians without necessarily destroying the entire human race. Truman was hell bent on it. And Eisenhower. New weapons. New kinds of weapons. A nasty business."

He speaks matter-of-factly, and it occurs to Emma that he knows a great deal about all of this, possibly more than he's saying. "Such as?" she asks.

"Oh Lord, oh Lord, let's see." He hesitates as if he's trying to recall. "Chemical. Biological. And psychological ones. Let's not forget those."

He takes the last bite of his ice cream. "Doubtless you're aware of some of the experiments at Fort Detrick that captured Senator Church's attention, experiments with which I believe your grandfather was not pleased."

"That LSD incident. Don't tell me Balfour…"

"No. No. No. Balfour had nothing to do with any of that. But we knew about it. And other things. I don't think we need to go into all that." She presses him, but he ignores her and rises. "Finished?" he asks, although she's barely touched the sundae. With her assent, he carries the two bowls over to the sink and begins to wind up the conversation. "I suspect it was an accident, an unfortunate misunderstanding." He is talking about her grandmother now. "She may have had access to some of your grandfather's files that were top secret at some point. Perhaps that's how she got the idea to contact the agency." He pours her leftovers into the sink and turns on the spigot. "Or it may have been some kind of fabrication," he says. "I imagine this is one of those situations where we may never know what happened. Never know the truth."

"But they killed her, Uncle Martin," she says, her voice firm and controlled. "Someone killed her."

"Do you think?" he says. "I'd wager that it was an accident. It wouldn't have been deliberate."

"Well, she's dead," Emma says as if that will somehow shake him out of his complacency. She is baffled by the casualness with which he is taking this news. She wonders if he knows more than he's letting on, if he might have been complicit in some way.

Martin Simon was born before her grandfather, so he may well be in his nineties, she is thinking, and he has a weary look about him. He seems to be fading in and out of the conversation. But she wants to ask about Alger Hiss, so she pushes on, moving over to the kitchen counter, standing next to him. He's washing the dishes by hand, then hand-drying each one with a worn dish towel.

"You worked with my grandfather during the McCarthy hearings, am I right?" He doesn't respond, doesn't even turn his head. She goes on. "I've had a visit from a historian, a professor. He's doing research on the Cold War era. He maintains that Balfour may have been involved in framing Alger Hiss. Do you think that's the wrongdoing Grandmother was talking about?"

Martin laughs out loud, a crackly, wheezy laugh that damn near knocks him over. He moves slowly back toward the kitchen table, catching his breath. The light coming in through an east-facing window crosses his face, making him look ancient. "Well your historian is barking up the wrong tree," he says, supporting himself with one arm as he sits. "Your grandfather did have a bit part in the Hiss drama. Of course, you would have no idea of that. Balfour was one of the companies that confirmed the authenticity of the microfilm—the famous Pumpkin Papers. We worked with Hoover and his people. Ah. Now there's a piece of history for you."

"Meaning Balfour? Balfour worked with the FBI on that?"

"That's no secret. But your historian must be confused. There was no framing to it. Simply doing our jobs."

"And Grandfather was somehow involved?"

"Nothing more than a messenger, a liaison. There was some confusion over the film and it had to be straightened out."

"Confusion?"

"As to whether the film was what the Chambers fellow said it was. And it proved to be."

"I just want to understand what Grandfather had to do with it."

"It was about Balfour. Not your grandfather. Balfour. The government just needed to confirm the dates, that the microfilm was what Whittaker Chambers said it was. And it proved to be just that."

"Are you sure?"

"Am I sure? Of course, I'm sure."

"I just want to know the truth."

"This is all in the public records, my dear girl. There's nothing secret about it." He walks back toward the counter, toward Emma. "There was no framing. There was no suggestion of framing. At least not among any of us. And, just for the record, your grandfather found J. Edgar Hoover to be untrustworthy. He didn't care for him." Then he stops for an instant and, shrugging with a slight smile, says, "Although I was actually rather fond of the man."

"But wasn't Alger Hiss an enemy of Balfour's?" Emma says. "Didn't he mount an attack against the company in the 1930s?"

He stares at her, incredulous.

"The Nye Committee," she says. "Those Munitions Hearings. Surely, you remember that."

"My dear girl," he says grasping her shoulders with his boney hands, sounding like someone lecturing a small child. "Look here— Hiss was a scoundrel. You can be sure of that. Accusing us of all sorts of things." He pauses. "War profiteering? Bull crap. Balfour is a business, like any other. We don't start wars. We don't have to. There are plenty of people out there capable of doing that." He's turned away from her and is walking in circles now, throwing a hand in the air. "Alger Hiss. Mr. Peacemaker. I imagine he was trying to feather his own career." Then he begins to compose himself. "But frame him? No, I don't think your grandfather would have had the stomach for such a thing. Besides, it proved to be unnecessary."

As she drives back to the estate, Emma is turning this all in her head—authenticating microfilm for J. Edgar Hoover, developing chemical and biological weapons for the U.S. government. The mention of Fort Detrick—"Things with which your grandfather was not pleased." Emma recalls the furor over the LSD experiments undertaken on military men at Fort Detrick, revealed during the Church Committee hearings, one of which resulted in a suicide. And there's this piece that would never have occurred to her, that she would never have imagined—that her grandmother called in the CIA. "It seems she was just in the wrong place at the wrong time," George Treadwell had said. By the time Emma leaves Martin Simon's kitchen, she knows full well that is a lie. She knows that her grandmother was up to something.

Somehow, as disturbing as they are, Emma feels liberated by these revelations. If what Uncle Martin says is true, it helps explain the disturbing collection of news clippings and their disappearance from her apartment, the charade of a house search by the CIA and the search warrant that followed. Whatever her grandmother was up to, she had somehow made a terrible blunder. "In the world of espionage, I imagine anything can happen, my dear." It seems clear to Emma at this point that Margaret Quinn has gotten herself killed by the very people she thought were her allies.

And what about Angus McLearan? She's thinking that this Hiss business is a dead end, irrelevant. That she's been misled. No, not misled. Played. If he has researched the Hiss case, she thinks, he knows full well the role Balfour—and her grandfather—would have played in the whole affair. Yet he'd said nothing of it. "Dammit," she says to herself. She had been imagining all kinds of possibilities. Perhaps her grandfather and this Muriel Markham, this secretary, had been engaged in some kind of subterfuge—forging documents, say, or helping the FBI. Perhaps they were afraid they would be exposed, that the truth would come out. That maybe the publication of *Perjury* had somehow triggered these events. It seems unlikely to her now. She wants to be rid of Angus McLearan—rid of him so she can contact this Muriel Markham unencumbered, talk with Annie and Lester, call this Bill Kidman, this CIA man who directs special projects, get to the bottom of this.

That afternoon, Emma will tell Angus McLearan that there are no papers. She'll take him into her grandfather's study and open every drawer and flip through the row of binders on the bookshelves and open the credenza to show him it's empty, that she has nothing to share with him. "Surely there's an archive," he will say. But, no, she will explain, there isn't, and she will suggest again that he contact Balfour Chemical. But, disinclined to alienate him, she will not confront him, still unsure of where the truth lies. And, shortly afterwards, he'll depart in a taxicab. "Headed back to New York," he'll say, and he'll make no promises, nothing about, "I'll be back in touch or call me if you need me." Just before he leaves, there will be a brief awkward moment at the front door where the two of them—Emma and Angus—seem propelled toward one another, toward an embrace of some kind, but they stop themselves. McLearan instead will deliver a firm handshake. And she will watch from the front door as the cab makes its way down the drive not at all sure when she'll see him again.

On Sunday morning, Emma drives the 20 miles north out the Concord Pike, past the Howard Johnson's where Roy Howard spent his last night, and the Carpet King and the Dunkin' Donuts where he'd bought his final meal—to arrive at a place called Pinehurst, in the hope of meeting with Muriel Markham. Lester had indeed driven Margaret Quinn out there on the second of February. "I waited in the car," he told Emma. "She said she was having coffee with an old friend." Wasn't in there long, he explained and said, yes, he thought it was odd, unusual. "Far as I know, she didn't have friends," Lester told Emma.

At this point, Emma has no idea what to expect. Based on Annie's comments, it seemed as if this Markham woman had had an affair with her grandfather. When pressed on the subject, Uncle Martin had been characteristically vague—"Anything's possible," he had said, and "She was quite a beauty, that one." When Emma asked Martin whether he'd kept in touch with her, he said, "Lord no. She was just a secretary. And I assumed she was dead by now." But Emma believes this is her best chance of understanding what exactly transpired in the weeks leading up to her grandmother's death.

Pinehurst is easy enough to find. Beyond a stretch of shopping malls well outside of town, it's a cluster of low-lying wooden buildings, contemporary, with smoke spewing from a few of the chimneys and rustic screen porches jutting out here and there. It looks more like a summer camp than a retirement community. Signs direct visitors to the main building, a '50s-modern, single-story, ranch-style at the center of the place. The man at the front desk—one Marius Bridgewater—is friendly, welcoming. He directs Emma to Ms. Markham's residence, as he calls it.

When she arrives, Emma climbs out of the old Mercedes onto a barren yard, more dirt than grass, sprinkled with pine cones and dried pine needles. There's no answer at the front door. Circling around to a small screen porch in the shadow of the trees, she takes the liberty of peering through the windows, where she sees no one. Afterwards, she sits in her car out front for a good 30 minutes, waiting expectantly, then drives back around to the main building, where Marius Bridgewater will call Ms. Markham's number and buzz the activity center and check in with the infirmary. But he'll have no luck. At a little after noon, Emma gives up.

By then, unbeknownst to Emma, Angus McLearan is headed north on the New York Thruway with Muriel Markham in the back seat of a van. And Serge Breuer, the man who has been following Emma around Manhattan for the past few weeks, is headed South on I-95 to the port of Philadelphia.

No. 34

Philadelphia, PA 3 p.m.

"Burn them," Serge Breuer says, walking in circles on the concrete floor of a near-empty warehouse on the edge of the Philadelphia waterfront. He is agitated. "Why do we not just burn them?"

Tina Dowd, transformed into something out of an L.L. Bean catalog, looks up from the stacks of news clippings laid out on the desk in front of her. "You're a fool," she says.

Serge stares down at her. "Well, I hear you say they have no meaning. So, do they have meaning or not?" He starts pacing again.

"I'm almost finished," she says and then, with a scowl, "Don't you have something else you can do? What about all these boxes? And that black book you keep talking about?"

"We have looked already," Serge says. Two men pushing a pair of dollies stacked with boxes nod their heads up and down. "We have looked everywhere. It is not here."

"Fine," she says, turning back to the clippings. Thirty minutes later, she picks up the phone, dials Hugh Grenville's Chevy Chase home, speaks. "I've read the news. Random shots in the dark. Meaningless." Serge reaches his hand toward the receiver. "He's not there," she says.

He grabs it anyway, adding this to the message: "We ship tomorrow." He starts to pass the phone back to her, then changes his mind, speaks again. "And I've told this lady here that we want to destroy all of it. We want it out of here. It's not safe."

He sets the receiver down and picks up one of the dozen glass paperweights that are lined up in a row at the front of the desk. He holds it in his hand, examining the red and black ribbon of glass swirling at its center.

PART II

A freight train makes its way from Philadelphia down the coast to North Carolina and along the banks of the Cape Fear River, stopping where it spills its waters into the sea. Scores of military transport vehicles are set one after another in an orderly row on a series of flatbed cars. The vehicles are boxy and jeep-like, with high, wide wheels and canvas tops, the color of desert sand. From a distance, they look like a string of toy trucks winding like a snake through the swampy countryside. The train is headed for Southport, North Carolina. Toward the rear there is a single boxcar loaded with 55-gallon steel drums stacked on steel pallets. The drums are hidden from view, but each one is clearly marked hazardous.

No. 35

Washington, DC

It's been two weeks to the day since Margaret Quinn died on Miller's Lane during The Great Blizzard of 1978. The storm's old news. Today, the front page of *The Times* is dominated by the story of a bizarre hostage-taking incident in the Middle East—Palestinian terrorists stormed a gathering at the Hilton Hotel in Nicosia, killing the editor of Egypt's leading newspaper, taking hostages, hijacking an airplane. An unsolicited attempt by Egypt to free the hostages has resulted in the death of 15 Egyptian commandos at Larnaca Airport in Cyprus. A bloody mess. By Monday morning, it's a full-blown diplomatic crisis. And it's a situation that's monopolized the attention of Carl Schmidt and Bill Kidman for most of the weekend. On Monday morning, they're called over to the State Department for another round of how-did-we-miss-this? Then Kidman is expected at an agency meeting about a situation unfolding in Iran. Margaret Quinn is the last thing on either of their minds. But, before they even make it over to State, Schmidt gets a call, the one he's been waiting for—from Max Frankel, Miriam Frankel's grandfather and the former chief of the division.

A few hours later, Schmidt heads into DC. There, not far from Wisconsin Avenue near the northern edge of the city's tony Georgetown neighborhood, a red brick wall taller than any man stretches from the Dumbarton Oaks Museum to the end of the block where 32nd dead ends into S Street. With its narrow streets, its elegant townhouses, its brick sidewalks, this is a rarefied corner of the world. Max Frankel and his wife live nearby in a three-story townhouse. They're just back from three weeks in Provence and, on Sunday evening, they'd entertained the family at the residence, something of a homecoming. Their granddaughter Miriam, of course, had been in attendance. It was a late night. Nonetheless, Max Frankel made it a point to call Carl Schmidt first thing on this Monday morning.

At noon, Frankel arrives at the entrance to Dumbarton Oaks in the back seat of a silver Mercedes Benz. Schmidt is already waiting beyond the red brick wall on a wooden bench beside a fountain. He has been waiting for nearly a week for this conversation to take place. He wants to ask Frankel about James Quinn and Balfour Chemical and Fletcher Skilling—the name scratched in pencil inside the Quinn file. He wants to delve into the past. At 84, Max Frankel has spent his entire life working in the intelligence field. He is short and stout, and since his retirement has taken to wearing a white beard that makes him look like a wise old man, although not a jovial one. He wears a brown felt fedora and walks with an umbrella that he uses as a cane.

At first, he passes Schmidt by, doesn't recognize him. They have met only twice before—at his son's wedding in 1955 and his grand-daughter Miriam's naming ceremony a few years later. It happens that Carl Schmidt's wife went to college with Miriam Frankel's mother, hence the connection. It's not a strong one. In truth, the two men have little in common aside from their experiences in remote corners of the intelligence community. It's been more than 20 years since they have had reason to inhabit the same space. The first time Frankel walks by, Schmidt imagines it's deliberate, a ploy of some kind. But no. It's just an oversight.

Frankel takes a second turn around the fountain and ends up facing the bench, looking at Carl Schmidt head-on. "Ah, it's you, isn't it?" he calls out and they exchange a few pleasantries. Frankel begins it. "I understand my granddaughter is now in your employ." And Schmidt provides a glowing report of Miriam's activities. But Max Frankel is not one for small talk and after that brief greeting, he gets right to it. "Tell me everything you know," he says, and Schmidt delivers a brief summary of the Quinn case, suggesting that they are "making some progress." Then he asks, "Did you know James Quinn or know of him?"

"No. I didn't," Frankel says, firm, direct. "But I do know that the company has been tremendously supportive of our efforts over the years."

When Schmidt presses him—"Perhaps you knew him through Fletcher Skilling?"—Frankel grows irritated.

"Look," he says. "The last thing we want to do is nose around in Balfour's business or draw attention to it in any way. In fact, I'm surprised you even followed up on the call from this Mrs. Quinn."

"But sir…"

"They're one of ours. They've always been. Since the war. Since the establishment of the agency."

Looking down at his feet, Schmidt is silent for a time, assessing his position. They continue along the brick pathway and deeper into the park, passing by the play area with its wooden swings and old-fashioned seesaws, and on to the topiary garden. It's a Monday. It's chilly and cloudy. The place is empty. After a moment, Schmidt raises another question. "What branch do you think they work with?"

And again, Frankel stops dead in his tracks, turning to face Schmidt head-on. "You're not hearing me," he says.

To his credit, Schmidt stands firm. "They may have killed one of our men, sir."

But Max Frankel does not relent. "That was your responsibility," he says. "Your mistake." Then, in as few words as possible, he tells Schmidt to take his people off the case. "Shut it down," he says and turns away, heading back to 32nd Street, leaving Schmidt standing alone in the cold.

No. 36

Langley, VA

When Emma arrives at CIA headquarters not long after noon, she's ushered upstairs by Todd Wilson. She recognizes him immediately as one of the men who searched the estate a few weeks earlier, the one with the gun and the faux leather jacket, the one for whom she'd developed an immediate distaste. But today he seems different, fresh-faced, younger, less ominous. He re-introduces himself, respectfully this time, his eyes welling with curiosity, bowing slightly as he directs her to the sofa opposite Kidman's desk, tells her to have a seat, that Kidman is tied up, and it may be a while.

She's dressed all in black, in the only thing she could find in her closet in Delaware—a black cashmere coat and black wool dress purchased in the mid-sixties and worn only once, to her grandfather's funeral. She'd paired it with her brown leather boots and black tights. Sitting cross-legged now on Bill Kidman's sofa, visible through a wall of windows, she presents a curious picture, that of a bereaved widow perhaps, unpolished, an outsider.

Nonetheless, today, Emma knows a good deal more than she did the first time she met Bill Kidman. She knows from her Uncle

Martin that her grandmother contacted the CIA, and from George Treadwell, that someone else died that day near Miller's Lane—the man who abandoned his vehicle in the storm. But she has no clue as to who he was, why the man died or how he might be connected to the mystery surrounding Margaret Quinn's death. She suspects that the CIA has emptied out her grandfather's office, that they broke into her apartment, and that they are either hopelessly off track or engaged in some kind of cover-up. She has plenty of questions. She's arrived un-announced, and she'll wait three hours for Bill Kidman's arrival.

After his grilling at State, Kidman hasn't the stomach for any more tap-dancing around issues. He's forthright, direct. She's full of questions, beginning with, "I understand a body was found on the Old Mill Road the day my grandmother died."

"One of our agents was killed that day. Shot in the head," he says, and pauses to let the impact set in. "Between your home and the old powder mill."

"Is there some reason you didn't tell me that the night we met?"

"We didn't know it. We hadn't found his body." He hesitates again, deliberately. "And after that, because we didn't know whether we could trust you."

"But you knew that my grandmother had contacted you."

"Yes. Our man was waiting for your grandmother. She had arranged the meeting."

"So, she did contact you."

"Yes," Kidman says and slips his desk drawer open. He pulls out a notepad and flips through a few pages. "I spoke to her myself," he says, stopping in mid-sentence to look directly at Emma for a moment, "when she called the agency. Let me tell you exactly what she said." He starts to read from his notes. "She said, 'I know who's selling all these weapons…'" But he's interrupted by Todd Wilson, who tells him that Carl Schmidt is waiting in the adjacent room, that he needs to talk to him, that it's urgent.

"Dammit," Kidman tells Schmidt, when he gets the news. "God Dammit." And then—"You gotta be kidding me."

"It's over," Schmidt tells him.

"And what do you propose I tell the granddaughter who's sitting in my office as we speak. That we've just decided to let it pass?" Kidman shoots back, his voice rising.

"Just tell her it was a wild goose chase," Schmidt says. "Tell her that her crazy grandmother called us with a crazy story. That we responded. And that it ended up getting both of them killed."

"Okay. So, she's not dumb. She's going to want to know who killed her grandmother," Kidman says.

Schmidt sits quietly for a moment. "Tell her it was a foreign government. That they got wind of it. Thought it was for real. That we are pursuing it through diplomatic channels. That it's over. That it was a tragedy."

When he returns to his office, he sees that Emma's face has fallen in a manner that suggests some failure of the muscles, a slackening— that, when he left the room, he had left her stunned. "Sorry about that," he says. "Where was I?"

"If I heard you correctly, you said—I know who is selling all these weapons…"

And he picks up where he left off, editing his notes slightly, but giving her a good sense of it. "I know who's selling all these weapons that are killing innocent people all over the world," he reads. "And I have proof." He stashes the notepad away.

"That's it?" she says. "Surely you didn't take her seriously." She's picturing all those news clippings in her mind, her grandmother frantically documenting all those incidents, the weapons, the violence, and she imagines a kind of mania taking hold.

"Given that your grandfather was in the business of producing weapons, we felt compelled to at least explore the possibility that she knew something that we didn't."

"My grandmother had a history of mental health issues. Are you aware of that?"

"No. We were not aware at the time." He exhibits no sign of remorse or concern.

"So, who killed her?"

"Apparently, one of our adversaries got wind of the meeting and killed her." He's watching her closely as he speaks.

"That's preposterous. You don't really expect me to believe that, do you?" She's agitated now, but Kidman remains calm, level-headed, as if unfazed by any of it. "It appears that a foreign intelligence agency was involved."

"Are you aware that someone cleaned out my grandfather's study? Took all his papers?" He doesn't react. "And someone broke into my apartment, you know that."

"It seems your grandmother had an overactive imagination," Kidman says. "She managed to trigger an unfortunate series of events." Observing her, he adds, "They were very thorough."

"And how on earth did they find out about this phone call from my grandmother?" Her mind is wandering to this woman, this Muriel Markham, but she suggests something else altogether—"Perhaps someone in your offices?"

"When we searched your house, we found a bug on your telephone. An old one. Dating from the 1940s or 1950s. It appears someone has been listening in on your family's calls for quite some time."

Why would her grandparent's estate have been wired? And who in the world would be watching them, listening to them for thirty years? She knows the answer lies somewhere in the files that have disappeared—and she confronts Bill Kidman.

"Look," he tells her. "We didn't break into your apartment or steal your grandfather's papers. I'm assuming this foreign agency did—in search of this so-called proof, we assume." She presses him for more information, but he tells her the case is closed. "It's over," he says.

"They killed my grandmother and you're going to do what? Nothing?"

"There will be consequences for the people who are responsible for this. You can be sure of that. But keep in mind—your grandmother set these events in motion Miss Quinn." Emma bristles, and he goes on. "She had no proof of anything, as far as we know."

"Well know this," Emma says as she rises, looking him in the eye. "I don't believe you." For the first time, she knows that there is something of substance behind these events. "If there is proof," she says to herself, "I will find it."

***

Bill Kidman feels off his game. Late in the day, after his meeting at the State Department, his run-in with Carl Schmidt and his sit-down with Emma Quinn, he pours himself a glass of whisky, nursing it as he walks around the office. He's trying to figure out who is responsible for this—what agency, what corner of the intelligence service, which one of Max Frankel's minions created this mess. In an effort to shake it off before the day's out, he makes a circle through his department. Wandering over to the fax machine, he picks up a feed from Reuters, a duplicate of a brief story that was buried in *The New York Times* that morning, an issue that drew everyone into Conference Room B earlier in the day for a meeting that lasted no more than 30 minutes.

Teheran, Iran, Feb. 19 (Reuters)—Six people were killed and 125 injured in anti-Government rioting in the city of Tabriz in northwestern Iran yesterday, the official news agency reported today. It said the rioting had been incited by Islamic Marxists.

The agency said the rioters had set fire to four hotels, and stormed movie theaters and banks in Tabriz, the capital of Azerbaijan province. One of the theaters was also burned, the agency said, and many cars were set ablaze. Eleven policemen were said to be among the injured.

There were demonstrations in eleven other cities in Iran over the weekend but not a single analyst or intelligence officer at their morning meeting was aware of the scope of these protests—the fact that demonstrations are spreading, getting more violent, harder for the police to control and contain. No one in the CIA is aware that Iran's military is about to step in to suppress the uprising. Certainly, no one is imagining that, within a year, the Shah of Iran will have been deposed. Kidman himself knows little beyond the news report that he's holding in his hand. That very weekend, he'd read a piece in the *Atlantic Monthly* where a member of the administration corroborated the prevailing wisdom within the CIA that, with his enlightened policies, the Shah has "preempted revolution." Certainly, nobody at the CIA is expecting the monumental transformation that's about to take place, the Islamic-led revolution that will unfold in Iran in the months ahead.

But Bill Kidman recalls Colonel Hariri's comment about Mossad and the Iranian Jews and is troubled by the general sense that the department is out of touch with what's happening over there, the lack of manpower, the lack of good intelligence. His instincts tell him something's not right, but he doesn't really trust his instincts at the moment. He's had a bad day. He needs this drink far more than he should. Before he leaves for the day, he bums a cigarette from Todd and slips back into his office, turning everything in his head. He makes a couple of phone calls. And he reminds himself to contact Mahmoud Hariri, from the Deputy Chief of Staff's office, to follow up on his comments at the interagency meeting, to pursue the matter.

Quinn Estate

"I should have mentioned it," Annie says. "I should have mentioned it before." Emma is back in Delaware for a long weekend. For two weeks now, she's been engaged at school, immersed in her work, stepping back from the entire disturbing episode—to wait, to recalibrate. She is here to finish up the packing, take care of the last details, prepare for the estate sale and find out whatever else she can before the house is dismantled entirely.

In the weeks following Margaret Quinn's death, a consultant had come in and guided Annie through the process of preparing for the sale. The man, a wiry, perfunctory fellow in his mid-sixties, had made a schedule, an elaborate plan. "Our itinerary," he called it. First, anything the family wanted—meaning Emma or Annie—would be set aside, then the finest items were to be shipped to Philadelphia for auction. Emma had tagged each one—paintings dating from the mid-1800s, antiques that would bring a good price, many of them heavy, European pieces that she couldn't abide. Annie wanted very little. Emma's things weren't enough to fill a standard moving van—her four-poster bed; her grandfather's desk from the downstairs library; a chaise from her grandmother's bedroom; two oriental rugs, a good number of items from the kitchen and the case clock from her bedroom, with which, in the end, she found she could not part. That, and some random chairs and end tables, were going into storage for delivery to a new apartment on Riverside Drive, an apartment she had yet to find. The rest was either destined for the estate sale or for the Goodwill. "Don't worry. We'll find a good home for everything," the wiry man had said, although Emma hadn't been worried. She had grown eager to be done with it. She would make her own home, she had decided.

For now, her bedroom—and Annie's—are still in place. "We'll do the linens last," the wiry man had instructed. "You'll have your work cut out for you."

Annie had followed the schedule—this itinerary—meticulously in Emma's absence. Four sets of china are laid out on the dining room table for the estate sale, along with two porcelain soup tureens and a set of Imari plates that had decorated the massive china cupboard for as long as Emma can remember. Wine glasses and crystal goblets stand on the buffet in the dining room like rows of miniature soldiers lined up for battle. The living room, the large, square room at the center of the house with the painting of the dark, roiling sea, the room that no one ever used, is empty. Most of its contents have already been crated and shipped off for auction; the wooden floor with its ebony border stands bare, polished.

"My team will bring you some tables and cloths, so you can spread more of the goods here." That's what the wiry man calls his helpers, a rag tag bunch of heavy lifters, all of them strong and silent—my team—and he routinely refers to the contents of the estate as the goods. Emma doesn't like him.

She had been stunned when she'd arrived home that Thursday afternoon. The estate had been virtually disassembled. The umbrella stand by the front door was gone, earmarked for auction. In the library beyond, the bookshelves along the west wall stood empty, surrounded by boxes, already packed by the team. The rare books, the oldest ones, sets with leather covers inlaid in gold leaf, had been set aside, lined up on her grandfather's desk, ready for her to review. In her absence, the room was reconfigured to accommodate random furniture, and the Bakhtiari had been rolled up and sent off for auction. The team brought in a few throw rugs to liven it up, but it no longer looked like their library, like their home. That evening at dusk, the library—indeed, the entire front of the house—took on an eerie cast. So few table lamps, so little light. Emma had avoided the front stairs.

At some point in this dismantling process, there had been no place for Annie and Emma to sit, to visit, to relax and review this itinerary together, except the kitchen. The wiry man had his team bring down a few armchairs and a side table from the second floor to create a private spot for Annie and Emma, a refuge. That's where they linger now, next to the kitchen window overlooking the backyard, the azaleas around the garage sprouting buds, the boxwoods in need of a trim, the window seat cluttered with small appliances—a mixer, a blender, an antique ice cream maker, a few mortars and pestles, the giant stainless steel coffee maker big enough for company in a home where there would be no more company. Annie had obviously taken the time to clean each piece, to ready them for the sale. "And what would the blender bring?" Emma is thinking. "Two dollars? Worth less than the time Annie took to scrub it clean and dry it and set it aside." But Emma says nothing.

It is Friday. The late afternoon sun is pouring in through the kitchen window. The team is gone for the weekend. Flip is in New York with Jean Buchman. Just Emma and Annie. They had spent the morning going through boxes of photos and albums and family records in the attic, together. Among them, her parents' wedding album. Emma has brought it down with her, is leafing through it as the tea steeps in salvaged mugs, the kind you find at gift shops and trade shows, with logos on them or the names of random institutions. She is looking at black and white photographs of her mother and father taken in the garden beyond the very window where she now sits. Her parents were younger at the time than she is now, her mother in the lacy gown, slim-waisted, strapless, her slender arm through his, the ceremonial sweep of veil, obviously red-lipped, beaming. Her grandmother—elegant, ceremonious in a long, straight silver-grey silk dress and multiple strands of white pearls. Sophisticated, her hair swept up, half-smiling. And James Quinn looking rather serious standing to one side of the crowd, his champagne flute raised in the air. It is a toast. He is about to speak. "Or was this posed?" she asks herself, looking not at her grandfather but at her father standing opposite. He is smaller than she remembers him, just a few inches taller than her mother, and slight. His hair is parted in the middle, which makes him look rather like a matinee idol or like someone who hopes to look like a matinee idol. There is something slightly off about his face, as if one eye is larger than the other. His lips are thin and he is not smiling. Or perhaps he has been caught at the beginning of a smile that hasn't yet formed. He is looking directly at his new father-in-law with his glass raised in the air.

"Who are these people?" Emma asks, turning the page, as Annie delivers the tea. She cocks her head, moving in closer. "Oh Lord," she says. "That was their crowd. From Washington." The women were beautiful, every one, and terribly chic. And the men like something from central casting. "Debonair—that would be the word," she thinks. Wavy-haired men with broad shoulders and big smiles, their arms wrapped around one another's shoulders, cigarettes hanging from their fingers, clowning around in their dinner jackets and black ties, every one of them laughing. Every one of them white. The women, with a sense of irony, as if it were a game, striking various fashionable poses with their cigarette holders and a couple of champagne bottles.

"Oh, I'm sure they were having a big time," Annie says. "Drunk probably." The image was made all the more striking by the '40s fashions, the sepia tones of the photo.

"Very Hollywood," Emma says.

"Drama, drama, drama," Annie says. "That was their thing."

There's a photo of Emma's grandmother, her head thrown back, laughing, a short, black cigarette holder in one hand, the other pressed against the chest of a man Emma has never seen before, an older man, who has obviously cracked some sort of joke. "That was their boss. Some big wig from Washington. Your grandmother was taken with him," Annie says. "Your grandfather was not."

Emma shoots her a quizzical look. But Annie lets it go, sets herself down in the other armchair. "I'm glad it's over, this business with the CIA," she says.

Emma nods, but knows it's not over, despite what Bill Kidman has told her. She's known for a few weeks now that she's being followed. It could be one of Kidman's people, she thinks, but it seems unlikely. "I'm not sure it's over," Emma says. "I think they're looking for something—whether it's the CIA or someone else, I think they're still looking."

Emma asks then about her grandmother's diary and her grandfather's papers. "I didn't bother with Mr. Quinn's business," Annie says, adding, "I must say I was most concerned about the newspapers. Your grandmother was obsessed with the news, but it looked to be getting out of hand." As for the diary, Annie has no recollection of seeing it since James Quinn's death—"She might have destroyed it, you know. After all, he gave it to her. It was a birthday gift. I've known her to burn things."

They talk for a good long time—about Mrs. Quinn's habits, her reclusiveness, the visit to Muriel Markham, her determination to go out the morning of the blizzard and the facts as they now know them—that she was killed, that the CIA officer was killed, that the phone was tapped for all those years. As the conversation unfolds, Annie grows visibly uncomfortable, shifting in her seat and, finally, speaking slowly. "There is something I probably should have told you," she says. "There was a book, a small bound book with a black leather cover." She is staring out the window, as if she can't quite look Emma in the eye. "I tried to find it in all this"—she waves her hands in front of her—"all this mess. When I remembered." Emma is still, listening intently. And Annie is flustered, stammering, which is unlike her. She is a woman of grace and poise, somewhat dignified, with a confidence about her. But she is obviously shaken. "I think it was something important. With consequences," she says.

"What do you mean?" Emma asks. And Annie tries to explain. "I found it one day. I don't know what it was." She pauses. "Your grandfather was very upset when it happened. He took it. Hid it. Told me never to tell anyone about it." Then another pause before she speaks. "I think that might have been what the CIA was looking for." Then, looking up at Emma, "I should have told you."

"What was in this book?" Emma asks.

"Just lists. And numbers. It was a record book of some kind. Hardly bigger than an address book. That's all I know."

"Did you tell the CIA about it?"

"Of course not," Annie says. "No. Of course not," she says again.

"Where is it now?"

"I don't know," Annie says. "I never did find it."

SATURDAY, MARCH 4, 1978

For nearly two weeks, the black canisters from Philadelphia await authorization in a warehouse at the Military Ocean Terminal Sunny Point—MOTSU—the primary point of exit for Defense Department shipments. Then they are loaded onto a cargo ship. It's a sturdy, steel-hulled vessel that sits square upon the water, its hull wrapped in huge swaths of color—one thick red stripe, one black. The CS Antwerpen flies the Belgian flag, the cargo buried in its hull.

No. 37

Martin's Tavern has the dark, clubby atmosphere of a classic urban alehouse. Wood paneling, low lights, leather seats. It's 3 p.m. on a Monday afternoon and the place is empty. Angus McLearan is sitting in a booth toward the back, far from the windows facing out on N Street and Wisconsin Avenue in Georgetown, less than a mile from Dumbarton Oaks. He's waiting patiently for Bill Kidman. Of course, this is not the first time they've met. They've known each other since 1967 when they were thrown together to prep the Johnson administration for a hastily arranged summit between the Soviet premier and the president. On the U.S. side, the summit was intended as a step toward making peace in Vietnam, but the Soviets were more interested in discussing the Middle East.

At the time, Angus McLearan was in his late twenties, but he was already recognized as an expert on Soviet politics. Bill Kidman had just turned forty, with experience on the ground in both Vietnam and the Middle East. Like-minded souls, the two were cooped up in the Pentagon together for nearly a week strategizing, tossing around ideas. They formed a bond that stayed with them through three subsequent missions in the field. Bill Kidman was one of the reasons Angus signed onto the British intelligence force.

"You in?" is the first thing Kidman says when he arrives, before he even removes his topcoat, standing over his old friend. McLearan nods. Relieved, Kidman hangs it on the hook above the booth and sits. "Is this off the books?" Kidman asks.

McLearan shakes his head no.

"You're still on the payroll?"

McLearan nods. "We're all in," he says.

They order a pair of beers and toast one another. "To the Queen," Kidman says, "and her merry men."

And when the young waiter steps away, McLearan leans in. "She's safe, by the way. Although she doesn't have much to say."

"Fair enough." Kidman pulls out a pack of cigarettes, holds them out to McLearan, who shakes him off. This is new, this smoking. "You were right about the girl," he adds.

"She obviously had no idea about any of this."

"And she's completely transparent. I don't imagine she could conceal anything even if she wanted to."

"But tough," says McLearan. "Like something from Charles Dickens. Financial hardship—zero. Emotional hardship—on up there." He pauses, eyes the room without moving his head. "I don't imagine she's going to let this thing drop." Then he lowers his voice, surveying the menu and speaks casually, as if commenting on the selections. "She's being followed," he says. "I've sent the photos over to my people. Should know in a few days."

After they've ordered and the waiter brings them each a plate—steaks and fries—and after a minor hubbub involving salt and pepper shakers and assorted condiments, they eat in silence for a time. "Any ideas?" Kidman says finally.

"What exactly did the woman say when she called you?" McLearan asks.

By now, Kidman has memorized the lines. He unfolds a piece of paper from his pocket, passes it across the table. It reads: "I know who's selling all these weapons and chemicals and explosives that are killing innocent people all over the world. And I have proof. Written proof."

"No wonder you thought she was a crackpot," McLearan says, shoving the words in his pocket.

"Yeah. I think it might have been Todd. He said she probably got all the data on U.S. arms sales for the past 50 years."

McLearan responds with a cynical look.

"Good old U.S. of A. Always number one," Kidman says. And Angus thinks he detects a tinge of shame in his expression.

After a time, Kidman asks, "You going to reconnect with the girl?"

"I don't think that's wise. I wasn't sure how long the Hiss story was going to hold," McLearan says. "Now that you've gone and killed it, I'll just keep an eye on her."

When their plates disappear, Bill Kidman slides a device across the table, a portable phone and leaves it under his rumpled napkin. "Don't use it unless you have to," he says.

McLearan barely acknowledges the gesture. And when Kidman stands, McLearan speaks. "We have anyone else in on this?"

Kidman takes his time responding. He puts on his overcoat, wraps a black wool scarf around his neck, makes a few adjustments, buttons the coat. Then he throws one foot up on the edge of the booth as if he's tying a shoe, leans in toward McLearan. "I've hooked up with an Army man," he says. "Name's Hariri. Otherwise, it's just you and me." He lowers his foot to the floor.

McLearan throws him a nod. "And the queen," he says.

PART III

At midnight on March 6—the ship's second night at sea—the captain of the CS Antwerpen cuts the engine as is tradition in this particular fleet. For almost 30 minutes the ship floats free over the foamy swells under the light of the moon. The crew—seven men in all—climb up on deck in the darkness to see the stars and to watch as the captain shines a spotlight over the black sea. It magnifies the depth of the darkness surrounding them. There is silence. This will be their sole moment of silence over the course of the 19-day journey across the Atlantic Ocean. Nineteen days at sea.

No. 38

Upper Saranac Lake, New York

The Quinns' Saranac cabin is in a place called Slatterly. Set deep in the forest on the north shore of the Upper Saranac Lake, Slatterly is hard to find unless you know where you're going. It's smaller than many of the Adirondack Great Camps, rustic retreats built at the turn of the century. If an outsider came looking, he might easily lose his way. There are no street signs or house numbers, no exit ramps. Just a primitive sign bearing a single word—PRIVATE—at the edge of the forest. To compound the possibility of confusion, there are three Saranac lakes in the vicinity—the Upper, Lower and Middle Saranac. There is a village called Saranac Lake that overlooks Lake Flower and a town called Saranac about 30 minutes from there and not far from Lake Placid.

Built as private preserves, some of the Great Camps are more imposing than others, with grand cut-stone lodges and elaborate covered walkways. But the earliest among them, built before 1900, were communities of relatively humble dwellings—cabins and boathouses and recreation halls—crafted from indigenous materials, rough-hewn logs and timber, each connected by footpaths, reeking of authenticity.

Such is Slatterly. The Quinn cabin—or, officially, the Rothenberg cabin—was built by Margaret Rothenberg Quinn's family around the turn of the century and passed on to her when her parents died in the 1930s. It is one of more than a dozen cabins in Slatterly, set on a ridge overlooking the lake in an untamed natural forest.

In March, before Emma makes her way up to the cabin, she finally has to put Flip down. She'd brought him back with her to Manhattan, dedicated herself to trudging him out to Riverside Park first thing in the morning and late in the evening, to walking him on shaky legs although the life was obviously going out of him. She'd been scanning the classifieds for weeks looking for a new apartment, a place on Riverside Drive, something with more space closer to the university with easier access to the park, for Flip's sake, as if he would live beyond the semester.

For a time, the vet had managed to revive the dog with steroids, which made him jumpy and wild-eyed and ravenously hungry. But finally, as winter persisted, he'd succumbed one night—had some sort of stroke in his sleep and couldn't lift himself in the morning. The vet, a slight, soft-spoken woman with a cherubic face, had come directly to Emma's apartment bringing along a needle and a rubber tourniquet in a small valise and an assistant, long-haired and disheveled and identified only as Bill. Emma sat cross-legged on the floor stroking Flip's neck as they delivered the shot, the dog lying flat on his side, all four of his boxer-legs stretched out straight as arrows, unmoving, looking up at her wearily out of the corner of one eye until he slid silently away. Emma was sobbing when the vet gently lifted the buckle of his worn leather collar and passed it over to her. She held it tight as she escorted them to the door, the dog wrapped in a blanket, the doctor and Bill holding each end like a hammock.

Afterwards, Emma lay alone on the long, leather sofa in her living room clutching the collar, still for a time. Flip had served as kind of an anchor in the weeks after her grandmother's death, given her a sense of purpose, comfort, relief from the events that followed in its imme-diate wake. As she lay there grieving in earnest, shifting gradually into the fetal position, holding the collar against her cheek, she noticed the worn duct tape on its underside, gummy and grimy and flecked with dog hair. Picking at it, peeling it away, she found taped to the collar the spare key to their cabin on Upper Saranac Lake. Emma knew the moment her thumb ran across it what it was, how it had gotten there and why.

She knew that if she got in her car and drove the six hours up to the cabin and searched the house, she would find whatever it was that had led to her grandmother's death. But she waits the few days until spring break arrives. She doesn't rush off to Saranac or make a call of any kind to anyone. She decides to leave when it's appropriate. And she has to figure out how to slip away, because she doesn't want to drag her stalker along with her to the lake.

No. 39

It was Manny Fredericks, Emma's colleague at the research desk, who first noticed Serge, sometime in late February, gave him a name, one that made him seem less ominous, more comical. The Shadow, he called him, after the old radio series, transforming him into something almost campy. Twice in one week, Manny had seen him watching Emma in the library. The second time, she was standing at the research desk and he'd signaled to her with a nod of his head. "Guy over there has his eye on you," he'd said. It became a running joke. Whenever she arrived at the reference desk, he would whisper in an ironic sort of way, "Beware The Shadow." At first, it seemed like something Manny had cooked up in his head. But then she noticed Serge one evening lurking on the subway platform at 72nd Street. And, the week before Flip's death, when they were out on a morning walk, there he was again—sitting on a bench in Riverside Park in his designer sunglasses, smoking. Given that he kept his distance, that he did no harm, she thought that perhaps he was one of Kidman's people, stationed nearby to make sure she was safe or tracking her in case she found any evidence, some kind of proof.

She thought, too, that she saw Angus McLearan one afternoon at the top of the Low Library steps, but when she made it up there herself, there was no sign of him. She'd asked after him a few times at the West End, when she and her colleagues gathered there, but no one had seen him in weeks. "Probably back in Edinburgh," the Oxford Don had said, adding, "I'll have to look him up next time I'm home."

In fact, by mid-March, her stalker, this man Serge, had grown skeptical. It seemed likely to him that the entire incident with the elderly Quinn woman could have been avoided, that she may have been leading the CIA on a wild goose chase. "Perhaps she was crazy," Hugh Grenville had said on a recent call from his lair in Chevy Chase, creating the impression that the DIA was ready to lay the matter to rest. They had relaxed their surveillance of late, although cameras were still in place at the Quinn estate and at the entry to Emma's building on West End, and the tap remained on the phone in her apartment. Serge had told the team in Philadelphia to notify him only if her pattern changed, if she showed up in Delaware or her new friend—meaning Angus McLearan—showed up again or any more boxes or packages left the estate on Miller's Lane.

They had—Serge Breuer and his people and, by extension, Hugh Grenville and Tina Dowd—monitored the shipments to Sotheby's and staked out the estate sale. And they'd waylaid a truckload headed from the Quinn estate to the Goodwill—hijacked it altogether and delivered the contents to the warehouse in Philadelphia where they'd gone through a promising array of boxes and found nothing. "It is a black book, a record of our early shipments, you can be sure of that," Serge's father had told him. "I myself saw it many years ago," he'd said. But there was no black book among the things in the moving van destined for the Goodwill or the boxes retrieved from Emma's apartment or the contents of James Quinn's office delivered by the Defense Intelligence Agency—the DIA—to the Philadelphia offices of *Cargo Belgique Americaine* the night of Margaret Quinn's death. They can find nothing, and it's becoming clear to all concerned that Schmidt and his people at the CIA have eased up on the investigation.

Angus McLearan, however, has been tracking Serge Breuer for more than a week now. He has watched him watch Emma and followed him to and from her block on West End Avenue and to what appears to be his home—an apartment building on the Upper East Side overlooking Third Avenue near 83rd Street. McLearan has made notes like this: "To all appearances, he is nothing more than a young business executive." And this: "He frequents East Side discos and on at least one occasion, appeared on the arms of a model, quite a young girl, Czechoslovakian, at Studio 54." Twice Angus followed him to a midrise office building on Broadway, not far from 34th Street, yellow brick with an off-track betting location on the ground floor. The effort yielded nothing. And, on three consecutive evenings, he staked out his apartment from a building across Third Avenue, saw him watching a rerun of Saturday Night Live, laughing at the Blues Brothers, and observed him snorting cocaine with a young couple, obviously European like Serge. One evening, McLearan tracked him to an athletic facility off George Washington Parkway, where he played a game of indoor rugby with some other expats. At the end of the week, Angus makes this note: "The man seems to picture himself as hip. He likes living in the city, in America. I'm guessing he wants to stay and doesn't want to get caught in some immigration matter that will force his departure. He's not a pro, very sloppy."

On Friday, March 10th, Serge goes clubbing and McLearan finds his way into his apartment. He discovers surveillance equipment hidden in the bedroom closet—one watching the entrance to Emma's apartment building, the other at the entrance to the history building at Columbia. He finds voice recording equipment, presses a button and hears his own voice played back on Emma Quinn's answering machine. He discovers Serge's passport, sees that he is officially a resident of Belgium, learns his full name—*Serge Breuer.* Before he departs, McLearan puts a bug on his phone. He's had a track on his car since the rugby game. He's shot photographs and forwarded them to his office at MI6 in London, along with the name on the passport, via the front desk at the International House.

No. 40

Spring break is about to begin. On this Friday afternoon, it is difficult to move around the Columbia campus with ease. Winter has persisted well into the month of March with a steady stream of frozen rain and snow. Mounds of the stuff are piled up along the university's walkways. By noon, students eager to escape are beginning to depart for points south and west and north. Cars are lined up along Broadway at the entrance to the Columbia campus, their lights flashing. They are being pounded by sleet. This is the day Emma has chosen for her departure to the cabin at Upper Saranac Lake.

At lunchtime, she emerges from Fayerweather, her hair flying loose, dressed in a powder blue ski jacket, work boots and jeans, opening her oversized black umbrella against the last breaths of the storm. She exits the Columbia campus at Broadway and crosses to Barnard, where she makes the final arrangements from Jean Buchman's office, calling Manny Fredericks at his apartment, reconfirming their rendezvous. She has enlisted him in a game of losing The Shadow and he's all in. He has acquired on her behalf a yellow rain poncho and yellow rubber boots in a size eight, both of which are sitting in a bag in Jean Buchman's office.

Emma changes there, leaving the down jacket, her boots, the backpack and the black umbrella behind. She shoves her hair under a nondescript wool cap. Then takes the stairs to the basement where an underground tunnel runs the length of the Barnard campus. She follows it north to Milbank Hall at the college's outer edge.

Ten minutes later, Emma resurfaces at Milbank looking like someone else altogether. Outfitted in yellow vinyl, she emerges from the front door unfurling a Columbia umbrella that conceals her face and protects her from the frozen drizzle. She exits at the northernmost corner of the Barnard campus and crosses 120th Street in the slush, turning east across Broadway, moving along the clay-colored facade of Columbia Teachers College with its archways and elaborate cornices, hugging the edge of the building against the wind. Pushing her way to the end of the block, she thinks of her grandmother, wonders how she felt on the morning that she headed out into the storm, whether she experienced any fear or dread or sense of what was coming. Or did she just plow ahead with her plan, determined, clueless that she was out of her league?

At the northeast corner of 120th and Amsterdam, Manny Fredericks is waiting for her in a rented Jeep, packed with her things and paid for in cash. She climbs into the passenger side and they ride on in silence, Manny so excited by the entire process that he can barely keep his seat. Still, he's alert, monitoring the cars behind them and the ones that pass them by as they make their way north on Amsterdam. "It looks good," he says at one point. Otherwise, they barely speak. She has her eyes fixed on the side mirror. Ten minutes later, standing on the curb in front of his Harlem apartment, Emma fumbles a thank you, reaching out her hand to shake his, then accepts his hug. "We did it," he whispers in her ear, his jaw crashing against her chin, the edge of his wire-rimmed glasses jutting into her frozen cheek. By then the sleet has stopped. As she drives off, she can see him in her rear-view mirror throwing her a sloppy salute, grinning under his worn wide-brimmed hat, then turning away, his hair falling down his back like the wet tail of a dead raccoon.

No. 41

They meet at Twin Lanes outside Arlington, just off the Beltway, early on this Friday afternoon—Bill Kidman and Mahmoud Hariri. The place is nearly empty. Hariri wears a shirt that says Rutabagas across the back. "A guy on my team is from Beirut," he says. "I guess he thought it was funny. Beirut—rutabagas. I don't know." Totally disarmed, Kidman smiles. They locate themselves at a center lane, each take a few turns, then grab a pair of beers and sit for a minute.

"They shut the investigation down, right?" Hariri asks. Bill Kidman nods. "So why are you here?"

"Same reason you are, I imagine," says Kidman.

"That would be Roy Howard."

Hariri is what Kidman thinks of as a cool customer. Self-possessed, the kind of guy you want in the field, someone you can trust. "Who told you to stop?" Hariri asks.

"You know who told me—Carl Schmidt."

"But who told him?"

"I can only guess at that," Kidman says, although he knows full well it was Max Frankel.

"So, this is something we don't want to know about."

"Right," says Kidman. "Unless we do."

They sip their beers, still sizing each other up. Hariri works in the office of the chief of Army Intelligence, so he has access to any file, any record, any department on the Army side of the U.S. government. He's an invaluable resource. When they finish the game, he's won by a landslide. "So, what was that business about Iran?" Kidman says finally. Hariri looks confused. "At the interagency meeting."

"Just expressing my concern."

"Regarding what exactly?" Kidman doesn't want to talk in riddles.

"For one thing, DIA is the only real presence in Iran. Our intel is really weak. And Mossad thinks the place is going to blow."

"Which means?"

"Which means either nobody's paying attention—or the wrong people are paying attention."

"And what's that have to do with Roy Howard?"

"I don't know," Hariri says. He seems wary, hesitates, then continues. "But I do know—from sources in Israel—that they stopped a rogue shipment near Haifa last year. Headed who knows where and it had Balfour written all over it—and I don't mean that literally. High-grade explosives. With the situation in the Middle East right now, it could have been going anywhere, but it was definitely coming from here."

"Was it authorized?"

Hariri nods. "Papers came from MOTSU, so it went through the system. But the destination and contents were—let's just say misstated."

"Who signed for it?"

"Couldn't trace the records." He hesitates a moment. "But an operation like that could have everything to do with Roy Howard's death."

No. 42

It's late when Emma arrives at the entrance to Slatterly, exhausted from the tension created by her own watchfulness, the concern that she somehow would be followed. During the last leg of the trip, she hit a long stretch of empty road. A sedan behind her with its lights on bright, stayed too close for too long. She turned into a stranger's driveway just to shake him, and watched in the rearview mirror as the driver revved his engine, as if in frustration, finally set loose on the open road. Now, at last, as she makes her way slowly in the darkness, her headlights shooting through the woods, she feels as if she can let her guard down. The forest is deserted, primordial—a mass of trees emerging from a tangled floor of fallen branches and twisted root systems and the mulchy remains of dead animals and rotted leaves and shards of old tree bark. The cabin itself is remote, as it was meant to be, set a good five miles from the nearest paved road via a narrow gravel drive at the far edge of Slatterly. Even in daylight, from what is now Emma Quinn's property, the only sign of civilization is the camp's recreation hall and the clubhouse, a modest, low-lying building visible along the arc of the lake from the wooden dock at the foot of the ridge. Tonight, it is marked only by a light shining across the water like a thin red line.

It's well past eleven when she opens the cabin door. She tosses her keys into the basket on the mail table, flips on the kitchen light, and hears a skittering about, a rodent of some sort, wishes she'd called ahead and asked the staff to get things ready. That, of course, is what her grandmother would have done. The place has a dank, earthy, closed-up smell to it. While the family always referred to it as a cabin, it's not small—three private bedrooms and a long narrow sleeping porch facing the forest that accommodates eight or more children, cousins and guests. Emma's grandparents had kept the bunk beds in place, although by the 1950s, she was the only child vacationing there.

Wandering from room to room, she sees mouse droppings on the floor in the bunkroom, a few tiny drops of blood on the coverlets in the twin room that had been hers, exposed mattresses in the guestroom.

At the cabin's center is a Great Room decorated with ceiling fans and an assortment of hand-woven rugs and family photographs from another time. A pair of oars are crisscrossed on the east wall above double doors that lead to a second screened porch, this one over-looking the lake. The woods are deadly quiet. She turns on the porch light—hears the insects pulled toward it, bouncing against the screen, and sees the thin red line of light that runs across the water. The moon is a sliver, the sky a deep, dark blue.

Emma is very much alone. She knows that. She suspects there's no one else at the camp aside from maybe one or two people bunked in staff housing across the arc of the lake. She hustles her things into her grandmother's room, searches the kitchen cupboard for a bottle of whisky and pours herself a drink, wondering if maybe this wasn't such a hot idea. The cabin feels at once empty and full of vague, ghostly memories, and recollections of her grandfather that now feel cor-rupted somehow. She settles on the porch, sipping on the whisky. It's chilly, below 40 degrees, and she's lightly dressed. The whisky warms her and burns her throat. "What was I thinking?" she says out loud to herself, suspecting she will find out something else she doesn't want to know in the days that follow. Or worse still, that she will find nothing and leave the whole damn thing hanging there, unresolved.

She takes her time, then retreats inside, locking the double-doors behind her. From the kitchen, she flips on the three spotlights perched along the roofline, lighting up the surrounding forest. But then she thinks better of it, doesn't want to draw attention to the cabin. Instead, she finds the old Maxwell House coffee can filled with loose change that lives on the kitchen counter and creates a make-shift alarm system. The coins jangle as she sets it down at the foot of the kitchen door. Then, moving deliberately from room to room, she secures all the windows, stopping at the entrance to the sleeping porch and puzzling over it. There is no lock on either side of this door, made so for good reasons—safety, comfort, ease of use for small children. It takes Emma a good 20 minutes to slide a bulky pine dresser from the guest room through the hallway and against that door, in the interest of her own safety, doing damage to the hardwood floor as well as a muscle on her upper right side. "Shit," she says, wounded and weary, realizing she still has to make up the bed.

She sleeps poorly, dreams that she's swimming in a lake with her mother, but it's not this lake, not their lake. The beach is composed of large, rough granules of clay-colored sand, scratchy against the soles of her feet. Her mother stands waist-high in the water, draped in the bodice of the grey-green gown she wore the night of the accident, its baubles twinkling in the sun, her wet hair plastered to her head. Emma watches her dive below the surface, feeling her own smallness as she waits for the hair, the face, the shimmering gown to resurface. But there is only the flat black-green of the water.

Emma awakens covered in sweat and makes her way to the sofa in the Great Room in the dark, where she wraps herself in an old woolen throw and drifts in and out of sleep. She finds that she is not happy to be here, wary, off kilter.

No. 43

Angus McLearan is back at the International House with the shades drawn tight. He suspects he's lost Emma. Although she appeared to show up at her apartment around dinnertime wheeling a grocery cart on Friday, there was something about her that didn't quite line up. And when he raised his binoculars, he recognized the face of Jean Buchman from their night at the West End. "Goddammit," he told himself and waited until 2 a.m. to see if either Emma arrived or Jean Buchman departed. Now, early Saturday morning, he hears the relentless beep of an alarm and swats at the clock beside his bed. It takes a second for him to realize that it's the tracker on Serge Breuer's car, that Breuer's on the move. Feeling like a rookie, he rings up Kidman on his dedicated phone and leaves this message: "They've gone on vacation. Both of them. I'll let you know my destination. I've sent a gift. Should arrive this afternoon."

No. 44

Emma awakens to a bright, clear day. After throwing a few windows open to bring in the mountain air, she nurses her coffee on the screen porch wrapped in a bulky fisherman's sweater found in the main closet. The lake is sparkling, and her mood is shifting as anyone's might on such a morning. Buoyed by the sense that either she escaped from Manhattan unnoticed or there was no escaping to it, she starts right in on the search, beginning in the most obvious spot—a hidden space behind the map of the Adirondacks in the guest bedroom. It's not a safe, just a discrete shelf that holds a metal tackle box. There's no lock on it, but it's hidden and it's fireproof. And it's secret. Emma has known of it since her youth, when she watched her grandmother stash petty cash or jewelry or an extra set of keys behind the map, probably with an admonition such as "always protect your valuables, my dear," although Emma doesn't remember such words. She picks up the handgun that rests on the shelf beside the box. She examines it, checks to see if it's loaded, finds some comfort in seeing the small silver bullets in each chamber.

On her last visit, she'd left copies of her own car key and apartment key in the tackle box, just in case. Lord knows why she didn't leave them on the mail table with the other keys. Beyond that, the box seems undisturbed. Rustling through the papers at the bottom, she finds a duplicate of the Rothenberg family's deed to the land, dated 1889, a copy of the homeowner's insurance, and an ancient list of people to call in an emergency, including Treadwell and a few summer residents of Slatterly, old family friends dating from the 1950s and '60s—the Morgans, the Simms, Kitty Bradford—dead people mostly. She checks underneath the tackle box, examining its underside. No diary. No little black book.

There are a few unopened packs of Camels on the shelf, her grand-mother's stash, who-knows-how-old, some sort of insurance against a craving. Emma smiles when she sees them. She putters around the guest room, looking under furniture and inside closets and drawers, proceeding from room to room as the day progresses, keeping the handgun close at hand as she moves about the cabin.

It's late in the day when she comes upon a small book covered in a navy blue dotted Swiss fabric in the drawer of a corner cupboard in the hallway. She recognizes it immediately as her grandmother's diary. She's never seen its contents, but remembers it well from Margaret Quinn's bedside table. The diary has a closure but no lock and opens with these words in her grandfather's hand:

June 5, 1939
For my Margaret on the occasion of her 40th birthday
Love, James

Still standing, Emma reads the first entry, written two full months after the gift itself.

August 7, 1939
I am trying to remember when it began. This feeling that my life somehow exceeds my own grasp, that I can at times lose control of myself. My dearest James seems to believe that this journaling as he calls it may help me hold myself together. So I will try. I have promised.

August 9, 1939
Nothing to report. It's hot as the dickens.

August 10, 1939
Catherine went off today in a car full of teenagers driven by a young man. She was a bit sassy with me before she left. It's time for her to be off at school.

Emma is touched to read her mother's name and immediately grasps the irritation in her grandmother's tone. "It's time for her to be off at school." Then—

August 15, 1939
I am not myself today. Spent the morning in bed. Listless. Must be the heat.

Emma stops and flips through the pages to get a sense of what lies ahead. She lands on one dated June 4, 1940, beside it a little drawing of the Eiffel Tower. She wonders whether her grandmother could have drawn so delicate a thing. Surprised by it, she reads on.

They have bombed my beloved Paris. The New York Times says there are "gaping craters of death in the boulevards of what was once the city of happiness and light." I have cut it out and folded it and placed it in this book, so we will never forget.

Emma looks for the news clipping, turns the page, sees nothing but another entry dated June 23, 1940. "France has fallen," it says and there is a star-shaped dried flower pressed into the page. The writing itself is angular and smooth, perfect really, as if her grandmother was calm and careful and self-contained, despite this news. Emma is struck by the simplicity of the statement, the implied devastation, the matter-of-factness of it. *France has fallen.*

Leafing through the book, she finds only one newspaper clipping—shriveled and torn at the edge, yellowed with age. It's not from June and not about France. Far from it. The headline reads "Himmler Program Kills Polish Jews." It is the only one, the only clipping in the diary. From *The Times* and dated November 25, 1942. She stops reading then, moves to a damask-covered chaise in the corner of her grandmother's bedroom and throws her legs over either side of it. Setting the diary down gently in between them, she settles in, picking up where she left off—

August 15, 1939
I am not myself today. Spent the morning in bed. Listless. Must be the heat.

September 2, 1939

It seems Germany has invaded Poland, and all of Europe
has gone to war. James is beside himself. He is cursing the
Russians, who apparently have signed some sort of pact
with Hitler and cursing the Brits for what he calls their
foolhardiness. I said, we must pray that it doesn't turn into
another world war. But he says it is too late for that—and
that we're lucky that this Hitler is across the sea and not in
our backyard. Truth is, I can't bring myself to think too much
about it. After all, one can only absorb so much. And it is our
last weekend with Catherine. We are preparing a barbeque
for Sunday. Two dozen people are coming. We have quite a
bit of work to do.

Sept 4, 1939

Catherine leaves for Holton tomorrow. James is driving
down with her. They are going without me. I am trying to
imagine what I will I do without my little girl? My sadness
has no end. I cannot seem to leave the bed. And Annie—
Annie is treating me like a child. I am unnerved by it. Dr.
McIntyre told her that I have melancholia. I heard him
in the hallway. Last time he said hysteria. So which is it?
Melancholia or hysteria? Phooey on him. He is an ass.

Then there is a gap of nearly six months, like a gaping hole in her
grandmother's life.

Sunday, March 17, 1940

Everyone at church stared at us today as we walked down
the aisle. Let's sit in the back, James said. But no, I would
have none of it. I held my head up high. I am not crazy. And I

am smarter than the whole lot of them put together in a pie. Little chirpy birds they are, busy bodies, small minded little sparrows all buttoned up nice.

Here, she had drawn an odd little batch of blackbirds flying across the bottom of the page, which Emma turns to find this—

> **April 10, 1940**
> Today, James called Adolph Hitler "so deranged as to be certifiably insane." He has invaded Norway and Denmark. I asked if I was certifiable. Good God, no, he said, which was a relief. The both of us had a laugh over that. I do want to make a note: This new treatment seems to be working. James is optimistic. And I am feeling well. I wanted to make note of it in this diary. James says to do it, but I'm not always very good at that when I get busy.

> **May 13, 1940**
> My dear girl was here. For Mother's Day! She has grown into a true lady, with her bob and her flowered dress and her white heels, plopping at the foot of the bed and pulling them off and lying here beside me, stroking my hair on Sunday morning. But it left me wondering—Who has been shopping with her? Annie? Her father? Some friend or the mother of a friend down in Washington? I feel a failure.

On the facing page—a line drawing of a bunch of tulips in a glass vase drooping half dead. Then the diary skips ten days and her grandmother's frame of mind shifts—dramatically, Emma thinks, struck by the swing.

May 23, 1940

It was a beautiful day today, a perfect day. In the morning, I took the dogs down Miller's Lane and out along the ravine. The trees all full and green. Little sunbeams dotting the road, the slightest breeze. I stood at the old powder mill looking up at a stunning, clear blue sky and closed my eyes and felt the sun against my face. It was as if all the forces of nature had conspired together to make me this day. Then Elvin arrived in the car. I'm fine, I told him. I'm fine. But Mrs. Quinn you have a guest, he said. And indeed I did. I was delighted to find Tread waiting for me in the garden, right on time for his appointment. And Annie brought the tea and little petit fours, and we had a good long talk about the market and James' contribution to the war effort and Catherine's plans to stay in Washington for the summer with her friends. I explained that, yes it was a good idea, that I want what's best for her, that I will miss her, but I will be fine. I feel myself again. Truly. Dr. Amery says it's because the new medicine is working. But I know better. It's because of the weather. And because my James is coming home tonight and he will be so happy to see me up. And because all's right with my world.

May 29, 1940

The Germans are on the rampage. They are taking over all of Europe. James is just back from Washington. He says that at least the country is now engaged in building our military so we that can defend ourselves. Seems to me that it's so that we can defend Great Britain. This idea of neutrality seems to me to be pure hokum. I don't trust this FDR.

June 4, 1940

They have bombed my beloved Paris. The New York Times

says there are "gaping craters of death in the boulevards of what was once the city of happiness and light." I have cut it out and folded it and placed it in this book so we will never forget. It says this—that the "anger of civilized people will burn so fiercely that it will consume the hateful German system that has loosed these horrors upon the world." I read it to James—the entire opinion piece—at breakfast this morning. He said "Mark my words. We will be fighting in Europe before the year is out." And I told him it seemed as if the world as we know it is coming to an end. And he rose from the table and came over and stood behind my chair and wrapped his arms around my neck and kissed the top of my head and assured me that they will never come here. They will never cross this ocean, he said.

June 22, 1940

Prescott and Elizabeth Hines came back on the last ship from Europe. It was in the paper. On the front page. I am trying to imagine what that was like, to escape from the bombs or to think that you could not, to be fleeing. We are not letting everyone in. But citizens, of course. And apparently the boat stopped in Ireland and let some of them on board. It seems a German U-boat very nearly attacked the ship en route. There was a picture of Prescott and Liz on the front page. I'm going to give her a call before I leave for Saranac in the morning. Welcome them back.

June 23, 1940

France has fallen.

Emma stops to examine the dried flower. It is brown now, but it looks as if it was originally white and shaped like a star—much like the flowers that surrounded the pool at the estate, a flower that would have bloomed in the early spring and into the summer. She picks it up and the petals disintegrate between her fingers, crumbling onto the page like so many grains of sand.

June 30, 1940

I like this Willkie. James favors him as well. There are rumors that FDR will seek a third term. It feels rather like we are becoming a dictatorship. A socialist dictatorship at that. All this talk of the evil bankers and financiers. No one likes the Nazis, but it sounds to me like their rhetoric. That banks are controlled by the Jews and all that business. It is frightening to me. Thank God my father isn't alive to hear such nonsense.

Here, Margaret's writing becomes a scramble of words that crisscross and blend into one another, ragged and jerky. Emma holds the page close, so she can make them out.

July 1, 1940

I must have been up half the night packing. I've so much to do. And the day is almost over! It's Monday already. Only four days. We head up to Saranac on Friday. We celebrate the fourth at Longwood on Thursday so we will lose that day. Three days! How will I ever get it done? I've hardly slept. Enough of this. Back to work!!!!

The entries that follow have no dates—

I am so ashamed of how I behaved with Annie. Don't

touch me. Don't come near me. Rattled. Agitated beyond belief. I can barely think straight. It started with the swim. What's the harm in it? What's the harm in taking a midnight dip? But James would not be roused, so I went myself. And of course I took my clothes off. Of course I did. Who goes swimming in the night wearing a swimsuit and a bathing cap? What's the fun in that? But afterwards I don't remember much. I know Annie came out in the morning. Screaming bloody murder. As if I were some intruder on my very own property. And she left me there, on the chaise, trembling, frozen, with something about you'll catch your death of cold. And then James running down the hill in his robe and Annie trying to keep up with a stack of blankets and towels and dogs at her heels, all three of them barking like maniacs for all the neighbors on Miller's Lane to hear. As if we need that talk. And Dr. Amery with his barbiturates and his patronizing tone. Now just have some rest, Margaret. This morning I could barely lift my head. And now I fear there will be hell to pay. What is wrong with me? What is wrong with them? What's the harm in any of it. And, for God's sake, what have they given me because the day has passed and I am still barely able to hold this pen.

Thursday

We have delayed the trip. Catherine was beside herself. Angry at me more than anything. So they have gone to Longwood without me for the fireworks. And I have made myself a whisky sour and found a spot here by the pool to rest. I am not myself. I'm unsettled. This infernal summer just crawls on. I am trying to convince him that we must go to Saranac. We must. It's really the only place I feel safe.

Friday

James held me for forever last night. Cradled me in his arms. He says everything's going to be all right. And that he will take care of me always. What a sweet, sweet man he is. How grateful I am to have my James. He says we are going to fire Dr. Amery. I am much relieved.

No. 45

For as long as she can remember, she has known of her grandmother's illness, but not explicitly, not in a clearly defined way. Until the day she herself had left for boarding school, for Holton, she knew only that there was something wrong, but none of the specifics. On that day, Margaret Quinn had failed to get up out of bed, which was not at all unusual. But it was a big day for Emma, and as her grandfather emerged from the bedroom across the hall, she'd heard him say in an uncharacteristically harsh tone, "For God's sake Margaret, she's going away to school." Then he'd slammed the door shut and stayed behind it while Emma gathered up the last of her things. Finally, when he joined her in the back seat of the Cadillac, he seemed to feel as if it were time to explain things, and he'd gone on at length about the illness, describing her grandmother generically as "unwell, unstable."

At the time, Emma was far more preoccupied with what lay ahead—a new school, new friends, new surroundings, a faraway place.

Nonetheless, her grandfather had launched into a portrait of his wife, providing details Emma had never known. "She does the best she can," he'd said. "And she was brilliant. A beautiful woman. A little wild at times, which made me love her all the more. A bit unconventional." Emma had found that hard to believe. And he'd spoken about the trajectory of the disease in ways that Emma remembers only in fragments, these being the most illuminating—

1. "After your mother was born, it got progressively worse. Finally, when she went to school—when your mother went to school, to kindergarten—she had her first break. She spent some time in the hospital."

2. "The doctors said it could be worse. And sometimes she goes months without incident. Months when she is lucid and fully in control of her emotions. You've seen that, I'm sure," he'd added, although Emma had few recollections of such times.

3. "They've never quite put a name to it," he'd explained. "But she experiences her highs and her lows. Hard to predict what will bring them on." By that description, Emma came to believe that her grandmother had what was known as manic-depression. But it had never been confirmed for her.

4. He told her the obvious. "When your mother died, when your parents died, she had a major setback. As you know. It's only now that she seems to be coming out of it." Although Emma wasn't noticing

any signs of this coming out.

5. She had been surprised to find that her grandmother was medicated, taking a drug called Thorazine and that, according to her grand-father, "helps her a great deal." Emma couldn't see that either, perhaps because she was never permitted to spend any time with her.

6. He'd ended the conversation in a way that he'd apparently planned all along. "She's a strong woman, Emma. She may well outlive the two of us. If anything happens to me, George Treadwell has power of attorney and will see to her. She is not to be moved from home. There are ample funds to care for her. And I am determined that the burden not fall on you. Do you understand?" Emma clearly remembers that last part. And she had nodded in assent. She was 14 years old.

It was some time later, in the mid-seventies, when Emma was at Columbia and long after her grandfather had died, on one of her rare visits to the estate, that she'd seen the prescriptions for lithium and the canister of pills on the kitchen counter awaiting Annie's careful dispensation. It was then that she realized how ill her grandmother had been, how crucial Annie was and how wide-ranging her respon-sibilities, although she and Annie have never discussed the matter. Emma and her grandfather had talked about the illness just that once, so she held it close like a dark secret. And they had never, ever talked about her grandmother's family. No one had. About the fact that the Rothenbergs had become Episcopalians long before Margaret was born, probably before Grandpa Rothenberg was born. She didn't know exactly when, only that it had happened.

No. 46

Late in the afternoon, before the sun begins to set, Emma wraps herself in a blanket that reeks of mothballs and heads for the screen porch overlooking the Upper Saranac Lake. She carries a whisky in one hand and a pack of her grandmother's cigarettes in the other. The gun is stowed in an old leather satchel of her grandmother's, slung over her left shoulder, and the diary is shoved under the pit of her right arm. She has to do a good bit of juggling to unbolt the double doors and get out to the porch. She sets the handgun on a wicker table, to one side of the whiskey, before she settles in and reads on.

August 12, 1940
I am myself again. James has promised that we can go to Saranac for Labor Day and that he'll try to get the week off before and we'll all go. He has promised.

August 15, 1940
Today's paper says James Cagney and Humphrey Bogart are communists. Sounds like pure nonsense to me.

August 19, 1940

Willkie delivered a tremendous speech. We heard it on
the radio last night, after we arrived home from supper
at the Balfours. James was pleased. And I am glad that
he mentioned the European Jews. He called the Nazis
barbarians, spoke of their persecution of the Jews. Called
it medieval and tragic. The most tragic in human history, he
said. I don't know that FDR has ever spoken on the subject
quite so eloquently. But it is impossible to ignore really.
Anyone who says so is lying. Last fall, all over Germany,
there were flagrant attacks on Jews after that boy in France
killed that diplomat. And arrests that made no sense.
Breaking windows, burning buildings, then arresting the
victims themselves. It was all over the news. Jews arrested
for their own protection it said. They are fleeing Germany
and I don't blame them. Fleeing to Poland with nowhere
to go. Sleeping in the fields. I saw it in the newspapers. We
should not have gone to the Olympics. We should have
drawn the line there, just as Governor Earle said. Now it is
too late. When they took Czechoslovakia, they made the
Jews register. It was on the front page of the Times and I cut
it out and showed it to James. It said they were required to
register all their property in Czechoslovakia. They were not
allowed to acquire real estate. They are no longer allowed
in health resorts in Germany or the central park in Vienna,
Austria. A public park, mind you. That was when I realized
that the Germans are on a mission. And they will not be
stopped. I told James that we have waited too long to speak
out. I said this is not right, not civilized. Something terrible
is happening. He tried to calm me down as if I am a fool. He
reminded me that real Jews aren't allowed to buy homes
in this neighborhood or to join our clubs. Real Jews—that's
what he calls them, as if I am not one because of my mother.

Then to add insult to injury, he reminded me that when we visited Memphis the Negroes could only visit the zoo on Tuesdays and that, even here, they are segregated in separate schools. And finally he said "it's not the end of the world." But I don't believe him. I don't think he's right. I'm just grateful my father isn't alive to witness any of this.

August 25, 1940

Last night, Edward R. Murrow broadcast from the rooftops of London. We could hear the air raid sirens, the bombs, the guns. I didn't sleep well. I dreamed of it. I woke in the night crying out, trembling. James held me until I fell asleep. We leave for Saranac tomorrow. He says we need to leave the war behind us. No radios, no newspapers, he says. Two weeks in the wilderness. I cannot wait to see my beloved cabin.

November 26, 1940

Now they've walled them in. The Jews. In Warsaw. I dreamt that I was living there. I woke sweating in my sleep. To find James gone. He is setting up those plants around the country. Gone for weeks on end. His Thanksgiving visit cut short. It is abominable.

November 28, 1940

London has been under attack for months. We read only of blitzkriegs—bombings and more bombings. In Britain, they have sent the children off to the country to keep them safe. And, according to the newsreels, whole families spend endless hours in bomb shelters and underground tunnels. I find the idea of it both terrifying and exciting. To be on the edge of danger with your fellow men. I picture myself among them as on a crowded subway platform in New York. All of us huddled together, communing with one another, connected in some way. Elbow to elbow. Whole families protected together. It reminds me of the people who gather on the stoops of the row houses in Baltimore near the Italian district. We see them in the summers. I always found that so appealing. They look so happy all of them. But perhaps I'm romanticizing.

December

There are things your brain cannot hold, cannot absorb. So we go about our business. We ignore, we look past it, until sometimes it's too late. And now seems to be one of those times. James believes that we will be forced to enter the war if Britain cannot stand against Hitler. Never mind what FDR says. Most Americans do not want another war. We do not want it. But we are not neutral in the least. Our hearts are with Great Britain. And I, I despise the Germans. James of course concurs on this. We are producing tens of thousands of airplanes and sending destroyers to Great Britain. And that is as it should be. And we now will have universal service. Everyone on all sides has supported it. So I can be grateful for one thing—that my Catherine is a girl. When she graduates this year, she will go on to Dana Hall and not into the Army. And let us pray that these weapons alone will defeat the Nazis, because if they don't, we will be forced to send our men into battle. We must.

No. 47

Atlantic Ocean

The CS Antwerpen is within reach of land. It has been a smooth journey. Tonight, the crew will celebrate its imminent arrival at the port of Zeebrugge. They shoot fireworks off the bow into the windless night and share a bottle of whisky among them. The moon drifts behind a smoky wave of a cloud to the backdrop of singing. It is the Belgian national anthem, a paean to unity and freedom and to war.

> O beloved Belgium, sacred land of our fathers,
> Our heart and soul are dedicated to you.
> Our strength and the blood of our veins we offer,
> Be our goal, in work and battle.
> Prosper, O country, in unbreakable unity,
> Always be yourself and free.
> Trust in the word that, undaunted, you can speak:
> For King, for Freedom and for Law.
> For King, for Freedom and for Law.

No. 48

Lake Saranac

Emma spends Sunday morning clearing out closets and drawers, and spends the evening on the back porch, lake-gazing into the night, the handgun by her side. The afternoon she sets aside for the diary. She has abandoned her grandmother's cigarettes. Too stale, too old. And had her fill of whisky. She finds she's looking forward to hearing her grandmother's voice and following the events as they unfold. Sitting on the screen porch with a cup of coffee, she notices immediately that her grandmother has skipped two full years. She glances back at the preceding pages to be sure. The last entry had been December 1940. Her grandmother had apparently not picked up the diary again until November of 1942. Emma knows that in the interim, the Japanese had attacked Pearl Harbor and America had entered the war. She suspects that her grandfather had already gone off to work on the atomic bomb, but she's not certain. And she knows, at this point, her mother Catherine would have been very nearly grown but not yet married.

She starts with the page that's marked by the single newspaper clipping that has remained in the diary for these thirty-some years, the one about the Holocaust, the one with the headline "Himmler Program Kills Polish Jews."

November 1942

The government has absconded with my husband. Of course, not literally. But he has been gone for more than a week now at meetings in Washington. Part of the war effort I'm told. Confidential matters I'm told. Ten years ago we were the bad guys. But now they need our help and there are no more accusations flying. James has been tied up with building the powder mills all over the country for two years now. What on earth do they want from us next?

November 25, 1942

My God. There is an order to kill the Jews in Poland. Literally. They have used the word exterminate. They will exterminate them all, except those that can serve as slaves. Slaves mind you. Has everyone in the western world lost their minds? Have we no conscience? Is there no one to stop it? There it sits, on the pages of the nation's leading newspaper under a big headline. They are making no secret of it. I have cut out the article and inserted it here so there will be no confusion. So I can show James when he returns. In what they now call the Warsaw ghetto, only 40,000 people remain where once there were more than ten times that. Where did they go? It is all here in print. People being dragged out of their homes and killed in freight cars. Where they are suffocated. Dying from fumes. It is a mass murder. James returns tonight. For our Thanksgiving. He'll find me praying for the Jews of Europe.

The entries that follow are undated, frantic scrawls, one following the next.

I cannot sleep for the nightmares.

***

They are gone. Catherine. James. Here for just a moment for a bit of turkey, a sip of booze, a slice of pie. They left yesterday afternoon or perhaps the day before. I am not sure. I've lost track of time. I had another episode. He has cancelled the newspaper. He has instructed Annie to keep the radio off. And Dr. West was here with his sedatives.

***

He's no longer allowed to tell me where he is. Not even what state he is in. That is the truth. Even his own wife cannot know. Although one time he tripped up and told me he was in Kentucky. That car arrives to take him to the airport with that Muriel Markham in the back seat waiting for him. Do I expect him back soon? I do not. Meanwhile, here I am twiddling my thumbs. Catherine off at school.

***

What possesses me? I have wandered the dark halls looking for what, going from room to room, all of them empty. Where is my husband? Where is my little girl? The dogs following on my heels. So I invited them in, called them up onto the bed and there I found some comfort.

***

I am filled with dread. James is gone now for months on end and the war never seems to stop. We have no sugar, no gas, little coupons that tell us when we can shop and what we can buy. If James were here there would be special dispensations, I am sure of that. But Annie says even when she tells the grocer who she is, who we are, there are no favors. I am locked in this dreadful room like a caged animal. I believe it will make me crazy, if I am not already. Then I will prove all of them right. And when will he be home? No telling. I believe I will smoke this entire pack before the sun goes down.

Then there are a good 10 or 15 pages torn from the book, ragged as if ripped out in a rage. And it starts up again in 1945, the prose lucid, the penmanship rather different, less frantic, clearer and easier to read. As if she is writing slowly and carefully and thoughtfully. And the war is about to end.

Friday, August 17, 1945—Saranac

James is on his way. He tells me it is over, truly over. He left Washington this morning on the train headed home and says to have dinner ready tomorrow. Trout! I have been hiding up here since May. Hiding or hidden. I'm not at all sure which. But now the war in the Pacific is ended, I will be going home. I have been here for three months. Three months! Elvin drove me, for James has forbidden me to drive. And with the gas rations, I've not been allowed to return home at all this summer. Forbidden, mind you. I think my experience at the cinema was what did it. It upset him, so he decided to just send me off. Although I reminded him that had he not been away in Washington, we would not have gone to the movies. We would never have seen that odious newsreel, the photos of those camps. Death camps. That's exactly what they were. I had to the leave the theater and Catherine called James when we got home. She gave me medicine, put me to bed, as if I am not an adult entitled to an opinion about what is going on in the world. Not entitled to my feelings. Criminals all of them. Evil. I suppose I had a bit of a rant. Because I told them. I told everyone years ago. Did he think I didn't know what was going on over there? And now this, isolated up here with little more than a deck of cards and a bottle of gin. And the nightmares. Annie has been small comfort. We went to see Meet Me in St. Louis for God's sake. You'd think they wouldn't show such a thing at a family movie of that sort. I expected a cartoon. It was dreadful, all of it. And I am not making this up. It is the greatest evil of all time. People are lying when they say we didn't know. We knew. All of us. How could we not? And who was willing to open our doors to them? No one.

Saturday, August 18, 1945—Saranac

James arrived at six. We had a brief toast before dinner, but it was not a lively event. He did not bring the newspaper so I could see the headlines. America victorious and so forth. Thank God it's over was all he said, and then, the world will be a different place now, my dear. But not in a truly happy way. In a distant way like he was holding something back as he has been doing nearly every day since the war began. He says he will stay for the duration, through Labor Day weekend. Catherine and her new friend Robert will be up for a few days. Me, full of excitement at the prospect. James not the least bit celebratory. Despondent really. He retired early. Gave me a little peck on the forehead. For goodness sake, what does he think I am, an old woman? I am 47 and still have my shape and have been away from my husband for three months. And I've been writing in this damn journal quite long enough. And with Annie and Elvin here to see it. What will they think, that we are no longer in love?

Sunday, August 19, 1945

They've gone all of them over to the clubhouse for a drink. I have promised to follow. But I'm heartbroken. Last night, in the middle of the night, I turned over and James was gone. He had left the bed. When I got up, I could hear him out on the porch. He was sobbing. Just sitting in the chair sobbing like a baby. I moved toward him to comfort him and I think he was ashamed. He turned away, spoke into the air, facing the lake. Oh dear he said, I didn't mean to wake you, he said. I just went over to him and put my arms around his neck and asked him what was the matter. Just the war, my dear, he said. And I said—but it's over now and we are safe, all of us. And I took him by the hand and told him to come back to bed. But he wouldn't. He didn't. He said, I just need a moment. And he thanked me. But he never did come back to bed as far as I know. It's hard to watch a man cry.

Wednesday

I like this Robert. He is a small man, but attractive. He complements my Catherine and is well mannered, very. I don't think James was quite as crazy about him as I was. He is rather arrogant. A good bit of talk, talk, talk. Full of opinions about this and that. He said, in front of James mind you, we dropped the big one on them. That's what he called it—the big one—and James gave him a look that would have melted ice. Then, he explained to us that the surge on the Russian front could have ended it. That it wasn't necessary to drop a bomb. That Japan was ready to fold. James was his usual diplomatic self. Is that right? he said. Perhaps Catherine failed to explain who her father is. After all, she really couldn't care less about any of it. Unlike me, craving the least bit of news, which has been rationed out to me for far too long. When she wasn't flirting with Robert, she was fooling with the canapés, trying to make up something special as if Annie couldn't. Little mushroom caps filled with some kind of paté. As if she wanted to impress the man. After they left, James said something about why hadn't he fought, why hadn't he fought in the war. I don't recall him explaining. But he's been in the Army, stationed at the War department, some administrative post. He told us at dinner, after James asked, rather tactlessly I thought. And Catherine had chimed in with something about "he aided the resistance, father." But the young man shook his head just ever so slightly. He seemed to be silencing her. Probably just showing off, that's what James said afterward. Well, it hardly matters. In all likelihood, we'll never see him again. Catherine seems to flit from one boy to another with some frequency. Always has.

No. 49

Alexandria, VA

Tables filled with baked goods and used clothing and household items are lined up on the blacktop of the Warwick Elementary School playground in Alexandria, Virginia. It's a Sunday morning flea market, a benefit staffed by dutiful parents. Mahmoud Hariri arrives early and buys a stack of vintage record albums. He's stashing them in the trunk of his car when Bill Kidman drives up. Together, they head for I-66 going south in a rented vehicle.

He has with him a copy of the one-page report that arrived via Federal Express that afternoon concealed under the false bottom of a box of chocolates—real chocolates, Belgian chocolates that brought a smile to Sara Kidman's face before Bill grabbed them away from her. "They are Spy versus Spy chocolates, my dear," he said. "It's a trick box." And she'd laughed, not sure whether to take him seriously until he made it clear that he was. "Just let me retrieve the secret message first," he said, still acting as if it was all in fun, a joke.

Now, sitting next to Hariri in the rented car going nowhere in particular, he reports, "We found the shipper." Hariri flips the document open, eyeballs the headlines, then reads it through quietly.

CONFIDENTIAL

Cargo Belgique
The Breuers are an old Flemish family that entered the shipping business when King Leopold decided to make the Congo a royal colony in 1895. During WWII, they ferried copper between the colony and Allied ports. It's never been a family with significant scruples about what they carry aboard their ships and, today, in 1978, its tentacles reach deep into the Middle East. The company is run out of Antwerp by Serge Breuer's father Albrecht and was run by his grandfather before that. Serge Breuer's mother is from Istanbul, which gives him the tawny skin and dark hair of a Turk. That marriage, like his aunt's marriage to an Israeli

import/export agent based in Haifa, has enriched and expanded the family's shipping business whose most profitable cargo is weapons and whose clients include the German, French, British and U.S. governments, and their agents.

Cargo Belgique Americaine (U.S. subsidiary)
Cargo Belgique Americaine was established in 1949 for one purpose only: To enable shipments of various munitions— explosives, tank ammunition, land mines, grenades as well as an assortment of chemical weapons—from U.S. plants to foreign sites. Like its parent company, CBA handles shipments of steel and coal and grain and agricultural machinery. It transports building materials and industrial supplies. But that's a cover. Its core business, its reason for being, its profit center, is the weapons trade. Although we have no record of any current relationships, CBA has operated under agreements with the U.S. intelligence service.

When Hariri finally looks up, Kidman speaks. "CBA is working out of Philadelphia. Our guy went down there yesterday. Nosed around. They're moving goods by rail." Hariri is listening, thinking. "Can you explore?" Kidman asks. Hariri nods. "If it's going through MOTSU, I can."

No. 50

Saranac Lake

On Monday afternoon Emma loads up the jeep and heads into the village. She's found nothing incriminating among her grandmother's things, no evidence of anything aside from good taste and old money—a cache of cable knit sweaters in the dresser, a closet full of Barbour jackets and rain slickers, rows of Bean boots of various sizes, knit hats and cashmere scarves in every conceivable color—luxury necessities for the fall weather, which comes on early in the Adirondacks. Emma holds onto the few things that she herself might wear one day. But most of it, she's piled into big, brown leaf bags for delivery to the Goodwill in Saranac Lake. It's a half-hour drive south around the lake, then northeast along Route 3. She's glad to get out. It's cool and cloudless, and there's no traffic on the southbound stretch, just unbroken forest punctuated by a few random outposts—an old Dairy Queen, a run-down motel fashioned of pink concrete, a chalet-style restaurant built in the 1940s and virtually unchanged since, except for, repeatedly, its name. Elk Lodge, Rambo's, The Chalet are a few she recalls. All the parking lots are empty. No reason to stop. She plans to stock up at the A&P in the village.

Emma wouldn't know anyone who lives in Saranac Lake anymore, but the place itself is part of who she is. She has memories that reside in this village set off from the world. As a girl, she'd come in with her grandfather or Annie or even her parents, although she was so young then that she doesn't have any clear recollections of their presence. She associates the place with outings on summer afternoons, with firework celebrations and rambling walks along the lake. Arriving, she recalls a time in the mid-sixties when she came into town with her grand-father, thinks she must have been nine or ten. They'd seen a movie at the old theater, a mystery set by the sea. She can recall the dress she was wearing—a white sailor dress with navy trim, a favorite. Afterwards, they'd gone to the ice cream parlor, then on to the five and dime, a summer ritual. She can visualize the place in her mind, the rows of board games and art supplies, pencil cases and puzzle books laid out on long counters that filled the store. But the image she conjures is grey, colorless. She can't recall the name of the film, which frustrates her now. "A Hayley Mills movie," she thinks, "Disney, surely." She beats herself up trying.

Everything around her feels familiar, virtually unchanged since her youth and still a bit rough around the edges. She knows where everything is—the supermarket, the liquor store, the drug store. She knows that the old homes with their screen porches are the cure cot-tages from a time when victims of tuberculosis flocked here from the city, remembers that the very idea of tuberculosis had frightened her for years. Perhaps for that reason, one of the churches in a cluster at the center of town—The Church of St. Luke the Beloved Physician—is etched in her memory.

She makes a stop at the park where the village meets Lake Flower, walks along the cobblestones to the cement barrier that marks the shore. Sitting on an old wooden bench overlooking the lake, the blue-green water twinkling before her, she remembers her first trip to Saranac Lake alone with a young man, her first date really. She hadn't known him well. He was the guest of another family at Slatterly. When she asked about him one summer, she'd learned that he'd been killed in Vietnam. There is no thread there, just a vague memory of a first date, a faint sadness.

Shielding the sun from her eyes, she watches a man cross the lake in a red kayak, a lone paddler. The wind has picked up. She can see his navy windbreaker blowing up behind him. She wraps her arms tight across her chest and begins to wonder how she will use the cabin now that everyone is gone, whether she'll keep it and sustain the tradition, whether she even wants to come back again and again. And whether she will ever have a family to bring with her.

In time, sitting in stillness on the cold bench, the paint on its wooden frame cracking with age, the sense of familiarity turns into something else. She feels alien somehow, unattached, like a time traveler with no connection to the present and no plan for the future. The kayaker is moving fast, paddling with sure, clean strokes. As she rises to go, her sweater catches on a nail at the edge of the bench, unraveling. Her grandmother's diary, filled with darkness that swept the world so many years before weighs on her.

March 23, 1946

James was full of himself this morning. We were sitting in the dining room, just finishing up. He surprised me, throwing down the newspaper. Well damn, he said cheerily. Well damn. I had no idea what to expect. He flashed the headline at me, too quickly for me to actually read it and said—The Soviets are refusing to leave. And—Damned if the Iranian government didn't take the issue to the new United Nations Organization. That'll be a test, won't it? I agreed, of course, and I asked to be reminded what they were doing there—in Persia—in the first place. He explained that we were all there. All? Who is all? I asked, just so he would know I was paying attention, that I was clear-headed. Brits, U.S., Soviets. During the war. It was our supply route to Russia, he said. And he reminded me that Persia is now Iran. Of course, I should have known that. Then he said, matter-of-factly—And the Russians turned it into an occupation. Duplicitous bastards. What do you think of that, Maggie? He never calls me Maggie anymore. I was buoyed by it. He didn't notice. He just went on—They are trying to build a barrier around themselves. A barrier of states. Communist states. Just as they're doing in Europe. And they're using our equipment, U.S. tanks. Russians driving U.S. tanks around Iran to flex their muscles. Using equipment we made and leased to them. And they're refusing to leave. That takes some nerve. You know what they want, don't you?

And I had no idea what to say. The oil, of course, he said. Then he just turned back to his paper as if I weren't even there. I was just eating my breakfast, innocently enough, trying not to start anything. And this time he throws the newspaper down and out comes another expletive. Well, the way he said it, it sounded like an expletive. Jesus Christ, he said. And then—for God's sake, why don't we just give the Jews their damn homeland and let them be. And I said, Amen. And he smiled, a sweet, sweet smile at me. I'm glad to see him in a good mood. I think it's UNO, this new United Nations Organization. I think he's optimistic about it. I love my James.

There are a few more entries toward the end of March and a sketch of a handful of daffodils with a caption: "Saw these popping up today at the foot of the drive." Then she's back on the subject of the United Nations, the household wrapped up, it seems, in this new world order, Emma's grandfather vacillating between cynicism and idealism about the future of the world. And Margaret Quinn capturing the details, recording them with such precision. Emma did not know her grandmother, not this grandmother. Her astonishment grows with every passage. And she is touched by the one that follows.

April 8, 1946
James might have thought that I forgot. But I didn't. This morning, he pulls out the newspaper and tells me the United Nations Organization did it. They passed their first test, he says. He shows me the headline—something about the Red Army leaving Iran—and says—now that's a cause

for celebration. It feels as if he's teasing me. But he's not.
He's pleased and he's sharing it. And I'm okay. I'm all right.
I smile—that's wonderful news, I say. He still doesn't let me
read the paper myself. But he knows how much it interests
me and he threw me that little bone this morning. And then
he lit my cigarette like the gentleman he is.

June 14, 1946

Catherine and her young man arrived this afternoon en route
to New York. I think he's lovely, really, and smart. Wears these
sharp little outfits, rather dashing. Seems they're meeting
some of his friends from Princeton in the city. I'm beginning
to think this is serious. Catherine cannot keep her hands off
the poor man. She is smitten like a groveling pup.

June 15, 1946

I'm not sure I've seen James this happy since the war began.
There is a proposal on the table, before UNO, a formal
proposal, that would have us give up the secret to atomic
energy, destroy all our bombs and give over authority to the
new Atomic Energy Commission, an international commission.
It gives me hope, he told me as we walked in the garden this
afternoon. He said—It is brilliant. I believe we may have the
leverage to make this happen, to make the threat of atomic
weapons go away. I cannot tell you what relief I feel. His eyes
were welling up with tears when he spoke the words.

June 16, 1946

They were back—Catherine and Robert—on their way home
from their big weekend in the big city. She was beside
herself, aglow. They stopped here for supper then we
dropped them back at the station after. When they arrived

by taxi, Robert did the oddest thing. Annie had packed them a snack for the way up, packaged in tin foil. I don't know what it was, sandwiches I guess. And he saved the foil. He brought it right back to us, folded neatly, so we could use it again. I don't know anything about his family. But I thought that was very dear. I genuinely like the man, but he seems to have a knack for upsetting James. During supper, he made an off-handed remark about the Baruch proposal, this proposed Atomic Energy Commission, something about the Soviets can't be trusted and it will never work. I changed the subject, asked him about the trip, about his friends and so forth. I know what James was thinking—who does this whippersnapper think he is? But I believe we got past it. I certainly hope so. James is not an easy man to please. And Catherine appears to be taken with this Robert Gardner.

September 12, 1946

We are back at last. Although I use the word "we" loosely. James is spending a good deal of time these days in Washington working on this new Atomic Energy Commission. Apparently, he knows more about our nuclear facilities than anyone in the country. And even though UNO can't seem to get the idea off the ground, we are doing it ourselves. Turning all our nuclear facilities into some sort of public enterprise for the good of the nation. James seems quite optimistic about the entire endeavor. He says we need to use this new form of energy for peaceful purposes. It's breathed new life into him. At least I hope that's what's behind his enthusiasm. At any rate, what I'm saying is that I'm back at last. Back from Saranac. I have missed my journaling. I must remember to pack in a more organized fashion next summer.

Thursday

We have a television set! James came home tonight beside himself and Elvin carried in a large box. I had seen pictures of televisions but this is the first one I've seen close up. It is rather silly, like sitting in front of a radio. But they can truly transmit the pictures right into our home. Still, there is not much to watch. We get a channel on which a man reads the news in the evening. We have not discussed whether I will be allowed to watch it. And I certainly didn't bring it up. No matter. He is gone so much I will do what I choose. He's very excited about this television business. He says it's only the beginning.

October 15, 1946

I think I may lose my mind. James is in Washington again. Off with that Muriel Markham. They have been back and forth and back and forth. He is all caught up in it. But is he caught up in her as well? What does she know about atomic energy? I asked him last time they returned. Is there no one else to accompany you? I can't stand the woman. She tries to be so friendly when I see her. Too friendly.

The entries that follow are undated.

I burned today's newspaper. I got hold of it and stuffed it in the backyard grill and lit it on fire. You should have seen Annie come running. Now that was something. For some unknown reason, the Times decided to devote two full pages to the eleven men who will hang today. Outside the Palace of Justice in Nuremburg I presume. Nazi wretches. I did not read one bit of it. I don't want to know their personal stories. Are they to be treated like celebrities? I think not. Let the fires of hell swallow each one of them whole.

***

Damned if Annie didn't call the doctor. And there is nothing wrong with me. Nothing. He tried to give me a shot and I bit him, right on the side of his neck. Drew blood. That'll teach them.

Emma is stunned, imagining the doctor leaning over her bed, trying to hold her down, her grandmother fighting back, her grandfather out of town. And where would Annie have been in the midst of all this? Right there in the room? "Good God," Emma thinks, beginning to grasp the dimensions of this tragedy. She sets the diary down for a moment, walking circles around the porch. This journal is proof of all kinds of things—her grandmother's obsession, her insights, her volatility and unpredictability. She could certainly have created this situation with the CIA, cooked something up in her head. Just as Bill Kidman suggested—her actions could have triggered these events. But the diary is also proof of her deep connection with reality, her attention to detail, her ability to document and interpret events as they unfold. If there is a black book, she is thinking, then Bill Kidman is lying. And if Margaret Quinn is crazy, she may well be crazy like a fox.

When Emma turns back to the diary, almost a year has passed, quite a gap, she thinks. Emma now identifies these as periods when her grandmother must have been sedated or hospitalized. Then, she turns back to her writing, her journaling, as if nothing happened, as if it's all normal. Of course, there's no way Emma could know one way or the other. The gaps could be something else, meaningless breaks, times when she was too happy or too engaged to bother with it, or otherwise occupied. Never assume anything, she thinks. And as she reads on, another story begins to unfold.

August 1947

Big news—it seems Catherine IS in love with Robert. I knew it was coming, but she believes he's going to propose. She wants James to get him a job at Balfour, so they can leave the war department and live in Delaware near us. I am hoping for a house on Miller's Lane. That would be perfection. What more could I ask for? A wedding. I will be glad to get them out of that awful city. We talked about it tonight at dinner. James seems unsure of the young man. But I like him. I raised my glass to them. But James, James raised his glass to me. Said I was more beautiful than ever.

September 1947

They are closing down the war department and I've insisted that James bring Robert up to Balfour. But there has been no proposal. And James is concerned. He says Robert is in with the wrong people. I don't like his crowd—that's what he said. And I suggested the best way to get him out of the crowd was bring him up here with us. For goodness sake. Wrong people. Seems to me we tend to get confused about who the wrong people really are. If the war taught us anything, it's that.

October 1947

Now Robert has moved to the Army of all places, ordering supplies or something. A deadly job if you ask me. And it's all settled. The wedding is set for May. And I'm not at all happy with this arrangement. James is being quite stubborn.

The last entry is followed by a series of lists, notes scribbled and crossed out, random phone numbers written at the corners of the page, drawings of flower arrangements and random doodles. The diary has become sort of a frantic wedding planner. It goes on for quite a few pages. And picks up again in the spring, shortly before the wedding.

April 24, 1948

Oh dear. I don't know what we're going to do about this. They argued the two of them, fiercely. And with the wedding only three weeks away. Catherine's Robert insulted James. At first they were celebratory. We were in the Library, Catherine and I in one corner going over the final details. Apparently Missy Ketchum has gotten so big that her bridesmaid dress has to be altered and Catherine's worried that we might have to get her another.

    Across the room, they were having a toast, the two of them. With Robert, it's always the same subject—the Communists are taking over the world. He talks of little else. This time it was the elections in Europe. And the news is good. France voted against the Communists in the fall elections. And now, in Italy, the Communists have been defeated. Bravo! Robert was saying and lifting his glass— To democracy! James raised his as well, but I could see a shadow fall across his face, a lack of enthusiasm.

I could see it from across the room. Then Robert began his lecture, as he always does—Of course elections aren't very meaningful in Europe anymore, he said. The Communists with all their dirty tricks. They take over the police force, bribe the officials, arrest their opponents or kill them. We had to fight hard for this one, he said. I guess he meant in Italy, fight for the victory there. James didn't say a word. He looked up at us, suggested we all go in for dinner. Then I heard him tell Robert—I don't think this is something we want to talk about tonight. But Robert had already had three martinis. Why the hell not? he asked, belligerent.

We left the room, Catherine and I, but we could still hear them. James was speaking and I could imagine his face was turning red as he did—I know damn well what happened in Italy, and you do too. Dirty tricks, indeed. Robert said—I don't know what you're talking about. And James said, Of course you do. You spend more time in Washington than I do, or something to that effect. And I could hear Robert—Again, sir, I don't know what you mean. Then James—Ask some of your friends. Ask them what they did to influence the election. Radio broadcasts are one thing. But I heard tell they paid off officials. That's bribery. And they infiltrated the unions.

Robert didn't say a word. Then maybe you can ask them this—what's the point of fighting for democracy if we don't respect our own principles? Finally, Robert raised his voice angrily—How else do you think we're going to defeat these bastards? And James excused himself, disappeared up the stairs and it was quite a few minutes before he came back to the table. I was proud of James. He is right. That is no way for gentlemen to behave. We must remain on the right side of history.

Emma leans her head back, trying to absorb the meaning of this encounter—her grandfather's adamancy, and this sense that he is accusing her father or these friends—or colleagues—of bribing officials to influence the outcome of the Italian elections. Sounds like something out of the Soviet playbook, she's thinking. Not a piece of history of which she's aware, but well within the realm of possibility. An impression of her father is emerging, but Emma is seeing him through her grandmother's eyes. Wary of her grandmother's reliability, she is reminded of Martin Simon's comment—"She had an eye for the truth."

It's late in the afternoon. Emma looks out across the lake, eyes the clubhouse, imagining there might be people about, but sees nothing. She hears the rumble of an engine of some sort off in the distance, the motor of a boat, a chainsaw maybe. She knows the rule against cutting down trees. "One must have fallen," she thinks.

When she picks up the diary again a few minutes later, it's the summer of 1948. The wedding is over, her grandmother, perhaps too caught up in it to document the event itself. There is talk of her father's friends again, of his crowd, and something clicks. Emma recognizes these as some of the characters pictured in her parent's wedding album, the friends from Washington. She recognizes a name. She reads it through twice.

July 5, 1948

I don't know what James has been complaining about. Robert's friends are dashing. War heroes, some of them.

From the best schools. Of course, I'd met a few of them at the wedding. But yesterday the whole lot came up for our 4th of July—a dozen of them along with their wives. Catherine calls them the Georgetown crowd.

The men seem to adore her. They drank a good bit and at the end of the evening, after all the local people had left, a few of them ended up in the pool. Clowning around. With their clothes on mind you. They all seemed quite eager to talk with James. Particularly this Skilling fellow. Fletch they call him. He's a bit of a rogue. From Louisiana, I believe. They took their cigars into the garden for a time, disappeared. The funny thing was when I asked a group of them what they do, one fellow said, We're just spies, ma'am. They had a hearty laugh about it. And I can assure you, I didn't enjoy being made fun of in the least.

When I came upon a handful of them at one point, talking politics, strategizing, I reminded them that this was a party and enough of that. And made a point of introducing them to the Balfour people. Robert thanked me profusely for everything. It was his idea, according to Catherine. And I think we did quite well all of us with the out-of-towners. But James was not happy about any of it. Not the party. Not Robert's friends. And not the return of this Mr. Skilling, which surprised me for at the wedding they'd seemed to be so well suited to one another. Both so preoccupied with the world beyond. When I pressed him, he said something about his having an agenda, a hidden agenda. I'm not at all sure what he meant. He may have been a bit jealous. The man is a natural-born flirt.

Emma recalls the wedding photos she'd seen with Annie that afternoon by the kitchen window when they were packing for the estate sale. The beautiful women, the handsome young men, preening and posing with their cigarettes and champagne flutes. She wonders who Fletch Skilling might be, imagines that somehow he may be relevant to all this. A friend of her father's from Washington, a man who worked with government, someone her grandfather did not like. The young man's throwaway comment about spies intrigues her. And this idea, expressed in the diary, that her father was in with the wrong people.

There are no telephones at the house. Feeling as if she's finally onto something, she sets the book down and walks over to the clubhouse looking for the staff, for a phone. But there is no one in sight. Finally, she sees an older man, someone she's seen before—a man she knows as Boone. He's a stocky, bearded soul with the look of a backwoodsman, and he's employing a chain saw to break up some branches. It takes Emma a few minutes of waving and jumping—the loaded gun smashing against her hip—to get his attention. Once she does, she's nearly on top of him. Startled, he shuts the thing off. "No one here. Place is empty," he says, nodding toward the clubhouse when she asks about making a call. "Door's open," he says.

She knows the building, enters by the porch that runs along the side of it, the railing an elaborate web of logs and twigs, woven together and wrapped around one another. The main hall is filled with picnic-style tables, more substantial than is the norm, and long wooden benches. A set of rockers made of bent wood and bowed branches stand empty in one corner. A dozen gnarly chandeliers fashioned from the antlers of Adirondack elks hang from the ceiling. She heads to the back hall where there's a row of cubbies and private mailboxes, a small office, a phone. She has to dial New York information to get the listing for the Columbia Library and speak to the operator before she can reach Manny at the research desk and ask, "Someone named Skilling. Maybe Fletcher Skilling. Can you find out who he is?"

No. 51

Bruges, Belgium

Angus McLearan is in the break bulk terminal in the Port of Zeebrugge on the North Sea, searching the board for the landing information on the CS Antwerpen. It was expected this morning. Two of his colleagues from MI6 are working with him. Both on the ground. And they've got a helicopter on standby on the edge of the seaport. It's a huge facility, in the midst of an expansion. There's construction everywhere. It seems the ship has been at the pier since 5 a.m.

A woman's voice comes in on his radio. "Twelve containers marked CSW unloaded. They're headed for the trucking terminal."

Then a man. "We're good. I've got four trackers on them."

Then the woman again. "I'm looking at desert jeeps, U.S. military issue. Unloading now."

McLearan speaks. "Paperwork says they're going to NATO outposts. We've got the specifics on those. Just let them go."

It's two hours before he hears anything else. He's dressed simply in a lightweight jacket and twill pants. His ball cap sports the logo of a shipping company, so he looks like a transfer agent, like he belongs, a clipboard under his arm. He gets a coffee and settles in on a bench not far from the big board.

"Heads up," the woman's voice finally comes through again. "Special handling crew is here. I'm guessing this is our target." It's another thirty minutes before she follows up, clarifies, "We've got black drums marked hazardous coming out of the hull. They're set on steel pallets."

"Everybody hang tight," McLearan says. "Wings, I'll give you the signal."

The wait feels interminable. There are dark clouds coming in from the west. The woman remains above the pier, looking through her binoculars, shooting photos. The man moves to retrieve their van. They've got someone on the inside, on the handling crew. It's his job to place a tracker on the shipment without attracting attention. The woman is monitoring the situation. On signal, the helicopter sweeps over, distracting everyone, and the crewman makes his move, placing trackers on two steel palettes. Within ten minutes, the three members of the MI6 team, including McLearan, are in a utility van headed southeast.

No. 52

Manhattan

Four days have passed since Serge Breuer left New York for the Philadelphia offices of *Cargo Belgique Americaine*, or rather for his desk in their warehouse on the Philadelphia waterfront. On Tuesday evening, he returns to his Manhattan apartment to find that Emma has left the city. There had been some concerns about the shipment—that the CIA would interfere, that whatever Margaret Quinn had been carrying in her bag of tricks would get in the way somehow. But now it has arrived safely in Zeebrugge and will be transferred to *Poudreries de Belgique*. Serge knows nothing of its final destination. That's not his job.

Arriving home, he sees a full bottle of red wine sitting open on the kitchen counter and a frypan full of pasta on the stove. The remnants of a half-pound of shrimp—old shells and sand veins—lie in a pile on the kitchen counter. The smell is rank. "*Fok*," he says and tosses the pan angrily into the sink. He just looks past the rest of it—throws open a window, grabs a glass of the wine and heads back to the bedroom. The noise from Third Avenue below pours into the apartment.

Behind a pair of double doors, he settles in at the small desk hidden in what would seem to be a closet. There, he turns on the surveillance feed from the foyer of Emma's apartment building on West End Avenue. He had seen her leave the building on St. Patrick's Day, headed out in her snow boots, her jeans, her powder blue jacket. He'd seen her over the feed returning under the cover of her black umbrella later that day, pulling a small handcart behind her full of groceries. Reassured that she'd be around when he returned, he'd left the city.

Now he sits drinking his wine, watching the comings and goings from her building over the past four days. He sees a mix of people, residents that are by now familiar to him—the balding man with the little rat of a dog, the young Asian couple, the elderly and the nondescript males that he barely notices because he needn't. The camera is positioned to catch sight of them as the elevator door opens or as they emerge from the stairwell. It's easier to get a good view as they exit the building in the morning than when they return at night. Then it's all backs of heads and tops of hats and people's asses. Finally, he sees someone that resembles Emma Quinn on her way out on Saturday afternoon. He freezes the frame, rewinds. She's wearing sunglasses, a black wool coat. When he stops it again and blows it up, he sees a wedding ring on her left hand. He moves on, not knowing that it's Professor Buchman, who had slipped up to Emma's in her stead on Friday, spent the night and departed the following day as part of the elaborate ruse to throw The Shadow off Emma's scent.

By morning, Serge has viewed all the footage. He's checked the wire on Emma's phone. There have been no calls, as if her line were dead. And, back in Philadelphia, he'd seen the feed from the Delaware estate. The place overlooking Miller's Lane is virtually shut down. No one passing through at this point but cleaning crews and realtors and prospective buyers, including the entire governing board of an exclusive private school located nearby.

Finally, Serge heads down to the garage on 43rd Street where he finds Emma's Mercedes in its usual spot. He returns to West End

Avenue and monitors the apartment all day. But by nightfall it's become abundantly clear that he's wasting his time. She's gone. She hasn't been home in days and, worse still, she may have deliberately given him the slip. He worries that she knows something or has found something. He reaches Grenville on his home line in Chevy Chase, who in turn contacts Tina Dowd. There is some discussion, a bit of research, some speculation. "Saranac Lake," Dowd says. "Their cabin in upstate New York." And it's agreed that Serge will go.

***

August 17, 1948

Imagine if everyone in the world had what we have at Saranac. No one would ever work again. All commerce would cease. The stock market would tumble and we would soon die of starvation. It's so quiet here right on the water. The air is so cool and the water so clean. I feel myself again, being here. I don't think James quite feels the same. It isn't his home, after all. But there is nowhere in the world I feel more at home. This is where I feel safe, where I belong. I'm afraid I've had far too much scotch this evening, sitting by myself out on the screen porch. Annie will think I'm a lush. I cannot write another word.

August 23, 1948

I couldn't bring myself to leave yesterday. It's too tranquil. Today, I made a dozen trips to the raft from our dock. The swimming invigorated me. Then, this evening, I had cocktails over at the club with the Morgans. What a life. I wonder, sometimes, if this world really is safe from the

Communists. If not, they will surely come to Saranac first and ransack our houses and send us packing. They're right. Such privilege isn't fair. It's simply not. Sam Morgan talked about it at length over drinks. These infernal communists, he called them. But do you really think they're infiltrating our government, I asked. And we both agreed—this Alger Hiss does not seem at all the type of fellow who would be a communist. Although he was a New Dealer. James talks about it on occasion. As a threat to Europe, of course, to world peace. But not here. Never here, he says. It's an utter preoccupation with Wellie. He claims their aim is to take over the entire world, the Stalinists. First, the Eastern Bloc, which is done really. Then Western Europe will fall. They'll take Great Britain and Africa will be no problem. Those poor bastards, he says.

Emma is startled to see the name Wellie. She recognizes it as her father's nickname, the name her mother often used. But she's not heard it spoken since her parents' death and has no recollection of ever hearing it uttered by her grandmother. Wellie—after his middle name, Wellford. Robert Wellford Gardner. Wellie. And Emma is surprised to see yet another reference to his politics. It was her understanding that her father was nothing more than a functionary, an administrator. First, in Washington. Then at Balfour. But, if her grandmother is to be believed, Robert Wellford Gardner was a man with strong opinions, opinions that ran counter to those of Emma's grandfather, and, apparently, some rather strong connections as well. And there is talk of Alger Hiss. Intrigued, she reads on.

August 24, 1948

I grow lazy. Too lazy even to write. James has not been up since I arrived. I am withering away, happily. The other husbands are here, of course. Too old and rich to stay in the city in August. I feel as I did when Catherine was young. We'd all spend the entire summer here—Annie and Catherine and I. She was all so busy with swimming and canoeing and her craft classes at the clubhouse in the morning. Coming home with little hangers decorated with twine or some sort of felt hat or a batch of leaves turned into a work of art. Friends in and out all day long. Arriving bubbly and red faced at the end of the day, from the sun and the water and the play, and we would scoot her off to bed half in a daze. I hardly missed him, except at night. Then he would come in for the weekend, arriving late Friday night and sweeping me off to bed. Grand and handsome he was, my James. This is where I have been at my best always.

August 25, 1948

Well there was quite a hubbub today over at the clubhouse. They had the new television set on and it seems as if everyone in all of Slatterly had to be there. Ginny Morgan came and grabbed me or I would have missed it altogether. She was quite revved up. It was those hearings in Washington and the whole thing was on television.

The room was packed—not just the clubhouse, but the hearing room on the little screen, filled with people and cameras. Men and women. Mr. Hiss standing up to face his accuser across the room, the two of them on their feet, and Mr. Hiss admitting right there on the Senate floor that he'd known that man, this Whittaker Chambers, this spy, although by a different name apparently. They disagreed on when and how long they had known each other. Hiss estimated 1935. And when Chambers said "until 1938," the whole clubhouse erupted. The consensus seemed to be that Chambers is the liar. But afterwards, Sam Morgan said it doesn't look good for our man Hiss.

Whittaker Chambers actually lived in the Hiss's house at some point. And the Hiss family actually gave him a car. This Whittaker Chambers was apparently a certified communist at the time and a Russian spy. There was testimony to that effect. Sam says that changes things quite a bit. They definitely knew one another, and apparently quite well. But then, of course, this Chambers was going under an assumed name, which seems a bit nefarious.

It was interesting to see. Alger Hiss has a very formal way about him. His style of speaking seemed almost evasive. He was saying things like "Although I have not checked the records" and "based on my recollection." Sam Morgan says that's smart. That he's obviously studied the law. The Morgans still think he's innocent, that Whittaker Chambers is pathological. But I'm afraid Hiss's manner makes him seem guilty as the dickens.

August 26, 1948
James is coming up tomorrow and staying through Labor Day. Thank goodness!!! And next week Catherine and Wellie will be up for the long weekend. I'm thrilled!!! And James is insisting that I go back with him after Labor Day. Which is fine. I have had my summer.

August 29, 1948
We had the Morgans over for supper last night. And now James is angry with me. He says I don't need to

be watching these hearings on television. It's a shoddy, shameful business, he says. And he is adamant. He went on and on—UnAmerican Activities—phooey, he said. Yes he did. He used the word phooey. It made me laugh out loud. And that made him even angrier. I maybe had a little too much to drink.

After they left, he went on a rampage, raising his voice so all of Slatterly probably heard every word of it—You can't go around persecuting people for their politics, for their personal beliefs. That's what's un-American. We are not living in Soviet Russia with its secret police. We are becoming our own worst enemy. He said basically the same thing when those Hollywood people got themselves into trouble. I can see his point and I told him that and I settled him down.

Labor Day—September 6
There is going to be a baby! Coming in the spring. So now James will have no choice. We must get them back to town in a little house on Miller's Lane. Come hell or high water.

This entry is followed by a whimsical drawing of a car with oversized, round donuts for wheels. Emma holds the diary sideways to look at it. The car sits above a squiggly line that winds through what must be mountains, but they look more like teepees. And this line, this road, then turns into an arrow pointing to the word DELAWARE in all caps and underlined three or four times. Childlike and cartoony, the drawing takes up the better part of a page. Emma is amused by it. When she turns the page, the diary starts up again a few months later, all seriousness. And, true to form, the subject remains Alger Hiss.

December 2, 1948

We have now been drawn into this entire Hiss scandal. The FBI has called Balfour in to verify that this microfilm is legitimate. These Pumpkin Papers. James is involved in verifying the damn things. He's gone down to Washington to retrieve the canisters from the Committee. Not by himself of course. I'm sure Muriel went along, although we didn't discuss it. It seems it was Balfour film that Mr. Chambers stashed in that ridiculous pumpkin. We'll see what happens with that. Perhaps it will prove the man's innocence.

December 6

The news is not good for Mr. Hiss. James says the Balfour film is authentic, made in 1937 or 1938. Photographs of State Department documents. And I said—But does that really prove that Alger Hiss was the one who gave him the documents? Does it? And James said—Good question, smiling as he does when I use my brain. But there was this other matter, initially some confusion about the dates. Some unpleasantness. And he was quite troubled by it. I found him walking in circles in the library, with a scotch in one hand and a cigar in the other. It took forever for him to explain it to me. But it seems, at first, they thought that one of the cannisters was from 1945, that it was a fraud, that Whittaker Chambers was lying.

According to James, when Richard Nixon heard that, he was furious. He seemed threatened, angry. But then it turned out to be a mistake. Both sets were authentic; the evidence is valid, all of it. And Hiss is in trouble. James said there's a moral to the story—he says this Nixon is far too invested in Chambers' testimony. He's biased, James says, in favor of Whittaker Chambers, the spy, the Communist. Nixon's out to get Alger Hiss. And why would that be, he asked me. He was still pacing in circles, smoking that cigar.

I was sitting in front of the fire, almost sorry that I'd ever gotten involved in the discussion. But I knew exactly what he was saying—Notoriety I guess. That's what I said and he gave me a big smile. That's exactly right, he said. Senator Nixon isn't trying to find the truth. He's trying to make a name for himself. My James was outraged, said he wants to wash his hands of the whole sordid business. Of course, it's just like James to be self-righteous. It's his nature. And he went on about what he calls "our alarmist son-in-law" and how he is going to have a field day with the news that Hiss may be guilty. Communist infiltrators and all that business. As if that were the most important piece, Robert's reaction.

Emma recalls her conversation with Martin Simon about the microfilm. Her grandmother's version of events confirms his story—about her grandfather's involvement with the case, his inclinations, his politics. Emma's mind turns to Angus McLearan. She wonders again what exactly he was up to. Surely, he knows the precise nature of Balfour's involvement with the case. She wonders if the subject is addressed in Allen Weinstein's *Perjury*, resolves to get a copy. Then, as she reads on she finds that just as she begins to feel some kinship with her grandmother, a new passage touches a nerve and the uneasy relationship is set right back where it had been.

December 12, 1948

I read the Times today. After all, James is gone. Why not?

Annie must have left it on the dining room table. Careless. It says the entire situation is political nonsense. That they're going after Alger Hiss because he's a prominent Democrat. Of course, it's one thing to accuse someone of being a communist and something else altogether when government secrets are passed to a Soviet agent.

But I don't believe the Chambers fellow. I don't trust him. After all, he has admitted he was not just a member of the Communist party, but a spy. Why on earth would anyone believe him? He's a ruffian. And, apparently, a homosexual. Maybe, as Mr. Hiss' attorney has suggested, Chambers wanted to have a relationship with Alger Hiss and was spurned. Alger Hiss seems to be an honorable man, a gentleman. And has repeatedly denied the accusations. I just don't buy it. I think it is a vendetta. It's the only thing that makes any sense.

***

Serge, of course, has never driven to the upper reaches of New York State on the Taconic or the Sawmill Parkway, throughways that run north along the Hudson River. They are passageways to the mythic green mountains where Rip Van Winkle slept, and the headless horseman rode into the night. Upstate, they connect to the Northway that leads to the Adirondack Mountains. As protected land, most of the Adirondacks remain undeveloped, and there are places that feel as if Columbus himself might have canoed upriver here—mountains covered in dark rich greens, burbling trout streams, rustic architecture. Very New World—that's how Serge might have described it to his family back in Belgium.

As he makes his way to Saranac Lake, Serge is stuck in his own head. He's not at all sure how he's going to pull this off. His goal, of course, is to retrieve the book, which his father—and his grandfather before him—had described in some detail. Small, no more than three or four inches wide. Black leather cover. Less than an inch thick.

They had made it sound like nothing. "Don't make things complicated. You don't have to hurt anyone. Just get the book and get out of there. It's one woman in a remote cottage. She's sure to leave at some point. And you can slip in and out without incident."

But Serge knows full well that is a lie. "How does one get one's hand on a little black book without threatening or cajoling or injuring? How do we even know she has it?" he'd asked.

They had no answer for him. "We don't want another mess," Grenville had told them.

There was some talk about whether he should arrive on foot or by canoe. Or drive right through the front gates. Someone who knows the family, someone who had spent time in Slatterly, had provided them with guidance. There is a fishing spot on the north shore of the lake, above the Quinn cabin. He was to rent a boat, ride down along the edge of the lake in the evening, set up camp in the forest above the cabin and wait until she drives off. "She'll have to get supplies at some point. Be patient. Be discreet," they had advised. "Entry won't be an issue. It's a cabin, for Christ's sake," someone had said.

Written directions—mile markers, landmarks, a roadmap—were delivered to Serge's New York apartment by messenger on Wednesday morning. By evening, he expects to be in the town of Saranac Lake, where he will spend the night and prepare for his expedition into the woods.

***

Labor Day Weekend, 1949—Saranac

Is it not a holiday? A chance to relax? To enjoy the mountain air? But no, no—they were at it again the two of them. Obsessing about Albania of all things. And dominoes. And stopping the Russians before they take over the world. I just caught bits and pieces of it when they were standing over the grill nursing their gin and tonics, Catherine with that child down in the lake. And Annie running interference. She could barely get the dinner on the table. Here we go again, I thought. Thank goodness James put an end to it. We can't beat the Russians at their own game, you damn fool, he said, and—I will not hear another word about this nonsense. Then he just walked away. Thank goodness. I am beginning to worry about Wellie. He seems utterly obsessed.

September 14, 1949

They are here at last! We moved them into the little Victorian on Tuesday. And next week Catherine and I are going to do a little shopping, get a few more things. But it's already coming together, charming really. So I will have Catherine and little Emma right here under my nose. And Robert starts at Balfour tomorrow! I am giving myself a congratulatory pat on the back. I convinced James that we needed to get them out of Washington—needed to get

Wellie out of Washington—and that it will be better for Catherine. That baby is a handful. We need to find them some help. Catherine won't get a break until we do. I've made it a point to get some names from Annie. I have to say, I've never been happier.

September 24, 1949

Goodness. You'd think a meteor had struck the earth. There has been an atomic blast in Russia. I saw the headline this morning, although James seems to have snatched the newspaper again. So either they've exploded their own bomb or some other entity has attacked the USSR. I'm imagining it's the former. Apparently, he doesn't want me to know. He is still trying to protect me from reality. I don't think he will ever understand how strong I can be. What does he think I'm going to do? Jump off the earth? What choice do I have but to stay around and watch these fools try to outdo each other. There may be those who believe that I'm insane. But truly, two countries threatening to destroy each other. To literally wipe each other off the map. That is insanity.

Sunday, September 25, 1949

James insisted that we go to church today. Last night, he withdrew to his study, did not come out. He seems profoundly disturbed. Obviously, it's the bomb business. Although he won't speak of it. Then this morning he said we need to do some praying. He said it in a light way. But when James wants to pray, there is nothing light about it.

After church, Catherine and Wellie brought little Emma over for lunch and we played outdoors on a blanket in the sun, the three of us—the baby and Catherine and I. It was a beautiful fall day. And when we returned, the men were talking softly between themselves as if they knew secrets

they were unwilling to share. And what would those be,
do you think? That we are all at risk now. That these men
will blow up the earth. That it means the end of civilization.
I sent Annie out today for a newspaper and she refused.
Sometimes it feels as if they are all against me. Everyone.

The pallets are shipping by rail from Zeebrugge to a facility southeast of Brussels, one of 54 plants owned by *Poudreries de Belgique*, one of Europe's largest weapons manufacturers. The trip takes barely an hour. The flatbed car itself is released from the train and abandoned at a remote corner of PDB's property, an area not far from a local village and surrounded by undeveloped fields and forests. There is an airstrip 40 yards away. From this curiously idyllic setting, at 6 a.m. on Wednesday morning, the twelve canisters full of hazardous materials are loaded onto an official government plane by members of the Belgian Air Force. McLearan's team has followed the tracking devices there. They observe the mission as it transpires and witness the plane taking off from the PDB runway.

Shortly thereafter, Angus McLearan makes his way to London. When he arrives at the MI6 offices, he will send this message to Bill Kidman via an agent in Washington:

Our shipment consists of a dozen 55-gallon industrial drums, black steel, marked hazardous. No other markings. Arrived in the port of Zeebrugge in Belgium by boat at 05:00 AST from Sunny Point and moved on to a munitions plant southeast of Brussels by rail. The plant is one of dozens belonging to *Cargo Belgique's* oldest client—a company called *Poudreries de Belgique*. It is one of the largest arms manufacturers in Europe. Like

Balfour Chemical, *Poudreries de Belgique* began as a gunpowder company in the 18th century. And now it looks like both families have done business with *Cargo Belgique* for quite some time. In that regard, it seems that Emma Quinn and Serge Breuer are virtually related.

No. 53

Saranac Lake

Late Wednesday afternoon, Emma is standing at a phone booth at the corner of Lake Flower Avenue and Main Street, with the door shut tight. She has Manny Fredericks on the phone. "I've got a Franklin Skilling born in 1938. Worked at the State Department."

"No. No. That can't be right," she says. "I'm looking for someone older. Worked in Washington in the '40s. Probably born closer to the turn of the century."

"Let me switch gears here," Manny says, and the line goes quiet for a time. Then he's back. "Okay. How about this? Robert Fletcher Skilling. Born in 1906. Worked for the CIA. And before that—he was high up in OPC. One of its founding fathers."

"OPC?"

"Office of Policy Coordination. OPC."

"Tell me more," she says. There's another silence on the line. Emma digs into her bag for a pen and paper, cradling the phone against her shoulder and the receiver slips away, dangling by a thick, snakelike silver wire, banging against the transparent wall of the phone booth. "Dammit!" she says, grasping the receiver in one hand, the pen and paper in the other. "Manny? You still there?"

"Yeah. Hold on," he says.

Emma sets the receiver down. She's possessed of an ominous feeling, as if she's about to discover something unsavory about her family. And then the sensation that she's not alone. She feels in the leather satchel for the gun, eyes the street. It's virtually empty. A couple of kids playing jai alai in the park across the way; a man lingering outside the liquor store smoking; and a pair of women pushing baby carriages across Flower Avenue. She can see the lake from where she's standing.

Serge is not even close, hopelessly off track somewhere along the Au Sable well east of Saranac Lake, misled by a road sign, mistakenly headed for the town of Saranac. It's been a scenic drive and he has the radio on full blast, the sound of the Bee Gees—*Stayin' Alive, Stayin' Alive, oohoohoohooh*—blowing out his windows. He's shaking his head, singing along, rapping his thumbs against the wheel and halfway to Saranac before he realizes his mistake and pulls over to consult his elaborate directions. He's added an hour to the trip. Frustrated, he pulls over to the side of the road at the edge of the woods. As he steps out to stretch his legs, a rundown sedan blows by very nearly swiping his car door. He spins around. "*Klootzak*," he screams at the driver, shoving his middle finger into the air.

Emma is leaning against the side of the phone booth, the door closed, her pen at the ready. On the other end of the line, Manny clears his throat. "Okay," he starts up again. "Apparently, after the war, OPC was this agency that masterminded covert operations against the Soviets."

She is still now, absorbing it. "Like what?"

"Let's see. Propaganda. Psychological warfare. Political subterfuge." He's reading from his computer screen. "Okay. Like arming Chinese Nationals on Formosa." He pauses. "Training dispossessed Europeans to overthrow their new communist regimes. Hold on." Another rather long pause. "Looks like they did the stuff the CIA wouldn't touch. Maybe quasi-legal. It was all anti-communist operations…"

"And this Skilling guy. Is he still alive?"

"Died a few years ago."

"Hold on," she says. "Hold on. What dispossessed Europeans?"

"Albanian exiles, for one."

"Albanians?"

"Yup."

"When?" she asks, recalling the passage from her grandmother's diary.

"Late '40s, early '50s," he says. "Wait a sec. I gotta read it."

The operator gets on the line. Tells Emma to deposit some change. She rustles around in her pockets, drops in a quarter and Manny comes back on. "Emma? You there? Look, call me back collect. I'll accept."

Once they've reconnected, he goes on. "So, apparently, these Albanian rebels all got arrested and hanged and shot. For trying to put a fellow named King Zog back in power. You know what they say about truth being stranger than fiction. It says here the U.S. and the U.K. were working together, training a bunch of Albanian exiles on an island in the Mediterranean."

"Where?"

"Malta." Then he pauses again. "Wait a sec. He was one of the CIA guys that masterminded the 1953 coup in Iran. Wow. The one where we put the Shah back in power. The Shah of Iran. You know, that one."

"Fletcher Skilling?"

"Yeah. Fletcher Skilling."

Then Manny starts asking a lot of questions, personal questions like: What are you working on? And does this have something to do with The Shadow? And where are you anyway? Questions that she doesn't want to answer. After she hangs up, she pulls out Angus McLearan's card and dials his number at the International House on an impulse. She starts to leave a message, but she has no callback number to give him, so she just says, "It's Emma. Calling from New York, from Saranac Lake. I'll try again."

No. 54

The Belgian Air Force takes a night flight from Brussels to Qatar, arriving before dawn on Thursday at an airstrip near the water. Qatar is a small country, a tiny peninsula that juts out into the Persian Gulf like an appendage of its much bigger neighbor, Saudi Arabia. The tiny island nation of Bahrain floats nearby. From Qatar, it's a short journey by sea to Iran. The Belgian Air Force releases its cargo at 05:45 (AST) just as the sun is rising over the Persian Gulf into a cloudless sky. It's mild and breezy on the shore, in the low 80s. Under guard, the shipment is moved to a storage facility operated by the Qatari government, and the plane departs. Twelve drums of hazardous material have reached their destination in the Middle East.

No. 55

By Thursday afternoon, Emma has searched all the closets, all the dressers, every one of the cabin's rooms for something her grandparents may have been hiding from the authorities all these years. And still she's found nothing. She has begun to pack up for her departure and is reading now in the afternoon light on the screen porch overlooking the Upper Saranac. The diary starts up again on Labor Day weekend in 1953, at the cabin, a full four years after the last diary entry. The passages have grown long and detailed, as if her grandmother feels compelled to record these events, and from these passages, Emma's understanding of what transpired between her father—and her grandfather—begins to come together. She winces as she reads, knowing that her parents had only a few months left to live. And, as the diary itself draws to a close, it becomes clear to Emma, from the very start, that her father is unraveling.

Labor Day 1953

The weekend has been a nightmare. An absolute nightmare. He started drinking the minute they got here and made a spectacle of himself at the clubhouse. I don't even know how it began. But James was furious. Furious. They left this morning, Catherine tossing everything in their trunk in a rage. Screaming at James—how can you treat us this way? And that poor baby girl, that poor little Emma, wailing. You could hear it as they drove off. I wouldn't be surprised if everyone in Slatterly didn't hear the entire thing.

And how did it happen? I know exactly how it happened. Someone made a comment about Joe McCarthy on Friday night and Wellie got himself all in a tizzy. We were having a drink at the clubhouse. All of a sudden, he started making pronouncements, calling the man dangerous with his imaginary lists of suspects, he said. And calling the hearings downright anti-American.

So I asked him—I said—Aren't you the one who insisted that communists were infiltrating our government? But that didn't stop him. It's an outrage, he said—between sips of his martini, of course. And raising his voice so everyone could hear him. Calling McCarthy's behavior unconstitutional. It's gone on long enough, he pronounced. As if we don't know this. As if all civilized people don't know this, for God's sake.

They had just arrived and I was so looking forward to it—the start of the Labor Day weekend. Everyone was there. Everyone. And people were turning their heads, listening. What kind of country is this? He was waving his hands in the air. Have we no courage? When James approached him at the bar, the two of them talked quietly for a moment. I thought he was going to calm down.

Then he began describing an incident involving someone from his crowd. Apparently, Joe McCarthy had fingered a man at the CIA, a completely honorable man, a foe of Communism. Those are the words he used. He was calm at first, but then he began to raise his voice again, insisting that this friend of his was a good man.

Here it's hard for Emma to make out some of the words. Her grandmother was writing in her maniacal hand, recounting each detail, obsessing perhaps, her cursive rushed and ragged. But she reads on—

Wellie kept getting louder and louder—McCarthy tried to get him fired, he shouted. James just nodded and told him to settle down. Now that's enough, James said. You're among friends. Then Wellie got angry—I know this for a fact, he said.

And he just spit it out. It was terribly offensive and Catherine just sat there on the bar stool nearby, staring, wide-eyed, like a little doe.

Now I'm no fan of Joe McCarthy and those awful hearings. Nor is James. But at the moment, I'm no fan of Robert Wellford Gardner either. James tried very hard to be calm. He asked, in the most gentlemanly tone, but rather skeptically—And how would you know such a thing, Robert? From my associates, Wellie answered. And who would these associates be? James asked. But no answer.

He just got more and more agitated, said "He ruined Chuck Williford's career you know. Everyone knows that." Of course, none of us have any idea who this Chuck Williford is. James was circumspect—You talk too much, he told him, sternly, firmly and that ended it. I was standing nearby talking with the Bradfords. They just looked down at their feet. It was quite embarrassing. Wellie was in his cups.

I thought everything would get back to normal. Things seemed to be better on Saturday morning. Catherine and I took Emma into town to shop. And Robert said he was going out rowing on the lake. When we returned, all was quiet. Robert and Catherine took little Emma for a swim in the afternoon. It was lovely really. Robert throwing her in the air, Emma giggling like mad.

Here, Emma stops reading and retreats to the kitchen, pours herself a whisky and takes a sip, then makes her way to the guest room, where she pulls a pack of Camels from her grandmother's old stash before returning to the porch. Standing, looking out over the water with her cigarette and her glass, she pictures the family scene some 25 years earlier in this very spot. She's trying to remember splashing in the water, or whether she was able to swim at the time. She can't recall her father's face or being thrown in the air or the laughter, but she is trying to visualize it. Trying to imagine what it would have been like to have such a family. She would have been four years old, she thinks. Her father was drinking heavily. Her young parents won't live beyond Christmas. And, as she settles back in and reads on, her father remains preoccupied with matters that her grandmother obliquely refers to as international affairs:

> Around six, we dressed and headed over to the clubhouse for drinks and dinner. Again, at the bar, he started entertaining some of the others with stories about international affairs. It seems he has a direct line to his buddies in the foreign service. I have never been sure quite what they do, but James says they are somehow affiliated with the intelligence services.
>
> At any rate, he stepped over the line again—this time, regaling everyone with some tale about how the people who led the coup in Iran were muscle men—weightlifters and wrestlers and acrobats—members of some sort of Iranian exercise club. Apparently, these muscle men are idols of some significance in Persia. Everyone thought it was uproariously funny. And Wellie was acting it out, as if he were a weightlifter leading the monarchists. He was talking so loud that he was shouting—They love acrobats over there and that's what started the riot that overthrew the government of Iran. The parade of the musclemen.
>
> Everyone thought he was joking, but he wasn't. Truth,

I swear it, he said, and then he crossed his heart. By then, just about everyone in the room was listening. Then he said—From what I understand from my friends in the foreign service, they surged to the prime minister's home and he escaped by climbing over the wall behind it. Literally. Now the Shah is back in power. And that is apparently how revolutions take place in the Middle East. With that, everyone laughed. And Wellie took a deep bow.

In truth, it was an entertaining story. But James felt it was inappropriate—given that the Russians have openly accused the U.S. of leading this particular coup, of putting the Shah back in power. It doesn't help to talk as if our people were there on the streets, even though the tale itself was silly and outlandish. Well, James handled it, drawing him by the elbow into the dining room. By then he was so schnockered, he just ate his meal in silence. Catherine kept rubbing his shoulder as if that would somehow make things right. After we got home, I could hear him upchucking in the bathroom.

Again, I thought it would pass. But Sunday, Sunday, James went off the rails. He was fuming. They got into it early on and he pulled Robert back into the guest room. We could hear them arguing, all of us from across the house, James calling Robert a fool again, saying—Look at Albania. It was a fiasco, an embarrassment. And then, a few minutes later, I heard him say—If you have funneled any resources to these people, as I suspect you have, then we are finished here. You are to leave my house. And you are not to come back. Robert was insisting that he would never do such a thing—behind your back, he said. And full of apologies and saying—I swear to you.

That's when Catherine entered into it. I've had enough, she said. She went right back there and said—I don't like the way you talk to my husband. And she came out with

her suitcase. We're leaving. We're leaving now. And off
they went. Now James is positively morose. I have to
say, I'm rather proud of Catherine for standing up for her
husband. I didn't know she had it in her.

***

It's still daylight when Serge arrives and pulls his canoe in north of
Slatterly—positioning himself in the woods on a ridge above the
Quinn cabin. He has spent the day gathering supplies, but he is no
woodsman. He remains ill prepared for this adventure. He struggles
to pull the canoe up the embankment, slipping, nearly losing his backpack. And by the time he reaches the hill overlooking Emma's cabin,
he has fallen so many times his pant legs are streaked with mud, a
purple bruise is forming above his left kneecap, and his right hand is
scraped, bleeding. He curses, wipes his hands on his trousers, pulls a
pair of binoculars out of his backpack. He can see her sitting on the
screen porch reading. He watches her light a cigarette. Pleased with
himself for following the directions, finding the cove that is Slatterly,
he steps back and creates a makeshift encampment—a small tarp, a
sleeping bag, a backpack. And settles in for the night.

Emma has only a few pages left the diary, which starts up again
in 1954, one month to the day after her parents' death. There are only
a smattering of short passages in the ten years between that and the

final entry, many of them undated. But Emma can surmise the dates, imagine when they were written, knows what they mean—

1954
Go away! Go away. I can hear them, their voices rising all the way from the front hall. Do they not know they failed to close the door? Do they not realize their whispers are not whispers at all? Are they not aware that I have lost my only daughter and am plunged into deep despair. Is that not the normal reaction? And how will I go on from here. How on earth? Away.

**

I cannot raise my head. I cannot. Tell them all to go away.

**

Dammitalltohell.

The word is scrawled sideways in massive letters, filling a page.

February 17, 1954
Annie has found something disturbing. At the children's house. I don't know precisely what it is, but James is quite upset. He says our late son-in-law was up to no good. And he didn't sleep a wink, up and down all night. He stayed home this morning. I had to beg him to tell me what was going on. James, I said, you need to talk to me, I said. He told me there was no one he could trust. That he just needed some time to think and he went back into his office and has not come out all day.

***

> That girl. I cannot abide that girl. She is walking death. And
> James is with her every minute.

With that, Emma feels a chill pass through her. Stunned, her eyes filling
with tears, she sits very still for a moment staring straight ahead, taking
another sip of whisky, before lying down on the wicker sofa, stuffing a
pillow beneath her head. She doesn't read the last two entries until later,
when she's gone in to bed. Instead, she just lies there on the porch as the
sky darkens. Less than a hundred yards away, on the ridge overlooking
the cabin, Serge sits Indian-style on his tarp, trying to keep still, chewing on a piece of red licorice he bought at a roadside store.

Later, after she's closed up the porch and smoked one last cigarette,
and she's turned off all the lights, save the bedside lamp in her grandmother's old room, she will read these words:

> We have a routine. We have a routine. I tell her I will be down
> for lunch, but if I cannot bring myself to climb down the
> stairs, you will have to bring it up to me, I tell her. And they
> tell me nothing.

And these:

> **1964**
> Today the world ended. My world. This book. This book is
> closed forever.

Emma knows full well this would have been the day her grandfather died. Lying there in bed, the diary open face down on her lap, she imagines how it must have felt to discover him in the shower in that grand bathroom with its double sinks, fallen, not knowing why. Not expecting a heart attack. And the shower of all places. Coming upon him. Today the world ended. By the suddenness of the passage, she is jolted into experiencing it all over again. She had been at school preparing for exams when the call came in. Gone, in an instant, her anchor, her strength, her only family, really. And she is reminded by her grandmother's words just how much she grew to despise her, that Emma was no more to her than a walking reminder of her dear Catherine's death.

When Emma finally closes the book and sets it back in the drawer in her grandmother's bedside table, she knows more than she had before. She knows now, or suspects, that it was her father, that he must have been selling Balfour's weapons to his friends in the CIA or OPC. Doubtless his buddies in Washington, this Fletcher Skilling and his crew. She doesn't know if it was legal or illegal, but there's no proof of anything. The diary is filled with suppositions and innuendos and the suggestion of wrongdoing, but nothing tangible. She knows that her father defied her grandfather in some way. And that her grandfather, however guilty he may be, is innocent in this regard.

She guesses, too, that there will be no black book, although it seems as if it existed and that her grandfather had it in his possession. She's searched everywhere and found nothing. She feels some sense of resolution along with the predictable letdown, the sense that she may never know more, may never know the whole story. And the recognition that they are all gone now, and there is no one else to tell it.

Before Emma turns off the light, she tries for a moment to feel some kind of love for her grandmother. She recognizes her now as a woman possessed of a certain brilliance, as a brave and tragic figure. She feels a certain pride and respect that she's never felt before. But Emma struggles to feel affection. And as she drifts off, she reminds herself, as a form of reassurance, of comfort, perhaps to relieve her guilt, that it's not easy to love someone who cannot find it in themselves to love you.

No. 56

Arlington, VA

"That makes no sense." Mahmoud Hariri is talking to Bill Kidman in a low voice. It's Thursday night at Twin Lanes. There's a mixed tournament underway and the place is packed. The two men have found an empty lane at the far end of the room. Hariri is at the scoring table, with one foot up on the chair, leaning over to tie up a bowling shoe and reading a piece of paper that's under his nose. Bill Kidman points to the paragraph from Angus McLearan's most recent missive, the one that arrived the preceding day through someone at the British Embassy—

> Our shipment consists of a dozen 55-gallon industrial drums, black steel, marked hazardous. No other markings. Arrived in the port of Zeebrugge in Belgium by boat at 05:00 AST from Sunny Point and moved on to a munitions plant southeast of Brussels by rail. The plant is one of dozens belonging to Cargo Belgique's oldest client—a company called Poudreries de Belgique. It is one of the largest arms manufacturers in Europe. Like Balfour Chemical, Poudreries de Belgique began as a gunpowder company in the 18th century. And now it looks like both families have done business with Cargo Belgique for quite some time. In that regard, it seems that Emma Quinn and Serge Breuer are virtually related.

Mahmoud is digesting these new details. "It makes no sense," he says. "Why would Balfour be shipping explosives to PDB? They can make all the explosives they want. And why would we be selling them to Belgium?" Then he looks up at Kidman, realizing exactly what he just said. "Shit. They're laundering weapons, aren't they?"

"Looks that way." Kidman nods. "And maybe they're not explosives."

"Shit," Hariri says again.

"Landed in Qatar this morning," Kidman says. "You making any progress in finding an authorization at MOTSU?" Hariri shakes his head. "But this should help." He hesitates a minute, thinking, then puts it together. "They gotta be using false end-user certificates," he says. "Belgian Air Force probably thought they were shipping PDB product purchased by Qatar. And who knows where it's going from there." He's got both shoes on now. Reaching for his bowling bag, he pulls out a file and slips it under Kidman's jacket on the grimy plastic chair. "It's a duplicate," he says. Then he steps over to the lane and gets ready to play. Kidman eyeballs the document. It tells him that Robert Gardner worked at the War Department during the Second World War and that he moved over to the U.S. Army when they closed the department down in October 1947. That he held basically the same job in both spots.

Mahmoud Hariri knocks nine of the pins down, walks over to the scoring table. "You got that? Procurement." He turns, does the walk, bends forward swinging the ball behind him, lets it go and hits the final pin. Then he takes a wild kick at the air and goes over to the bar to grab another beer. By the end of the night, he's had four.

Kidman is reflecting on Robert Gardner's career. The next time they have an opportunity to speak, when one or the other isn't swinging a bowling ball or celebrating a small victory, he says, "So you think maybe he took his relationships with him to Balfour." And Hariri says, "Yeah. And maybe the connection is still in play."

Later, before he peels off from the parking lot, he tells Kidman, "I'll see what I can find."

Twenty minutes later, on Chain Bridge Road, a few miles upriver from the bridge itself, on the District side, Hariri hears the sound of a siren. By the time he sees the lights flashing behind him, he's slowed to a crawl. He pulls over, edging his car up to the balustrade. The uniform calls him "sir," asks for his ID, seems friendly enough. As soon as Mahmoud Hariri asks, "What's the problem?" he knows what's happening. Regardless of how many beers he's had, he can see it in the uniform's face. And before he has time to react, to reach for the weapon stashed in his glove compartment, the man's holding a gun to the side of his head and telling him to step out of the car. Mahmoud trips the door handle and swivels in his seat, imagining he can kick the car door into him, disable him for an instant. But it doesn't work.

"Seems like maybe you've had a few too many. Am I right?" the uniform says, as Mahmoud folds over onto the ground. The cop pulls him up, tells him to walk in a straight line. They're both parked in a spot where the narrow road edges along a steep incline that leads down to the Potomac. Mahmoud doesn't see the other man in the police vehicle. He's thinking maybe he can make a run for it, maybe leap across the low guardrail into the water. As he starts to move, he's thinking maybe he's mistaken, maybe the cop is legit. That's when the police car starts toward him, striking him down as he makes for the guardrail.

No. 57

It's after two in the morning when Emma is awakened by a rustling among the leaves. Something moving about behind the cabin. The sound of it sends a chill through her. Rising, gun in hand, she slinks out of the bedroom in the darkness, through the center of the cabin. Creeping toward the kitchen, she's jolted by the sound of the lid to the garbage can as it hits the back shed. "A raccoon," she's guessing, "drawn by the smell of rotting banana peels and empty yogurt containers." Peeking out the kitchen window, she can make out the shadow of an animal up on its hind legs. The trashcan rolling about, the sound of it muffled by the forest floor. She flips on the spotlight, and the thing goes running. A red fox. Emma takes a deep breath. Her eyes have adjusted to the darkness. Unsettled, she grabs her keys from the mail table and stuffs them in the pocket of the sweater. Wants to keep them with her, to be able to run, to slip out, to slip away if it becomes necessary.

In the process, she knocks the key basket off the mail table. There's the jangle of metal hitting the hardwood floor. Two tiny keys, conjoined, never separated, and removed from the house for one purpose alone—to check the Quinn mailbox at the clubhouse. She feels a fool.

"Of course," she says to herself, experiencing the kind of realization one can only have half-awake in the night, as if the subconscious is way ahead of the rest of the brain. "Of course," Emma says to the darkness, picking up the tiny keys. "The little black book. It's not in the cabin. It's never been in the cabin. Of course. She mailed it to herself. To Slatterly." What could be simpler? Safe in a locked mailbox. The keys sitting in the open just inside the kitchen door. "Easily fetched, easily found," she thinks, "as long as you know what you're looking for." Emma is so agitated by this epiphany that she hardly knows what to do next. "I'm an idiot," she says aloud. "I am an idiot." She stashes the mailbox keys in her pocket with her own keys, clutching them in her free hand as she makes her way back to bed, where she lays the gun on the table beside her and draws the covers close.

She can lie still as a stone, but her head will not be silenced. "No one can find me here," she thinks, reassuring herself. "I would hear a car. I would see a light." Then she wonders how the CIA would have found the place without explicit directions. She worries that her grandmother was carrying the directions to the cabin with her when she died. And that someone absconded with them. "They would have come by now. They would have found them. But no," she tells herself. "They wouldn't know about the keys. They wouldn't know about the book. They wouldn't come," knowing that of course they would. For nearly four hours, until the sun begins to rise over the Upper Saranac, she lies in stillness, sleepless, gripping the keys in the pocket of her sweater, fearful, wrestling with these thoughts. She is thinking about how carefully Margaret Quinn planned this and trying to imagine who would have gotten wind of it and how, as she finally drifts off.

No. 58

Serge awakens early, before the fog lifts from the lake. His hair, his sleeping bag and one arm of his jacket, exposed in the night, are covered in mist. He slept poorly on the solid ground. Awakened by the sound of an animal, he had watched the spotlight shoot out from Emma's kitchen, seen the fox fleeing into the woods, settled himself back in. But it took him nearly two hours to get back to sleep. Now he watches from the ridge eating trail mix and sipping on a warm Coca Cola, wishing he were in Manhattan, wishing this were over. He clears up the camp site and folds the tarp down on the ground. It crackles when he sits. He fumbles with the binoculars, settling in, monitoring the cabin. He plans to wait until she goes off somewhere, preferably in her car, then search the house. If it takes a day or two, so be it. He plans to wait it out. The last thing he wants is a confrontation.

It's after eight when Emma rolls over, feeling for the keys in her pocket, and fairly leaps out of bed. Operating on too little sleep, she fumbles with the coffee pot, drops the basket on the kitchen counter. Yesterday's wet grounds spill everywhere, along the counter, across the front of the cabinet and onto the floor. Cursing, she sops up the mess with a wet towel, throws it in the sink. Retreating to the back of the house, she searches for her cigarettes, going from room to room, finds them on a dresser in the hall. Serge sees her move past the guest room window and watches as she reappears on the screen porch overlooking the lake, the brown leather satchel thrown over her shoulder. She fiddles with the cigarettes and lights up—but the first deep inhale tastes like the inside of an ashcan, and she stubs it out and disappears again.

He doesn't have a clear view of the bedroom, where she's packing her things now, making up the bed, preparing for her departure. She dresses quickly, then lingers on the screen porch, sipping a coffee, nursing a container of yogurt, looking out at the lake. She's recalling what she now knows—that her father was up to something in the wake of the war, that only a few months before his death they had argued—he and James Quinn; that, in all likelihood, her grandmother was fingering her father when she contacted the CIA. "She carried that with her all these years," she is thinking. And she suspects it was old business, that no one would care now, that it means nothing. But she is reminded of what Bill Kidman had said: "Either she possessed proof of something or someone believed she possessed proof." She is eager to get hold of the black book.

There's a chill to the lake air, and Emma is fully dressed in lightweight boots and a jacket. When she rises this time, there's a momentum to her step and Serge senses that she's preparing to go. She disappears back into the house with her satchel in tow. Hearing the kitchen door slam shut, he rises and moves along the ridge above the cabin, watching in the shadow of a tree as she approaches the shed, rights the garbage can, throws in a bag of trash, heads back inside. Here, he's close enough to see her without binoculars. Then she's out of view.

Not long after Serge shifts back into position near the tarp, she emerges again on the porch, gathering up the cushions from the wicker furniture, hauling them into the cabin. It takes her two trips. He looks up at the sky, imagining that means rain. But, no, the sky is clear. And she's back on the porch a few minutes later, looking around, straightening up. It's clear to him now that she's closing up the house. She's planning to leave. She seems to be carrying her purse with her everywhere she goes, keeping it close. He wonders if perhaps it contains the black book. Panicked, he abandons his own plans. Leaving his gear behind, he begins to creep slowly along the ridge, his work boots rustling up the leaves. He's wishing that he'd sent his people, or rather his father's people. "This is not my job," he's thinking. "This is their job." When he's certain he's out of her line of vision, he begins to slip down the hill toward the cabin, stumbling, tripped up by the root of a tree, very nearly falling. Oblivious, she's packing the cooler in the kitchen, then making one last pass through the house. Her duffle sits by the kitchen door. And Serge stands at the corner of the cabin now, at the edge of the sleeping porch, out of view, not far from the shed awaiting her next move.

No. 59

"The girl's at Saranac Lake." Those were the first words McLearan had uttered when Bill Kidman picked up the phone early that morning.

"We lost Hariri" was Kidman's response.

"Well, that's not good," McLearan had said, speaking from his suite at the International House. He's just arrived from London and he picked up Emma's message first thing, then checked the signal on Serge's car to determine his whereabouts. "Serge Breuer's up there too. Arrived yesterday."

Now they're in a helicopter headed for the Adirondacks. "Fuck Schmidt." That's what Kidman said to himself when he had requisitioned the chopper. And when McLearan had called Annie Daniels to get a fix on where exactly he would find Emma, she'd said, "I already told you. Didn't you write it down?" McLearan didn't answer or argue, and she'd proceeded to give him precise instructions as to how to get to the cabin by boat.

Coming in from the southeast, the region looks like nothing but puffs of greenery wrapped around a string of dark puddles. From where they sit, the town of Saranac Lake reads out-of-scale—more like a city than a village—that is, until they get close enough to see the spires of the old Victorian cottages and the fading copper rooftop of the sanitarium. They make landfall on the blacktop at the town's center not far from the phone booth where Emma spoke with Manny Fredericks a few days before, and then go directly to local law enforcement. They're moving fast. "We've got someone in immediate danger," Kidman tells the troopers. McLearan rides with the Sheriff, who knows exactly how to get to Slatterly. Kidman takes the chopper.

No. 60

Emma leaves by way of the screen door on the front porch, heading down the wooden stairs toward the dock, then up along the narrow footpath that follows the arc of the lake. By then, the midmorning sun is sending a dappled light across the gravel drive toward the back shed. Serge hears the slam of the door, watches her standing lakeside, shielding her eyes from the sun, looking out over the water, still for a moment. Then raises his binoculars, follows her with his eyes until she disappears into the woods.

When she arrives at the clubhouse, Emma weaves her way through the dining room with its wooden picnic tables and its high ceiling and its massive Adirondack chandeliers and goes directly to the back hall, to the wall of mailboxes. She slips the tiny key into the lock with a certainty that, when it opens, a small black book, perhaps the size of an address book, will be sitting there waiting for her. But these mailboxes are as deep and wide as your average shoebox, designed to hold mail for months, seasons even, until their people return. She hasn't been up to Slatterly since the preceding summer and she's certain no one else has. The Quinn mailbox—technically the Rothenberg box—is crammed with envelopes and flyers and magazines of various kinds.

She grabs the stack and moves to a card table on the east side of this small foyer, facing a wood-framed window that looks out to the forest beyond. Standing, her back to the foyer's entrance, she lays the leather satchel down at her feet. The porch, the dock, the lake, the Quinn cabin are all behind her.

Meanwhile, Serge has rifled through her car, tossed the contents of her duffle onto the kitchen floor, searched the cooler and the small box of mementos she had planned to take home with her. Her things, all of them, are strewn all over the kitchen floor when he abandons the cabin and sets out on the footpath.

At this point, she is tentative and remarkably calm. Leafing through the mail piece by piece, tossing most of it in the trash. She comes upon a glossy magazine with a distinguished-looking older white man on its cover, smiling, knee deep in a trout stream in his waders and his blue plaid shirt and a ball cap, his vest festooned with flies. *Adirondack Life,* it says. Beneath that lies a puffy brown envelope. The return address is 10 Miller's Lane, Wilmington, Delaware 19807, the handwriting unmistakable. She locates a tab on the back, pulls and the little black book is in her hand.

She's not sure what she had been expecting, something more incriminating, clearer, perhaps. It is, in fact, just as Annie had described it—a book of lists. On each line—a series of dates and what appear to be destinations, followed by a series of codes and numbers. The earliest entries read—

12/7/45	Ghent	N — 2	
3/14/46	Rize	X — 25221	72.5
8/5/47	Haifa	RB — 2560	101.86
9/6/47	Port Said	NI — 2725	81.9
9/8/47	Ghent	SR — 2726	-
9/8/47	Ostend	NC — 2727	66.5
10/2/47	Cyprus	SR — 2800	10.2

The lists begin in December 1945, shortly after the end of the war, and continue until December 1953, just before Christmas and her parents' death. Emma had imagined the information would be more current somehow. But of course not. How would her grandmother have anything current? She leafs through maybe 20 pages. The writing is minuscule and sometimes hard to make out, all in the same hand. There are dozens of empty pages toward the back. On the very last page, Emma finds the information that's easiest for her to interpret.

R.W. Gardner—her father's name—followed by a series of what appear to be phone numbers. Two of them scratched out, replaced with a third.

The name M. Frankel—also followed by a series of phone numbers, three of which are scratched out and replaced with a fourth.

Then—A. Breuer, Cargo Belgique, 71 Sint-Paulusstraat, Antwerp, Belgium +32 (0) 3 231 16 21

She's still for a time, leaning against the table, reading through the book again, thinking through it. There are clear lines of delineation, points at which the notations, the format, the contents seem to change. This first happens in October 1947, when it begins to look like this—

10/31/47	Ghent	250/BMV	#47-712
11/17/47	Malta	312/MM1	#47-631
11/22/47	Haifa	250/M14	#47-712

Then in September 1949, changing to this—

9.12.49	Rosslare	10/PTN	$1,500
9.15.49	Vadso	120/ALUM	$2,000
9.15.49	Ghent	80/PTX	$650
		100/PVA	$840
		50/D	$600
		20/HQ	$400

It's not much to go on, but based on what she knows, she assumes that these are shipments, shipments of munitions of some kind or maybe chemicals. And proof that her father was involved. She slips the book into her jacket pocket, glancing through the rest of the mail, setting aside a handful of notices from Slatterly, throwing away the balance.

Out of the corner of her eye, she sees a flash of movement across the window at the opposite end of the corridor. Startled by it, she hears the voice before she sees the man. "Hello in there," he says. "Is that you, Emma?" She sees no sign of a weapon, just the threat of the man's presence. She recognizes his face. Sweat begins to bead on her forehead and she's thinking as fast as she can, running through scenarios in her mind. He is positioned at the entrance to the foyer. There is no exit route, no simple one, no way around him.

"Who are you?" she says, and he holds out his hand to shake hers, fluid, civilized, moving toward her. She's expecting—or rather hoping—that he'll say he works with Bill Kidman, but he doesn't.

He says, almost cordially, "Serge Breuer. My grandfather worked closely with your father. Our families have been linked for more than a generation."

"Meaning?" Her brow wrinkles as she speaks, and he can hear the note of anger in her voice. His eyes are on the satchel at her feet.

"We've worked together. I am from Belgium," he says, as if somehow that will explain anything. "I believe you've found the black book, the record of transactions between my family's company and your family's. Surely, you have no need of it."

"And what does your family do exactly, Mr. Breuer, aside from stalking people?"

"I am not a stalker, madam."

"And I'm not a member of the Balfour family," she says.

Serge is inching toward her. "I have not threatened you in any way," he says in a soft voice. "I just want to take the book off your hands. Surely you don't want this responsibility."

"What book is that?" she says.

Again, his eyes dart to the satchel. "What is your plan? To incriminate your own father?"

"I don't know what you're talking about."

"There seems to be much misunderstanding." He speaks slowly, articulating every word. "We—you and me—we are on the same side." And he grins then, revealing a darkness she hadn't grasped initially. She puts both hands on the plastic chair beside her, trying to imagine how to reach the satchel without putting herself at risk. He shifts his strategy. "I am prepared to pay you a substantial sum."

"I have nothing to sell you," she says. Then, for a moment, they seem frozen, uncertain how to proceed. As if someone has given each of them the wrong part in a play. Miscast, they have no idea how to bring this business to a close. "You have nothing to gain from holding on to it."

"I don't have any book," she says, as she reaches down to swoop up the satchel. "Or anything else that would incriminate my father."

"This is unfortunate," he says, angry, springing toward her. She reacts swiftly, swinging the satchel at his head, the full force of the gun striking his temple. He buckles. "*Sheeeps,*" he cries, his hands covering his eyes. "*Sheeps.*" She knows then that this man, this man crumpled on the foyer floor gripping his bloody nose, is the one who invaded her apartment and disassembled the shipping boxes, the man who stole her grandmother's papers and her grandfather's paperweights. And, of course, she knows that he's The Shadow.

Standing over him, she slips her hand inside the satchel for the gun. But he reaches for the leather bag, yanks it away and the handgun goes flying, bouncing against the wall and falling a few yards from Emma. Her scream comes out in sentences as she makes for the gun. "You son of a bitch. You broke into my apartment." And he grabs at her leg, holds her fast by the ankle, pulls her to the floor. "Let me go," she screams struggling, kicking at him with heavy boots, stretching toward the gun—these two sleepless souls, children from a long line of bandits, engaging in their own private battle. "Let me go," she screams. "You killed my grandmother. You killed her."

In fact, she has been screaming since she took her first swing at him. And Serge, still reeling from the knock on the head, is only half-fighting at this point. When Emma finally grabs the gun and flips over, pointing it at him, she looks up to see Boone, standing at the entrance to the foyer with a rifle in his hand. "Let her go," he says flatly. "Or I will kill you."

What follows is an arrest of sorts, Breuer held at rifle point until the authorities arrive, McLearan and the Sheriff being the first to get there. "They won't hold him long," Kidman tells McLearan when it's over. "He wasn't even carrying a weapon. We'll have to put him in the chopper, take him to Albany, make it formal." Then he'd left Angus there with Emma, left the helicopter in a small clearing near the clubhouse, and gone back to the village with the Sheriff and Breuer.

No. 61

There is no coolness between them now. When he had arrived, Angus greeted Emma with a full-on embrace and made no effort to conceal his relief. Nor did she. Now as they make their way through the woods toward the cabin, they both have their hands in their pockets, glad to see each other but uncertain how far this will go. "And who are you exactly?" Emma says, hoping to clarify things.

"I am Angus McLearan," he says, putting the stress on the word *am* to make things perfectly clear.

"And you're researching the Alger Hiss case?" she says, knowing otherwise.

"Well, no. Obviously a red herring."

"You mean a lure," she says. Angus smiles. He likes her, likes the fact that she has a brain. "Come on," she says. "The truth."

"Can I trust you?" he says it lightly, almost as if he's teasing her.

"I think maybe that's a question I should be asking you."

He stops then and turns to face her. "Seriously," he says. And she just looks at him, steady, unintimidated. "How could you not?" she says.

"I am Angus McLearan," he says again. "I did write *The End of Communism as We Imagined It.* And I do teach at Edinburgh, which is just as gloomy a place as it's made out to be."

She stops and turns to face him. Looking at him, fearless, knowing that's not the whole of it. "And?"

Then, quietly, almost as an aside, he says, "I sometimes work as a consultant."

"A consultant?" she says. "Really?" She smiles. But his facial expression remains fixed. She doesn't press it. "And you and Mr. Kidman are…"

"Friends. We've known each other a long time. He called me shortly after the two of you met." He doesn't flinch. "Asked me to help him with this."

"Because of your expertise in…"

"History. This era, of course."

"And…"

"And, then there's the fact that we trust one another."

She shoves her hands back in her pockets and starts walking again, turning it all in her mind. "So, I guess you'll be able to explain what's happened here, won't you?" she says finally. And once they've arrived at the cabin and climbed over the various items strewn across the kitchen floor—"It's the same man who broke into my apartment," she tells him. "I can see that," he replies—and she's picked a few things up, including the diary, which Serge had thrown across the room in anger. And once they've put on the teakettle and settled on the screen porch—"Lovely up here," he says—she hands him the diary. "See if you can make any sense of this," she says.

He flips through it, scanning a few sections, but she doesn't give him time to read. "It wasn't my grandfather. It was my father."

Thoughtful, he looks up. "That makes sense. He was in procurement—first with the War Department when the intelligence services were just getting off the ground. Then with Army. Then it seems he went on to Balfour and kept the operation going."

"You've known all along?"

He shakes his head no. "I've known since this morning," he says.

"It seems they befriended him. This Fletcher Skilling and his band of spies."

"I imagine the connection started as something aboveboard. When your father was with the War Department, he probably worked the back channel that sent arms to OSS—which would have been the wartime intelligence service, supporting the resistance, that sort of thing. Then maybe as OPC and CIA came into being, and he moved over to Army, he probably supplied munitions for covert operations. That would come out of a different sort of budget than defense, again a back channel, under the radar. Then he gets close to Skilling's people at OPC and goes to work for Balfour, he takes his bag of tricks with him. Maybe they courted him, hard to know. He becomes a resource for weapons for some of these activities. Again, off the radar."

"You make it sound so innocent."

"They were good men, you know." She gives him a skeptical look. "Well, everything's relative," he says.

"And what about this Mr. Breuer, who's been following me. Is he a good man, too?"

"Serge Breuer. No. No, he's not a good man. But you could have done worse. He came into battle without a weapon. Apparently underestimated you. I think it's safe to say he's a bad guy. But his father's worse. And his grandfather was worse than that. He was in league with the Führer himself. They'll ship weapons to anyone in the world. Their business involves profiting from the pain of others."

"And how is that so different from Balfour Chemical?" she asks rhetorically.

"Like I said, everything's relative," he replies.

Sometimes it's easier not to think, to deliberately stop your brain, to shut it down. That's what happens next. They both know Bill Kidman has left for town, and there's a sense between them that this may well be the only time they have together. At some point, after they discover a bottle of wine in the kitchen cupboard and before they make up the double bed in the guest room, she asks him one more question. "So, this Breuer, he killed my grandmother?" And he replies, "I wouldn't think so. I don't imagine he'd have the stomach for that. We suspect it was his father's people. A rough lot. Based in Philadelphia." Then there's no more need for talk as they turn their attention to other matters, to each other.

He is watching her closely as she opens the wine, recognizing her timidity, the distance she likes to keep. Then smiling. At this point, it doesn't require any discussion or any particular effort to get her consent. Just a shift in his body weight toward her, his breath against her neck, his hand on her waist, and she turns and folds into him. It couldn't be more natural, the weight of his body fully against hers as they're swept up into it. And there's no coyness or awkwardness as they move toward the Great Room, the sofa, wrestling with each other's clothes until they're naked, giddy, like a couple of kids. Then more like two adults who know precisely what they're doing, that this is serious. By morning, he's taken to calling her Quinn and she's taken to calling him Angus. And any pretense that they're not attracted to each other—all that is behind them.

At some point in the night, when the two of them were half awake in the double bed in the guest room, Emma had raised a question. She was lying flat on her back staring at the ceiling, and he was on his side with his arm across her waist. "Tell me about Albania," she said out of nowhere. Surprised by it, he laughed out loud. And she smiled. "Some sort of operation in Albania. After the war. My grandfather called it a fiasco."

"He was right about that." McLearan said, edging up onto his elbow, resting his head on his hand. "It was part of a push to see if we could train disaffected citizens in Western Europe to overthrow these Communist regimes." He shifted his weight, hesitating a moment. "We started it. In Albania, anyway."

"We?"

"The British. Training Albanian refugees in Libya. Armed them, took them to the border and dropped them into the mountains to start a revolt. Eventually, we got the U.S. involved. They moved the training ground to Malta and it went on for years. It was an ugly business. Your grandfather was right on a number of counts. For one thing, the refugees were a motley bunch. Nazis and criminals among them."

"And?" she said. "For another?"

"Most of them got killed."

She rolled over then, looked him in the eye.

"You've heard of Kim Philby?" he said.

"The famous spy? The double agent? Of course."

"Well he was in on the entire operation. So the Soviets got wind of it every time a rebel crossed back into Albania, every time they made a drop. Every single mission. Those poor sons of bitches all got executed. It *was* a fiasco." Then he lay back down, speaking as if he was thinking out loud. "The Americans were so naïve, so idealistic. So new to the whole business. They couldn't compete with Russians. Subterfuge is a way of life for the Russians. You can't outfox those foxes."

Emma had begun to drop off. She was still facing him, but her eyes were closed. "That's the history anyway," he said softly before he fell off to sleep.

No. 62

There is the whirring sound of the helicopter overhead. The two men—Angus McLearan and Bill Kidman—are in the two front seats, shouting at one another, saying words Emma can't hear. She has stopped wondering where they are going, stopped trying to think of all the questions she has for both of them. She feels safer, less confused, more secure than she has since the entire episode began.

When Bill Kidman arrived at the cabin that morning, she'd given him the black book, privately, when Angus was out of earshot, in the back taking a shower. Once Kidman had looked through it, she'd drawn his attention to the back page, to her father's name and to the name A. Breuer. And then asked, "Who is M. Frankel?"

Kidman gave it some thought before he spoke. "Just forget you ever saw that name," he said. And when she pressed him, when she asked him why, he said only, "Because it's not relevant."

Frustrated, she'd raised her voice then. "If it's not relevant, why did they kill my grandmother?" And that's about the point at which Angus appeared, freshly showered and shaved, looking like a new man.

"You need to forget everything you've seen and heard until we're sure we know the answer to that question," he said. The two men looked at each other. "I promise you," he told Emma. "We will get to the bottom on this. And when we do, I'll tell you everything. In the meantime, I'd like to keep you alive."

"C'mon," Kidman said. "We have someone we want you to meet."

Now, they've been in the air less than an hour, scuttling across upstate New York, running parallel to the Canadian border, approaching the Great Lakes when Kidman prepares to land. From where she sits, Emma can hear nothing, but the view's a stunner—the Finger Lakes spread out beneath her, looking for all the world like long black eels wriggling toward Lake Ontario. As the copter approaches the first of them—Skaneateles Lake—the landscape below transforms into a glorious patchwork of fields and farms, browns and greens, furrows and forests. Square and rectangular and oddly-shaped patches of cropland, each as distinct as the next. He brings the bird down in an open field of mowed grass that slopes gradually down to the lake, not far from two buildings. They're small, each one resembling a trailer, but they're not trailers. They're finished cottages, with pitched roofs and front stoops and flower boxes at the windows, although they lack a sense of permanence, as if they were dropped from the sky.

When the blade stops spinning, Angus takes Emma's hand, helps her disembark, guides her out of the way so Kidman can take off again. Emma looks confused. "We can't leave it out here," he says. "This is a safe house." She sees the woman then, slight and elegant, handsome really, her grey hair pulled up in a knot behind her head, emerging from the larger of the two cottages. Hard to tell her age, but she's probably in her seventies, dressed comfortably in a white blouse and beige cashmere sweater, a pair of light wool slacks, flat shoes. She reaches both her hands out toward Emma as they approach.

"Is it? Is it really?" she says. "Little Emma Gardner. Oh, my dear. Come. Come." Emma is speechless, overwhelmed. "I knew you when you were knee-high to a grasshopper," she tells Emma, grasping hold of her hands. "And your mother. What a beauty she was. You favor her, I think." A sadness passes across her face. "And I knew your father. As I think you've learned, he wanted very much to be something of a hero."

Angus is grinning. He's obviously developed a fondness for the woman. "This," he says, "is the infamous Muriel Markham."

"Oh dear," Muriel nods. "I thought you knew. I'm going too fast, aren't I? I'm just glad to see you. I was so disappointed I couldn't meet you when you called me. They wouldn't let me. They wouldn't even let me call you."

Angus eases them into the cottage, which is simple, well-tended. "It's only temporary," she tells Emma. "Why don't we sit?" Angus says, and they crowd into a space that feels rather like the inside of a trailer, long and thin and somewhat dark.

Miss Markham offers water. "I'm not really equipped for

entertaining," she says, and they sit, the three of them.

"I'm afraid you and I have both been thrown for a loop by your grandmother's death," Muriel tells Emma. And McLearan jumps in. "We were concerned that this lady might easily become a target," he says. "Since someone was tracking your grandmother and following you."

"But how did you know?" Emma asks.

"You led me to her," he says. "That may well have saved her life." When Emma looks utterly baffled, he goes on. "As I think you already know, someone had access to voice recordings from your grandmother's phones—for quite a few years as far as we can tell. We believe they picked up her call to the CIA and took it quite seriously. That, of course, would have led to her death. They may well have picked up her call to Miss Markham. We don't know. But we were fairly certain that if you had gone to meet her—and you'd found her at home—it would have put her at risk."

"So they brought me here." Miss Markham looks over at Angus. "Temporarily, correct?" And he smiles, nods.

"My grandmother," Emma says. "Did you meet with her right before she died?"

Muriel nods. "She came out to Pinehurst. Told me she was going to the CIA, that she was going to report Balfour to the authorities. She must have thought I knew something." She stops a moment, gathering her thoughts. "Your grandfather and I were close." She hesitates again. "As you know, your grandmother was not always—how should I put this? Well, available to him. We were friends, your grandfather and I were friends. We both worked for Balfour." She shifts in her chair. "Maybe it would be best if I told you what little I know, if that will help." And she goes on to speak in a steady stream.

"After your parents died, your Annie found a little black book at your house—at your family's cottage on Miller's Lane. She was cleaning, packing, clearing things out. Until then, James—or rather, your grandfather—had no idea that your father was involved in this business. When he found out, he was devastated. He felt betrayed."

"Help me understand," Emma says, looking at McLearan. "Would his activities be considered illegal?"

"Probably," McLearan says, "If—as it appears—your father established a relationship between Balfour and the clandestine services that hadn't existed before, that was off the books, going to covert operations outside regular channels—I would think so. It would be unethical at best. Balfour's a public company. Shareholders—and possibly even senior management—may have had no knowledge of it. If your grandfather was the man I think he was, I imagine he would have been upset by that."

"Terribly upset," Muriel goes on. "The Balfours knew nothing about it. When he showed me the book, I'd never seen him so angry—angry at your father—who, of course, had just died." She lowers her gaze, shakes her head. "It's important for you to understand—it wasn't just what Robert was doing, the subterfuge, the deception of it." Here she seems to confirm what Emma read in the diary—this battle between the two men. "James believed that your father was participating in something that was morally wrong. At that point, he was disillusioned with Balfour. The bomb, these new chemical weapons they were working on. The war itself had changed him. I watched it happen. He had no interest in participating any longer—and of course, that's why he retired. He knew full well where your father was sending those weapons. He knew what Fletcher Skilling's group was all about—fomenting uprisings, supplying arms for anti-Soviet missions, outright propaganda."

Emma is intrigued and impressed by this woman. She's watching her closely, and having no difficulty imagining why her grandfather was drawn to her. She leans forward, listening intently.

"James was a smart man, a thoughtful man," Muriel says. "He was vehemently opposed to their tactics—he called them no better than the Russians. And he always said we couldn't beat them at their own game." She becomes more and more agitated as she speaks. "He didn't know whether to report Robert. His own son-in-law. He didn't know what to do. Of course, he ended up just leaving the company. He didn't want anything to do with any of it anymore." She stops for an instant. "I think I'd better have a little of that water."

McLearan stands, his head almost brushing the ceiling and squeezes his way between the two women to get to the miniature sink. He has to open more than one cabinet to find the glasses, as Muriel goes on. "After that he asked me to keep an eye on Balfour, to let him know if these underground activities continued after Robert's death. Your grandmother may well have known that. Which is probably why she called me." Angus hands each of them a glass, then moves toward the other end of the small room, sitting a few feet away in an old bentwood rocker.

"Did they?" Emma asks. Muriel looks confused. "Did they continue?"

"Well, it certainly looks like it now, doesn't it? I had no way of finding that out, with the work I did. I told him that." She gets up and moves about the small space, carrying her water with her, looking out the window above the tiny sink as she speaks, then turning back to Emma. "I worked for your Uncle Martin. He may be odd, but he'd have had nothing to do with all this." She takes another sip of water. "We were on the agrichemical side."

"How well did you know my grandmother?" Emma asks then.

"Well enough to know she was very bright, very engaging. Just a bit erratic, I'm afraid. And withdrawn at times. That was hard on your grandfather."

McLearan gets up then, goes outside. He can hear the helicopter approaching. He wants to give them a little time alone. Not long afterwards, when Emma prepares to depart, she and Muriel embrace, both tearing up. Emma welcomes it. And as they let go of one another, before Muriel says goodbye, she tells Emma, "I promise you, I had no way of knowing your grandmother was in danger."

Outside Muriel's little house, the field stretches down a broad slope of well-trimmed grass to the lake below with a panoramic view of the private docks and swimming rafts that dot the shoreline, pristine cottages and what appear to be substantial estates. A few sailboats sweep across the lake. The spire of a church rises at the edge of the town of Skaneateles, visible in the distance. Idyllic. Set apart from the outside world. The three of them—Emma and the two men—stand for a moment taking in the view.

"She was quite something, wasn't she?" Emma says. "I hope I can see her again."

Kidman shakes his head. "Not gonna happen, I'm afraid. And forget you even know her name."

"Are you serious?"

"We're about to change it," he says.

McLearan jumps in. "Maybe you can find her a nice place in London."

After another few minutes, Emma says, "So why did they kill her?" Then she answers her own question with a question. "The black book?"

"That's what it looks like," Kidman says.

McLearan goes further, speaking slowly, hesitantly. "We knew—in Britain, we knew…"

"Wait. Just wait a minute," Emma says. "Who is we?"

"The British government," he says. "We knew Balfour was moving product through Europe. We tracked a couple of shipments that ended up in the Middle East—weapons with fake serial numbers and false end user certificates. Shipments that were intended to slip under the radar. We found them on random ships—one off the coast of Turkey. We didn't make the connection with *Cargo Belgique* until now. And we hadn't encountered anything shipped by air before. So, we've gained crucial information because of your grandmother's actions."

Kidman appears anxious, as if he wants Angus McLearan to stop talking, but he continues. "There's always illegal arms trading going on. This is something that's not quite as clear-cut. These are off-the-books transactions. And it appears they were authorized by someone in the military or intelligence community. At some point, they may have been sanctioned by an administration. We don't know. But this has obviously been going on a long time." McLearan shoots Kidman a look. "That's just about all we can tell you. In this case, it looks like somebody's stockpiling weapons in the Middle East."

"Why?" Emma asks.

"Because they can," McLearan says. "Look, this administration is talking about cutbacks in arms sales. They're cracking down on covert ops. Somebody obviously feels threatened." He looks up at Kidman, again, adding, "That would be my guess, anyway."

"So it's someone on the inside, that's what you're saying, isn't it?" Emma says.

"Hold on," Bill Kidman jumps in then, puts an end to the conversation. "Point is, your grandmother did the heavy lifting here. She put herself at risk to alert us, to get this information into our hands. And so did you. We know that. But you're going to have to let this go for now. We're going to find out who did this. It's just going to take us a little time."

No. 63

"His generation is spoiled, not prepared for this work." Albrecht Breuer is on the line with Hugh Grenville, who is alone in his Chevy Chase study rolling a squash ball between his thumb and his forefinger, gazing up at the painting of flying geese that hangs over the mantle, his stocking feet crossed at the ankle and resting on his desktop, the birthmark across his face fully exposed.

Breuer goes on, his voice somewhat distant, his accent pronounced. "We are grateful that they didn't question him. He has been deported. He is home."

"Ah," says Grenville, leaning in slightly. "Perhaps you gave him too much responsibility."

"I suspect I didn't give him enough responsibility."

"So, what does he have to say?" Grenville asks, probing.

"They found nothing. No evidence."

"And this black book you kept talking about."

"Nowhere to be found," Albrecht Breuer says, a calm and confidence to his voice.

"No names?"

"No names."

Grenville sits up now, removing his feet from the desk, setting the squash ball beside the speakerphone. "I understand you closed your offices in Philadelphia?"

"Yes," Breuer says. "And New York."

"So," Grenville says. "Let's lay low for a time. Let this pass." He hesitates a moment, then adds, as if it's an afterthought, "What about that last shipment?"

"On hold in Qatar."

"Fine. And the other?"

"In Jordan, not far from the Iraqi border."

"Good," Grenville says, reaching for the speakerphone, preparing to disconnect. "Let's hope this is over. And keep your boy at home. Where he's safe."

POSTSCRIPT

The United States is the largest arms dealer in the world. Between 1970 and 1978, with the U.S.-backed Shah in power, Iran purchased more than $20 billion in weapons and military equipment from the United States, all sanctioned by the U.S. government. The Shah's reign ended with the Islamic Revolution in January 1979, which also marked the end of the country's alliance with the United States. In 1980, Iraq attacked Iran. During the eight-year war that followed, both the U.S. and British governments poured a steady stream of advanced weapons and military equipment into the region, much of it through circuitous channels to avoid detection. Shipments from the United States ended up primarily in Iraq.[1] The British sent munitions and equipment to both countries. Neither the British Parliament nor the U.S. Congress sanctioned these sales. Various government agencies laundered everything through friendly banks, friendly companies and "conduit" countries, all of which were complicit in what has been described as the first global arms scandal.[2] It was a massive effort. In many cases, these activities were hidden from the management and shareholders of the companies that were involved.

In the end, some 700,000 Iraqis and Iranians died in the Iran–Iraq war that began in 1980, and 1.8 million people were wounded—all at the hands of weapons provided by the governments of the United States and

Britain, as well as other European nations, the Soviet Union and Israel.[3]

This is not fiction. It is true. The facts have been well documented.[4] And,

of course, it is only a small fragment of a much larger story.

1. While the U.S. arms went primarily to Iraq during the 8-year war, famously, in 1985, the Reagan government agreed to sell arms to Iran—including anti-tank and surface-to-air missiles—in exchange for the release of hostages being held in Lebanon. The deal was exposed in 1986 and is known as the Iran-Contra Scandal, because the funds from that sale went to the Nicaraguan rebels or "Contras."

2. The U.S. and British governments used a variety of tactics to conceal the shipments. As described in Nikos Passas' Foreword to the 1997 book *Arming Iraq*, these included "the use of friendly countries (e.g., Jordan, Egypt, Saudi Arabia) as conduits, the systematic use of false end-user certificates, the breakup of the production and transfer process by the involvement of numerous companies, the deliberate false description of shipments in official documents, and the use of trusted companies that kept 'black books' on 'joker contracts' to deceive even their own employees, managers and shareholders."

3. *Arming Iraq* by Mark Phythian, Northeastern University Press, 1997, 3.

4. *Arming Iraq* by Mark Phythian, Northeastern University Press, 1997.

ENDNOTES

The following cover headlines and stories are quoted or referenced in the text. They are listed in order of appearance:

Birney Lettick, "The CIA: Mission Impossible," *Time*, February 6, 1978, cover.

Claude Salhani-Sygma, "The World: Terror and Triumph in Mogadishu," *Time*, October 31, 1977, cover.

Terence Smith, "Terror at School," *The New York Times*, May 16, 1974, 1, 18.

"The World: Northern Ireland: The Bitter Road from Bloody Sunday," *Time*, February 14, 1972, 18-25.

United Press International, "Arab Guerrillas Kill 31 in Rome During Attack on U.S. Airliner, Take Hostages to Athens, Fly On," "Grenades Hurled," *The New York Times*, December 18, 1973, 1, 18.

"Belfast Bombings Kill At Least 13 and Wound 130," *The New York Times*, July 22, 1972, 1, 4.

United Press International, "Mideast Massacres," *Time*, May 27, 1974, cover.

"Middle East: Bullets, Bombs and a Sign of Hope," *Time*, May 27, 1974, 24-32.

"Hiss: A New Book Finds Him Guilty as Charged," *Time*, February 13, 1978, 28-30.

"Six Die in Iranian Riot Against Government," in "World News Briefs," *The New York Times*, February 20, 1978, 10.

Adam Smith, "The Arabs, Their Money…and Ours," *The Atlantic Monthly*, February 1978.

James MacDonald, "Himmler Program Kills Polish Jews," *The New York Times*, November 25, 1942, 10.

"Paris," *The New York Times*, June 4, 1940, 22.

ACKNOWLEDGEMENTS

The idea for *The History Teacher* sprang from my interest in the Alger Hiss case. Over the years, I've read much of what has been written on the subject, including a good bit of *Perjury: The Hiss-Chambers Case* by Allen Weinstein. Originally published in 1978, it has been updated and remains the landmark book on the subject. The scope of *Perjury* boggles the mind. I can't say that I've read every word, but it was an invaluable resource. In my mind, the Alger Hiss case remains unresolved. I think the best description of its status remains Hiss's own obituary, published in *The New York Times* on November 16, 1996.

I also want to acknowledge Mark Phythian for his remarkable book *Arming Iraq: How the U.S. and Britain Secretly Built Saddam's War Machine* and Evan Thomas, whose book *The Very Best Men* provided insight into the activities and nature of the early CIA and Office of Policy Coordination (OPC).

The History Teacher is a work of fiction that takes place against a backdrop of historical events. In some respects, Balfour Chemical resembles the Delaware-based DuPont Company. The DuPont Company was engaged in the Manhattan Project and the company was investigated during the Munitions Hearings in the 1930s, where Alger Hiss was among the attorneys on the government side. I want to thank Gerard Colby Zilg for his book *DuPont: Behind the Nylon Curtain,* which was a great source of background information and context on Delaware, the DuPonts and the times. That said, Balfour Chemical is a fictional company and the events depicted in this story are fictional. In addition, with the exception of well-known historical and public figures, all the characters in this book are fictional. Finally, I inherited a stack of weighty, oversized volumes from my grandparents—YEAR books, co-published by Year Inc. and Simon & Schuster—that are photographic records of the time. I was enthralled with them as a child and used the 1948, 1949, 1953 and mid-century editions for this project. They gave me a window into the news of the day and how it was interpreted in its own time.

I also want to acknowledge—and thank—all these people, without whose support this book would not exist.

— My indefatigable copy editor and longtime friend Pam Hamilton, who always has the right answers and is always there when I need her.
— Carol Buchman and Paula Kovarik, my sisters in crime here

in Memphis, both of whom read the manuscript early on and encouraged me along this road and all others.

— My dear, dear friend Nancy Bogatin, who remembers many of the events described in this book because she lived through them. She was one of my earliest readers and greatest supporters.

— Abby Rosenthal Johnson, poet and writer, mentor and counselor on all things literary and sometimes not so literary.

— The many friends and advisors who read and commented on the manuscript at various stages, generously contributing their time and ideas—Kelly Brother, Emily Wyonzek, Barbara Nixon, Ellen Klyce, Tom Pittman, Olga King and my old friend Catherine Cotter, whose insights are always invaluable.

— Everyone in the Lofts book club, who never cease to inspire and entertain, and weighed in on all kinds of issues. I especially want to thank those who read the near-final manuscript and joined in that discussion—Manisha Rea, Carol Ann Fila, Priscilla Hernandez, Juli Eck, Cam Armstrong, and, again, Emily.

— Two consultants who handheld me through the publishing process—Arielle Eckstut and Eva Natiello, both consummate professionals and delightful people.

— And three people who helped me with the final revisions, bringing fresh eyes and masterful skills to the process. The brilliant Jim

Kovarik, who provided a spot-on critique; Danielle Costello, who did a thoughtful and concise final edit; and Cameron Sandlin, who did a yeoman's job of proofreading to the finish line.

A huge thank you to the people at Design Positive. I couldn't have asked for a more professional creative director on the production side than Patrick Worley, who specializes in print and digital publications. Taylor Martin, the firm's chief creative, designed the cover and everything else associated with this book as well as my identity in the digital realm. Taylor is my go-to person for all things design and marketing related, my favorite collaborator and a trusted friend. I am grateful for his help on this project. I couldn't have done it without him.

Finally, I am blessed with many wonderful friends and a wonderful family, without whom this life would not be nearly as much fun. I want to thank all of you for all you do. Including my wise and incomparable brother Brud and sister-in-law Liz, and their hilarious and charming daughters, Eliza and Julia. My two amazing sons—Alex and Max—who enrich my life beyond measure and their equally amazing spouses, Mindy and Michelle, who do the same. And, for the grand finale—ta-da—my grandchildren, Evie and Owen, to whom this book is dedicated. They are my greatest joy and my biggest fans.

A NOTE FROM THE AUTHOR

Many thanks for reading *The History Teacher*. I hope you enjoyed it. I'd love to hear from you. Feel free to drop me a line, write a review on Amazon and/or GoodReads, or just spread the word among your friends.

For book clubs, you'll find reader's guide questions here and on my website. Post photos of your book club discussion of *The History Teacher* with the hashtag #historyteacherbook. Go to susanbacon.com to find out about scheduling a Skype book club visit with me, and join my mailing list for updates on upcoming events and my next book.

Thank you for your interest and support. And happy reading!

THE HISTORY TEACHER
BOOK CLUB QUESTIONS

1. What do you think is the meaning of the title of the book? Who do you think is the history teacher?

2. Were you surprised by Emma's reaction to her grandmother's death? What do you think about her relationship with her grandmother? Did that affect your feelings about Emma?

3. Why do you think the author chose to spotlight the Alger Hiss case? How is it relevant to the underlying themes of the book? Do you have any thoughts on whether Hiss was innocent or guilty?

4. What did you think of Margaret Quinn? Did your feelings for her change as the story unfolded? How would you describe her?

5. Why was Emma so upset by her initial meeting with Angus McLearan? And what are your thoughts on how their relationship evolved and his role in the story?

6. How is Emma's privilege reflected in her behavior and thoughts? Why do you think she was so uncomfortable with her family's status and position in society?

7. What are your thoughts on Annie's role in the family and in the story? And that of her son Lester?

8. Who do you think are the villains of this story? Are some more obvious than others?

9. Were there historical events or news stories in the book that surprised you? Did any of those change your perspective on history or politics?

10. Do you think *The History Teacher* is different from other spy stories or political mysteries? If so, how is it different?

11. How do you think this story relates to what is going on in the world today?

12. Who do you think was the most engaging character? The most interesting character?